Alder Gulch

ERNEST HAYCOX

Alder Gulch

G.K.HALL &CO.
Boston, Massachusetts
1984

Published in Large Print by arrangement with Jill Marie Haycox.

G. K. Hall Large Print Book Series.

Set in 16 pt Times Roman

Library of Congress Cataloging in Publication Data

Haycox, Ernest, 1899–1950.
  Alder Gulch.

  "Published in large print"—T.p. verso.
  1. Large type books. I. Title.
[PS3515.A9327A73 1984]   813'.52   84–15842
ISBN 0–8161–3550–9

Contents

I: Escape

ONE MOMENT he was a cool man who viewed his chances for escape and found them full of risk; and then a night wind moved over the river with its odors of dark soil warmed by summer rain and the resin scent of firs and the acrid taint of brush fires, and when these rank flavors came to him he knew at once he was done with caution. He belonged to the land and the land summoned him. Before midnight came he would go over the ship's side, no longer caring whether it would be as a living man or a dead one. He stood on the foredeck and laid a hand on a capstan's bar, and excitement rushed all through him and sweat made a dry nettle-stinging on his face.

The Bos'n was a short black shadow hard by the foremast pinrail. The Bos'n said: "Pierce, come down from there."

This square-rigged ship, the *Panama Chief*, wound slowly at midstream anchor, bowsprit pointed on the streaky glow of Portland's

1

waterfront lights two hundred feet removed. One street lay against a ragged backdrop of buildings, beyond which the dark main hulk of town ran back into a mass of firs rising blackly to rear hills. All sounds travelled resonantly over the water — the crack of a teamster's whip, the scrape of feet on the boardwalks, the revel of a near-by saloon.

"Come down," repeated the Bos'n.

The ship's bell struck five short ringing notes. The moon's quarter-full face dimmed behind a bank of clouds and the color of night at once deepened so that the surface of the river became a vague-moving oil surface into which a man might quickly drop and quickly vanish. Pierce bent and unlaced his shoes. He kicked them quietly off, moved to the break of the deck and descended the ladder.

He went by the Bos'n, passed the galley and paused near the mainmast shrouds. Mister Sitgreaves, the First Mate, stood against the starboard rail and Canrinus, the Second Officer, was in the same sentry position on the port side. The Captain was above them on the aft deck, his cigar bright-burning in the shadows. "Mister Sitgreaves," called the Captain, "come here."

There were two named Sitgreaves on this ship, the Mate and his brother the Captain. The Mate retreated and went scuffing up the aft deck's ladder. On the amidships hatch cover the rest of the *Panama Chief's* crew

2

silently and sullenly waited for a break to come, hating the ship and its master and its officers.

The Captain said in his bold, steady voice: "If any man tries to jump ship, Mister Sitgreaves, knock him down. This crew is signed from San Francisco to Canton and return. I'm no hand to lose my men."

The Captain was afraid of losing his men, as well he might. All of them, excepting the two Mates and the Bos'n, had been shanghaied aboard at San Francisco by force and knockout drops. There had been, Pierce remembered, an amiable man beside him in the Bella Union saloon. The amiable man had suggested a drink and presently he, Pierce, had died on his feet, to awaken on the *Panama Chief* at sea.

"Bully boy," said a murmuring voice from the amidships hatch cover.

The Captain moved to the head of the ladder and he stared below him and gave the crew his hard, short laugh. "You'd like me down there, no doubt, to start a confusion whereby you could make your escape. I'll not please you till we put to sea. Then, by God, I'll give you confusion."

On the hatch cover men softly and bitterly murmured. The First Mate, Mister Sitgreaves, clanked down the ladder and took his station again at the starboard rail. The Second Officer hadn't moved from the port side, the Bos'n remained deep in the fore-mast's shadows. All these men were armed, and it was six months to Canton and back, by which time this year of 1863 would be gone. The *Panama Chief* was no better than the Confederates' prison at Richmond, of which Pierce had his undescribable memories.

He closed his fingers around the rail and his body, lank in the shadows, bent backward until all weight rested on the balls of his feet. Mister Sitgreaves saw this and smoothly said: "I wouldn't do that."

The men on the hatch cover stirred and rose up. Brought aboard by violence, starved and bruised by iron discipline, they caught the clear wild smell of freedom and suddenly all of them were shifting softly along the deck. The Captain issued a sharp call: —

"Who's that by the rail, Mister Sit-greaves?"

The Mate said: "Pierce, sir."

"Knock him down, Mister Sitgreaves."

The Mate moved forward, his boots sibilantly chafing the deck. Pierce let his arm drop to the cool round top of a belaying pin, seized it from the bitts and took one quick side step. A sound at his rear warned him that the Bos'n now was moving forward to slug him and a man in the crew called out, "Watch back!"

The Captain roared, "By God, don't you know who's master of this boat?" and came

4

down the ladder in long jumps.

Pierce gave ground and retreated to the hatch cover, thereby avoiding the Mate and the Bos'n who now joined shoulder to shoulder and moved slowly at him. The crew shifted toward Pierce, making a cover for him; faced with this unexpected resistance, Mate and Bos'n paused.

The Captain said, "I'll show you how to handle mutiny, Mister Sitgreaves," and came on, bold and black in the night. Some man groaned, "You're done in, Pierce!"

Pierce gave ground as Bos'n and Mate moved at him, backing toward the port rail. The Captain wheeled to block Pierce's way. "You're a sea-lawyer," he said. "I am going to make you cry like a dog."

These three, Captain and Mate and Bos'n, were pinching him in around the galley, circling it to the starboard side, and reached the mainmast stays. He had shaken Mate and Bos'n but the Captain had outguessed him; the Captain was before him, softly laughing in his throat. Pierce saw the Captain pluck a pistol out of his pocket and lift it for aim, and all this while the steps of the Mate and Bos'n pounded behind him. Pierce, never wholly stopped, wheeled aside. He caught the flat explosion in his face and felt the violent pain of his eardrums, and brought the belaying pin down on the Captain's head in one sweeping blow. The next instant he took his tumbling dive over the ship's rail, with a second shot from another gun following. Deep under the water he heard its echo.

He stayed under and drifted with the current until his heart began to strike its hammer blows on his ribs, and came up to see the dark hull of the ship slipping by. The water was half warm from spring rain and bore the silt of a hundred valleys and hills far away. He heard Mister Sitgreaves calling: "Lower the boat!"

"There's his head!"

A bullet whacked the near-by water and sent him down. He swam breast stroke until he thought he had cleared the boat completely, and rose again. The stern of the *Panama Chief* was an edgeless shape upstream. Mister Sitgreaves issued his orders, very cold and very even, and the blocks of the davit falls were squeaking. He heard the bottom of the lifeboat hit the water. Mister Sitgreaves said, "Let go," in a softer and softer voice. This man, Pierce remembered, was the Captain's brother.

The current carried him downstream. Somewhere on the water another rowboat traveled and a lantern bobbed close by the water's surface. Pierce angled shoreward, feeling the down-dragging weight of his clothes. He swam overhand, putting his strength into his long arms, and as he swam he had a very strange recollection of a shallow

Virginia creek he had crossed two years before under the fire of Confederate sharpshooters. All around him the creek had run red.

Mister Sitgreaves had lost him. It was so quiet aboard that he heard Mister Sitgreaves say conversationally: "Hold it, while I listen." The pilings of a wharf stood before Pierce and water splashed steadily from it to the river. He had the thick odor of sewage around him as he cleared the wharf's end and put his feet down upon yielding mud. A voice called from wharf to ship. "What's the trouble out there?"

He faced a low crumbling bank and dropped into the wet silt to fight for wind. The Mate's answer rode over the water from the *Panama Chief*. "Man jumped ship. Where's your police?"

Pierce drew in a mouthful of water and spewed it out. He came against the bank and climbed it, to face the played-out end of a street on the ragged edge of town. Sheds and barns loomed before him. The wharf was to his left and in that direction the main part of Portland seemed to lie; a wagon rolled by, two men idly arguing on the seat.

There was no more sound from Mister Sitgreaves and no further inquiry from the watchman on the wharf. But as he lay flat on the edge of the river bluff with water draining from his clothes, Pierce realized the town was no more safe for him than the ship had been. Sitgreaves would notify the police and the town would be searched. What he needed was dry clothes, a meal and a quick means of leaving Portland.

He moved away from the bluff, past the wharf and through broken piles of lumber; he crossed the pure mud surface of a street entirely dark and empty, pursued an alley not much wider than wagon's length and found himself at a small, triangular square. Across the square a saloon shed light from every window, and beyond this saloon the main part of the town apparently lay, hard by the river, its stores open even at this late hour. Along this street supply wagons steadily moved. The name of the saloon was the Oro Fino.

He left the alley and walked directly over the small square toward the flaring lights of the saloon. A string of freight wagons crawled out of the darkness and passed between him and the saloon and somewhere a river boat whistled. Paused at the edge of the square while the freighters rolled by, he observed a man ride up and come to a halt before the string of wagons. He was in high boots and rough clothes, he wore a shaggy beard and he had the stain and the smell of a miner about him.

Pierce said: "Where's gold country around here?"

The man gave him a look and a moment's

study. "Upriver. Away up. In Ideeho."

"Just came from the California diggings myself."

"Hear they're played out. You look damp to me. You could stand a drink."

"I am a little shy of company," said Pierce.

He had judged his man rightly. The miner's lawless spirit instantly arose and prompted him to say: "Stay here and I'll get you a drink." The string of freighters had now gone on; the miner crossed the mud, dismounted before the Oro Fino, and rolled the swinging doors aside with his shoulders.

There seemed to be a sharp dividing line in town. Before him light glowed and warmth moved, regardless of the hour, while behind him in Portland's quieter quarter the solid and respectable citizens slept the sleep of the righteous. At that moment Pierce heard a quick call and turned to find Sitgreaves pointing to him. Behind Sitgreaves was the Bos'n and two citizens who were undoubtedly police.

"That's him," said Sitgreaves.

Pierce wheeled across the square to the alley's mouth. There was perfect darkness here for the length of a full block. Running down the loose mud, he heard the halloo of voices and a command from one of the police, "Hold up or I'll fire!" The alley played out in the middle of the block, dissipating itself into a series of between-building pathways and Pierce took one of these in full flight, to arrive at a street all dark except for a corner house whose lights shimmered on wet pools in the street's mud. He swung close to the face of the buildings with the racket of the pursuing gentlemen steady-continuing to his rear. He cut across the mud to the far side of the street; he ran through the beam of light from the corner house, and curved into another street — and heard a woman's voice say: —

"Wait!"

He came to a dead stop, he whirled half around to face the dark side of the house. The woman was a shadow against the house and he saw only the motion of her shoulders in these shadows. "No," he said impatiently. "No, I'm sorry."

She came nearer. "I had a look at you when you came across the light. You're wet." She put a hand against his chest and drew it away. Back on the other street Sitgreaves' dead calm voice was very distinct: "He went that way."

The woman said: "Come with me."

She went ahead of him at a light run, so that he had to stretch his legs to keep up with her. Half a block onward she darted behind a building and paused to catch his hand. "Careful with your feet," she said, and led him on. Somewhere in the heart of this complete darkness she stopped again, threw open a door and pushed him into a lighted room. She came in after him, closing the door.

It was a bare and worn and unlovely room with a stove in its center, a counter in the corner, a clock on the wall, and a huge man-shaped woman sitting unsurprised in a rocking chair. She had iron gray hair and a tremendous figure and her eyes were thoroughly unsympathetic as she looked at Pierce and read his story. "Jumped ship, didn't you?" she said. Then she turned her attention to the other woman and her expression changed, as though she saw something she didn't understand. "What are you doing in this end of town, Miss Castle?"

Pierce wheeled to have a look at this Miss Castle and met a pair of gray-green eyes dead on. She had black hair covered by a kind of shawl that woman sometimes seized on the spur of the moment for both hat and cloak. It sat like a cowl on her head and came down about straight shoulders and a strong, rounded bosom. The night had brought color to her cheeks and her glance made a good job of investigating him. For a common woman she was well gotten out in a maroon dress which came snug to her throat. A cameo pendant hung from a fine gold chain about her neck.

The big woman in the rocker said: "Ladies never come here. What kind of menfolk have you got to let you be such an elegant fool? If

11

you were seen you would be compromised."

Miss Castle shrugged her shoulders. "You have two fugitives instead of one, Madame Bessie."

"How would a lady like you know my name?" demanded Madame Bessie in clear displeasure. "And how did you know my door?"

"From my menfolk, of course. You're talked about over Portland's supper tables."

"Is that what the best part of town talks about?" asked Madame Bessie. "In mixed company?" She got up from the rocker and took a lamp from the counter, and trimmed and lighted it. She was, when she faced Pierce, both taller and heavier than he; she was a formidable creature with a square jowled face and a bit of a mustache. "Your menfolk ought to keep such things out of their houses."

She led them down a dismal hall scarcely wider than her shoulders and flung open a room's door. She put the lamp on a marble-topped dresser and stepped back, again watching Miss Castle with resentment. "I don't understand this. I shouldn't permit it. You're a fool for being something you shouldn't be. Usually it is money or a man that turns a girl. Your people have got money enough. So it must be a man."

"We won't be spending the whole night here," said the girl.

"That makes no difference," said Madame Bessie. "You are compromised now. But I suppose it is the same falling from a high place as from a low place." Thus far ignoring Pierce, she now turned to him. "Be quiet if you hear trouble outside. Get out of those clothes and I'll find some dry ones. All these ship jumpers land here wet to the skin. You'll be getting the last one's clothes. The next one will get yours. I'll take four dollars now."

"Two," said Pierce, "is my stake."

"You think I do this for the fun of it?" asked Madame Bessie sharply. "You can get out now. I won't be cheated."

"It's all right," said the girl. She produced a little purse from somewhere and laid a half-eagle into Madame Bessie's waiting palm. Madame Bessie gave the girl one look of scorn. "To go with him is bad enough. To pay his way is worse. He'll use you and lay you aside. Don't you know you can't buy a man for very long?" She closed the door behind her with a harsh jar; her heavy body went audibly down the narrow hall.

"Fugitives," murmured the girl, "can't be particular."

"Don't spend your money on me," said Pierce. "I have no way of paying you back."

"Perhaps," she answered, "a way will present itself. What is your name?"

"Jeff Pierce."

"Mine is Diana Castle. You were

13

shanghaied aboard ship at San Francisco, I suppose, and made a break tonight."

"That's it," he said. "How would you know?"

"I saw the *Panama Chief* drop anchor in the middle of the river. When a boat stays out from the dock it usually means she's got a shanghaied crew. Men escape frequently from these boats. It is an old story to us. You can hide here until your ship sails and then walk abroad a free man. Our authorities are not much interested in recapturing seamen for bully shipmasters."

"For a lady," he said, "you have uncommon knowledge of the hard side."

"I told you I was a fugitive also, didn't I?" Then she lifted her hand to keep him silent; for there was the sound of men suddenly arrived in Madame Bessie's office, and uncivil talk. Pierce looked carefully around the room, saw a window and went to it. He raised the window and put his head and shoulders through the opening. There was an alley black as a tunnel running beside this building; he drew back but left the window open. Out in Madame Bessie's office a first class quarrel raged with Madame Bessie laying her voice around like a club. "If they come down the hall," said Pierce, "we go out this way."

It was her lack of excitement that puzzled him more than anything else. She was, as Madame Bessie had said, a lady from the

14

proper quarter of town and had no business being here; this cheap lodging house was for the other kind of woman. There were only two kinds. This was the thing that unsettled his judgment of her and made him resent her steadiness, as Madame Bessie had resented it. Either she was too ignorant of this muddy side of life to feel shame or she was a woman turning bad. He could not really tell. She was a strong shapely girl with full red lips firmly controlled and with a cool expression in her eyes. She was sober, yet he had the idea there was a laughter in her which she deliberately hid from him. On her left hand a diamond burned its single spot of white fire.

The sound of bitter brawling died and the searchers apparently departed. The girl said as an idle thought: "Madame is outraged by my conduct. I have noticed that her kind of woman always has the strictest sense of propriety. Why is that?"

"She knows what good and bad is."

"What is good and bad?" asked the girl. "Do you know?" She gave him a sharp glance, she shook her head. "You do not approve of me," she murmured and shrugged her shoulders. "I'm afraid it will do you no good."

Madame Bessie came into the room. She closed the door behind her and stood with her great shoulders against it, more formidable than before. "They're gone," she said. "Now

15

you both get out of here."

"How about that change of clothes?" asked Pierce.

"No," retorted Madame Bessie. "I'll call no trouble down on myself." She put both large arms across her bosom and locked them together, and a clever thought came gray and sly to her eyes. She turned on Diana Castle. "You're paying for this man's trouble, ain't you? It will just cost you a hundred dollars to keep my mouth shut. I could always call the police back."

Diana Castle said: "What has happened?"

"This man," said Madame Bessie, nodding at Pierce, "killed the Captain in the fracas."

II: The Second Fugitive

DIANA CASTLE stood before Madame Bessie and watched the woman. She matched Madame Bessie's stare. She was cool and she was very thoughtful. Madame Bessie said: "You can get that hundred dollars for me, Miss Castle."

"You want to keep out of trouble, don't you?" asked the girl. "What if I were to step out on the street and start screaming? Suppose I said you had dragged me into your place? I think you'd be in the penitentiary a long while."

Madame Bessie watched her a considerable interval, not so much with anger as with a reluctant admiration. And she said finally: "All right, Miss Castle. I guess you know what you want."

"Now," added Diana Castle, "could you get him some clothes? And he needs a drink, Madame, and we are both hungry, aren't we?"

17

Madame opened the door and cruised through it and turned. "Miss Castle," she said, "you are too calculating for a proper lady. Wherever did you learn to be smart?" With this, she departed.

The girl walked to the open window, her back to Pierce, and placed her hands on the window's sash. Her shoulders dropped and became round at the points and then she came slowly about and he saw that her face had a shadow on it. Her confidence was momentarily broken, leaving her tired or weak or a little afraid. He liked her better for seeing it. It took the calculation and the chill out of her.

"Did you have to do that?" she asked in a small voice.

"When I made for the rail he came against me and fired a shot. I knocked him down with a belaying pin and went over the side." He shook his head; he made an odd motion with his hand. "Not to be helped."

She was watching him and he discovered that she was afraid of him for the first time. "What?" she asked in a distant voice, "would you like me to do?"

"Nothing. You'd better go out of that window now."

She let out a sigh and moved toward him. She was almost smiling, her fear vanished. "For a moment I thought I had made a mistake in you. But I have not. You are not one of those murderous Sydney ducks coming off a ship with your teeth broken in, cunning and half inhuman." She paused, not quite through with her thoughts about him, and added in a softer way, "I can still hope."

He said: "Why should you hope?"

"Because I need a man. That is why I stopped you on the street. You are to help me get out of this town. There are four thousand people in Portland. I can't appear on the street or get on a California stage, or take a boat, without being recognized. A woman traveling alone in this country is under handicaps."

"I do not know about that," he said.

She checked him in with a gesture. "You're in trouble and you know nothing of this region. You cannot take any road from Portland without being spotted in the back country. But I know how you can drop from sight."

"How?"

"Do I go with you?"

"How do you go with me?" he asked.

She drew a breath and her pleasant lips came momentarily together. She looked down at the floor and so avoided his eyes. "As your wife."

"No," he said. "Not as my wife."

She said: "There will of course be no marriage. We must make the best of it before people's eyes until we get to the place we're

19

going. Is it so much to ask? Are you already married?"

"No," he said. He moved back to the window and he stood there watching the yellow lamplight shine in her eyes. She had a fair, smooth skin and a round face pointed by a firm chin; she had an enormous certainty in her, she had a positive will. What confused him was that light in her eyes which seemed to hold back some kind of laughter from him. In a way she liked this touch-and-go business; it had an exciting effect on her. Madame Bessie stirred heavily in the hall and time went fast on and he looked at her and made this decision. "All right," he said.

Madame Bessie came in with a suit of clothes and a pair of boots over one arm. She had a whisky bottle under the clothes, and carried a pitcher of coffee and a loaf of bread in her other hand. She threw the clothes on the bed and deposited the rest of her burden on the washstand. "There's a miner from the Owyhee dead drunk in one of my rooms," she said. "This is his suit."

"Give him mine in the morning," said Pierce, "and tell him he fell in the river."

Madame Bessie nested both fists against her ample hip line and scanned these people with her dismal experience of the world's worst side. "You're a cool lot," she said, "the both of you, and you want your way and mean to get it."

"Yes," said Diana Castle, "we mean to get it, Madame."

"Mark me," said the Madame, "you'll get something else. You will get hurt." She turned out and lifted her shaggy eyebrows in faint surprise when Diana Castle followed her into the hall and closed the door. "You start with modesty," Madame commented in her tart, disbelieving voice. "You will end with something else. You will never keep him."

"I don't want him, Madame. Not for long."

"So you think," retorted the Madame. "Cool as you are, you are still a fool. The game you play will make you cry soon or late. He will break your heart and you might break his."

"What game, Madame?"

"For a woman there's only two — money or a man. You have money, so it must be a man."

"There's still another game, Madame."

"Is there?" countered Madame Bessie. She moved her massive shoulders forward and laid her gray chilled stare on Diana Castle. "I've seen a lot of girls start as you start. You know where they are now? Up on the second floor of places like mine, waiting for trade." She put her face quite close to Diana Castle, darkly murmured, "Women are weaker than they think," and moved heavily down the hall.

Pierce removed the cheap sweater and pants that had come out of the *Panama*

Chief's slop chest and stood stripped in the room's center, drying himself with a towel. He was lank-bodied top and bottom, with long flat muscles; his ribs showed when he lifted his arms and two bullet scars made white nipples above his left hip. He had sandy red hair and a heavy-boned face, and his eyes sat broad and deep in their sockets. His mouth was full at the center, and habitually held steady. When he had gotten into the miner's clothes — trousers and double-breasted blue shirt and high boots — he said: "You can come in," and took time to wash up at the stand.

She came in; she stood against the wall, waiting. When he turned to her she noticed that he had the bluest and darkest eyes a man could possibly own. They were penetrating and reserved rather than friendly, and he had an alertness to his body motion, as though keyed and cocked for the unexpected. He was thinner than he should be and she had not yet seen him smile. She supposed he was around twenty-eight.

He put on the miner's coat and took a water glass from the washstand. He filled it half with coffee and half with whiskey; he tipped his glass to Diana Castle and waited a moment. She had that smile somewhere behind her eyes when she said: "Luck." He drank his coffee and whisky straight down.

He had been cold, and presently was warm.

He broke the bread with his hands and offered her half the loaf. She shook her head and watched him eat. He had a ring on his small left-hand finger that interested her, since it seemed to be a woman's ring, but she pushed the obvious question away. He put his hands in the miner's coat and pulled out a pipe, a letter, a small bullet mold, and a buckskin pouch. The pouch, when he loosened the pucker string, held three or four ounces of coarse gold nuggets.

She watched him now with complete troubled interest. He looked down at the pouch and hefted it between his hands, and laid it on the washstand beside the other articles. "What's left of a large bust," he commented. "Madame Bessie will probably see that he never gets it." He went to his wet clothes in the corner, retrieved his two dollars and put them in the pocket of the borrowed coat. The girl released a held breath. "You're honest," she said.

"Up to thirty dollars," he answered, dryly. "What now?"

"The steamboat *Carrie Ladd* leaves the foot of Washington Street at five in the morning for Lewiston. A thousand miners come through here every month bound for the mines upriver. When you get there you'll be out of sight."

"Neither you nor I," he pointed out, "will walk up that boat's gangplank at five in the morning without being stopped. The police will watch it."

"I know," she said, "but we have to get on that boat."

"Where's Washington Street?"

"Two blocks south of here. Then turn left and go two blocks to Front."

"I'll go take a look."

She came toward him. She had her small purse in her hand. "As long as we're together," she said, "this is yours."

He let the purse lie in his palm, feeling its heaviness. "Maybe honesty doesn't go beyond thirty dollars."

"I've got to take that chance, haven't I? When I left the house tonight, I left for good. There's six hundred dollars gold in the purse."

He turned to the window and had one leg through it when a thought arrested him. He looked back to her. "You married?"

"No."

"Not that it would have made much difference," he said in the same dry way. "But I have never run off with a married woman."

"Otherwise?" she asked.

He gave her a good and sudden smile. "Or any woman," he said.

The window let him into a pitch-black alley which he pursued to a street bordered by little frame shops long since locked up for the night. He halted on the sidewalk, listening to the thinned-out voices of men drift over housetops from the waterfront; and presently crossed the mud and advanced another block and saw the flare of lights on Front. Keeping to the shadowed walls, he moved toward the river and now began to pass late-closing establishments whose lights made successive yellow pools out upon the loose mud. There had been a driving rain recently hereabouts, turning the air damp and sweet. Coming to Front he put his back to a saloon for a moment's observation.

Directly across from him stood the Pioneer Hotel, and beyond that was a dock to which a steamboat lay tied, pilothouse and single stack showing against the night sky. Men trotted from boat to dock, loading freight, and a barrel of tar burned on the dock's end, its smoky yellow light darkly dancing on the river. A line of waiting wagons bent around the corner of the Pioneer House as far as the dock.

He was in poor position here, with men moving past him, in and out of the saloon; and so he crossed through the line of wagons and took position on the shadowed side of the hotel. A runway tilted downgrade to the lower deck of the boat, and at the foot of the runway a big canvas-topped wagon stood, its driver half asleep inside a blue army overcoat.

"Hard sleeping," said Pierce.

The driver pulled himself awake. "Been here three days. Damned boat is booked solid. I'll get on tonight, though."

"Coat looks familiar."

"Third Ohio," said the driver.

"First Michigan myself," offered Pierce.

"Ah," observed the driver, "it is a hard war, and a long one. Buy your way out?"

"Wounded and discharged," said Pierce. "My wife and I are trying to get upriver. There isn't any space."

"Be lucky if you get away inside of a week."

"That would be too late," said Pierce. "It is damned serious." He came forward and stood close by the wagon. A heavy piece of machinery crashed on the deck of the *Carrie Ladd* and four men rounded the corner of the Pioneer and came to a stand behind Pierce. He was in a the shadow cast by the wagon, with his back to them, but he recognized Sitgreaves' voice at once.

"We will watch this boat until it sails."

"Hard man to give up, ain't you?" said one of the others.

"Why yes," stated Sitgreaves in a steady voice, "I reckon I am. I will get him tonight, or in the morning, or next week, or next year. Let's try the alleys again."

The four departed. "Somebody killed," commented the driver with disinterest. "Well, I guess we seen a lot of boys killed, ain't we brother?"

"You've got a cover on your wagon," said Pierce. "If my wife and I hid inside they couldn't see us."

The driver revived himself sufficiently to pack and light his pipe. He lowered the match until he caught a clear view of Pierce's face. He laughed easily to himself. "That's one way," he said. But he gave Pierce one more sharp appraisal before he said, "Come later when some of these lights go out."

Sitgreaves and his three partners were fading into the darkness up Washington. Pierce moved back into the first available shadows beyond the saloon and took station there, watching the driver of the canvas-topped wagon with a degree of suspicion; the man's gesture with the match was on his mind. The driver settled down inside his big coat for a chilly rest and, half an hour later, Pierce made his way across town to Madame Bessie's, let himself through the window to the lodging-house room, and found Diana Castle sound asleep on the bed.

The strain of the evening had been greater on her than she suspected. She lay curled on the bed's gray top-blanket, her arms around her chest and with both fists doubled, and her face had a softened expression, as though she dreamed of pleasant things. Pierce pulled out the edge of the blanket and brought it over her and stood back, and suddenly he was displeased both with himself and with her. She had no right to want the things she seemed to want. She was laying the false light of romance over her night's adventure, she was touching the borders of an existence meaner and harder and dirtier than she could conceive. She did not even realize her present danger, asleep and unguarded in the shabby room of an ill-reputationed rooming house, in the presence of man she knew nothing about. She had too much faith.

He took a helping from Madame Bessie's bottle and stood with his back to her, feeling the damp night air move through the window. Far past midnight, the town had fallen asleep at last. Deep silence lay on Portland, broken at long intervals by a distant voice or the hollow knock of some lone traveler's boots on the near-by boardwalks. A plank squeaked in the upper part of the house; he heard a body shift on the dry springs of a bed. He ate the rest of the bread and drank the cold coffee and tilted himself on the room's only chair. He thought of the dead Captain with a slow pity but without regret, much as he had once thought of those butternut-clad Confederate infantry who came running out of the summer wheat fields in Virginia and dropped at the crack of his gun. Pity was something he remembered in a far-off boyhood, never since recaptured; it was just a memory.

Long later he got up from the chair, observing that the black night's square at the window began to tremble slightly with gray, and touched the girl on the shoulder. "Time to go," he said.

She was up at once, frightened. She stared at him and her arms came up in a quick pushing gesture; and then the shock passed and relief softened her and for the first time he saw her smile. "I would have been asleep in another moment. You weren't gone long."

"You have been asleep for three hours," he said irritably.

She said in a little voice: "I don't ever mean to cause you trouble."

"You have a good home. You have people. You have friends and money and nothing much to worry about. You don't know what you're getting into. It is like leaving a warm room and going out into the rain. You'll never get dry again."

"So you have a conscience," she murmured. "But let's not argue. If you hadn't turned the corner of this house a few hours ago some other man would have. I would have taken him."

"All right," he said. "We go out through the window." He gave her a hand through the window, seized the gray blanket from the bed and followed her. It was still black in the heart of this block but overhead the stars had lost some of their electric brightness, and a thin river mist moved against them. Diana Castle took the lead, reaching back for his arm, and in this manner they reached the nearest street and went along it, their footfalls running sharply ahead.

The remnant of a tar-barrel fire guttered crimson and black on the dock and the superstructure of the *Carrie Ladd* traced a skeleton shape against the night mists. The girl suddenly pulled him to a stop before a building's door. She had, he saw, a letter in her hand and now bent and slipped it beneath the door. Looking up, he noticed a sign that said: "Castle and Tipton, Wholesalers." Diana Castle faced the door, and her voice contained the first regret he had so far heard from her. "I am telling my father not to worry. I am telling him that this is my own doing."

Somewhere footsteps made a breach in the town's stillness. The girl whispered, "That will be them," and seized his hand and led him down a between-building gap. Fifty feet from the street, once more in the sightless heart of a block, he pulled her to a stop. Back of them, at the mouth of the opening, a lantern made its diamond-bright flash, and men were talking.

"There was a racket up this way."

"She'd not be walking the street at this hour, Harry. It makes no sense."

The first man's voice came back, hard-used and very tired. "None of it makes sense. I'm going to knock on the door of every house in town."

A third man added his word: "You have seen all her friends. Now I should not like to offend you, Mr. Castle, or you, Mr. Wyatt. But we must be practical about this. Was she fond of any other man?"

"If you suggest that again I'll be forced to knock you down," said the tired voice.

They moved on, their steps long echoing back from distant quarters. Light made a first thin pulse in the sky and the river mists began to show clearer. "One was the marshal," whispered Diana Castle. She had his hand again, leading him on through quarters she seemed to know well. "One was my father. I am sorry for my father."

"That leaves Mr. Wyatt," suggested Pierce.

"I'm not sorry for him," she answered. They came presently to another street along which low-burning night lights showed out of glassed shop-windows. The square edge of the Pioneer Hotel stood directly to their right, and a man lay on the boardwalk wrapped in a tarp, and the line of wagons waiting for the boat made a black curve around the hotel's corner. The girl moved over the mud to the farther walk. They passed along a building's side, thus coming to the dock at which the *Carrie Ladd* lay and softly groaned against the piling. A light burned in the purser's cabin.

"What do we do now?" asked the girl.

The foot of the runway was near them and the teamster who had been in the Third Ohio slept soundly on the seat of his wagon. Deep

31

in the hull of the *Carrie Ladd* iron fire doors slammed and woodsmoke drifted in the heavy river air. Light appeared from a window of the Pioneer and steam curled from dew-damp housetops and back of town the Oregon fir forest began to break through, silvered by mist. There was nobody at this moment visible on Washington except the sleeping teamster. Taking the girl's arm, he moved toward the Ohio man's wagon, pulled the canvas open at the rear and gave Diana Castle a hand up. Following, he found himself sprawled on a load of sacked potatoes, with scarcely more than breathing room between the potatoes and the canvas top.

The teamster, wakened by the motion of their entrance, put his head through the front apron and withdrew it. Pierce heard the girl say, "You are resourceful," and saw her face dimly near. This situation would be uncomfortable and in some degree risky, for although the canvas lay tight-lashed against the bows, all down to the wagon box, there was an opening at the rear into which anyone might look. He thought about this, and settled himself half on his knees, shifting the potato sacks to block off that view and also to create a space in which they might better lie. He spread down Madame Bessie's gray blanket. "Yours," he said, and watched her slide into it.

It was light enough so that he now saw her

face. She wasn't smiling but the effect of excitement was in her eyes, as though she had far pleasanter thoughts than she wanted to show. "Thank you," she whispered, "for being thoughtful."

"It is Mr. Wyatt I'm wondering about," he said.

The teamster left the wagon. Daylight came and the odor of coffee drifted out of some near-by door and people began to stir around the corner of the Pioneer Hotel toward the *Carrie Ladd;* and presently the boat's whistle sent a great warning blast bounding back through Portland. People tramped steadily along the gangplank, and a woman said, half in tears, "Write, won't you?" And over and above the growing confusion he caught a voice that belonged to Sitgreaves. "You've gone through the boat, cabin by cabin?"

"He's not on board."

"We will watch."

The girl touched Pierce's arm. She looked up and her lips moved and he saw the steady brightness of her eyes; and once more he got the idea that this was all something which pleased her in a way that no other thing could. The Ohio man stirred on the wagon seat and kicked off the brake; the wagon moved downgrade and struck the *Carrie Ladd's* deck. A boat's officer shouted his constant orders and all round there was the rising clash of voices on dock and on board, and other

33

wagons groaned across the deck. "Plank's in, sir!"

"Cast off bow and spring!"

The whistle flung out a second warning and bells jingled in the *Carrie Ladd's* engine room. "Cast off stern!"

"All clear astern!"

The deck trembled to the thrust of the *Carrie Ladd's* big Pittmans. The paddles slowly threshed and the nose of the ship swayed as it turned into the channel, and out from the dock floated a woman's voice, now openly crying: "Write — write from Lewiston!" and a cheer went up from the passengers of the *Carrie Ladd* and the whistle let out a final long hark of farewell.

The girl's hand still rested on his arm; he felt the pressure of her fingers and he looked at her and saw she wanted to cry. She gave him a glance then he never understood, wide open and crowded with strangeness and sadness and wonder. This was the one moment when her self-control wavered, for she said: "Be tolerant of me won't you, until we reach Lewiston? It is my father I'm thinking of."

She was warm under the blanket, and the steady steaming sound of the bow cutting water soothed her. She lay with her face toward the canvas top, listening to voices on deck and to the restless march of feet round and round the deck. It would be a crowded boat, as all upriver boats had been since the discovery of gold in Idaho and Eastern Oregon. Portland, which had been a raw village crowded between the fir hills and the river, suddenly woke to find the restless men of America moving in from their mysterious origins and departing to the distant recesses of the Blue Mountains, the Salmon River gorges, to the Bitterroots. They came and had their day on Front Street and were gone, scarcely more than shadows. This man beside her was one of them.

She said: "Are you hungry?"

He didn't answer. Turning, she found him asleep, his head cushioned on an arm and his body awkwardly adjusted to the lumpy potato sacks. After his flight from the *Panama Chief* and his all-night wakefulness he simply dropped away from the world, giving it no more thought. He was a clean-shaven man, now with a day's stubble giving him a dark cast; but asleep he lost the guarded alertness which was so noticeable on him. His life, she guessed, had not been easy; but once he had been a boy, and somewhere he had learned what manners and morals should be. His convictions were very definite and very strong. Now he slept dreamlessly and had no care at all.

She saw nothing of the outside world, but was familiar enough with it to picture the great and high and black walls of the gorge through which the *Carrie Ladd* moved; five hours from Portland the boat nosed ashore and the wagon moved off to a rutty, piece-meal road. Jeff Pierce stirred and said in a half-asleep voice: "Where are we now?"

"We've left the *Carrie*. We're driving around the Cascade Portage to the middle river boat — the *Oneonta*. We'll be in The Dalles tonight."

He fell asleep again. The wagon turned down an incline and struck the middle river boat's deck; and in a little while they were under way, steaming through the great Cascade Gorge. During the afternoon sun beat on the canvas top so that she grew warm and felt the gritty dust of the potato sacks. But it didn't matter. She was away from Portland, she had made the great break of her life, and had long ago decided that whatever this new life would be she would never complain. She thought again of her father and sadness came back to her and for want of support she put out her arm and let it lie on Pierce's chest, comforted by the knowledge of his nearness. He had walked out of the night and she had stopped him and had gone with him because she would do nothing else. And then he had laid the gold pouch on the washstand and after that she had been reas-sured. He disapproved of her now for what she was doing, being in that respect as strait-laced as her father; and because he was that kind of man, he distrusted. He shared Madame Bessie's beliefs concerning women — Madame Bessie who placed all women in two classes. Madame Bessie was a sinful one, but she knew what goodness was; so did this man know, and in him was one streak of tenderness which had made him think of the gray blanket.

Dusk came and with it the smell of food; and darkness fell. Pierce was awake and lay silent beside her, and somewhere in the early night the *Oneonta* whistled and turned into The Dalles landing. The wagon moved up a long grade and town lights streaked the side of the canvas and there was music from a saloon and rough voices cheerfully calling. Then the wagon stopped and the Ohio man rapped on the canvas. Pierce moved the potato sacks and crawled out, assisting her to the ground. They were, she discovered, on a quiet back street.

The Ohio man said in a rather shrewd voice: "Both you folks seemed a little shy, so I thought I'd unload you privately."

"I am grateful," said the girl.

The teamster nodded, and gave his attention to Pierce. "I could make a good guess as to your bein' on my wagon," he said. "But army men stick together, don't they?" He got on the wagon, lifted a hand to them and rolled away.

Pierce moved to the street's corner and

looked toward the heart of this river town. He said: "What's next?"

"The Umatilla House is on that corner. We are halfway to Lewiston. The upper river boat leaves in the morning."

He gave her a long, straight look. "I'll have to see about space on that boat. Meanwhile we'll need a room and something to eat. I expect we register as man and wife."

"Yes," she said. "Yes — if you don't mind."

"It is too late to mind now, isn't it?" There was no particular inflection to his words but as she took his arm and moved with him toward the Umatilla House she had an unexpectedly painful thought: His judgment of her character was unsure. She wished it were not.

III: The Wicked and the Bold

THE DALLES' principal street paralleled a river whose lava rock margins lay jagged and black in the quarter-moon's light; and a soft wind brought in the balsam scent of a thousand miles of pine hills and sagebrush desert, giving the air a thin and vigorous pungency. Coming up to the Umatilla House with Diana, Pierce observed the freight outfits loading for their long slow run into the back country, and the shaggy shapes of men who prospected the hills, and the sharp-eyed and half-wild cowhands in from distant ranches. Indians — these of the proud and intractable Plains tribe, so different from the slovenly fish-eaters of the Coast — stood by the hotel wall, and army men roamed by in their dusty blues. Pierce and Diana Castle made way to the desk through a crowd of citizens and boat passengers. Pierce said: "A room for myself and wife." A neat, grave man dressed in black broadcloth and white shirt turned from the desk and slightly collided with Diana, and was quick to lift his hat in apology.

"There's been some confusion," Pierce said as he signed the register. "We have lost our luggage and my wife is considerably fatigued. Could you bring up a meal?"

"Yes," said the clerk, and handed Pierce a key. "Four. Up the stairs."

Pierce walked as far as the stairway, there handing the key to Diana. "I'll see about passage," he said, and turned back through the crowd to the street. Rain had dropped here recently but there was no mud underfoot; the fine powdered soil of the street glittered by lamplight and would make, in another dry day, a steady pall of dust. An auctioneer stood on a box beside a tar flare calling up customers in a tireless voice and a woman came against him and looked at him with a laughing face. He stepped into the office of the navigation company, near the hotel, took place in line and eventually found himself at the counter. Beside him was the grave and neat man who had lifted his hat to Diana.

"Passage to Lewiston for two," said Pierce to the clerk.

"Thirty dollars," said the clerk.

"My wife is in poor health," added Pierce. "This includes a decent stateroom?"

"All gone," said the clerk. "You are buying deck space, and not much of that. It will be a full list inside of half an hour.''

The neat man had been listening. Now he said: "If your wife does not mind sharing a stateroom with my daughter, I should be happy to accommodate you."

"That is handsome," said Pierce. "We will see you in the morning. Pierce is my name."

"Temperton," offered the man. "Will Temperton." He was courteous but did not extend his hand. Pierce paid for two passages upriver and moved aside, hearing a woman's voice attack the clerk with a good-natured malice. "One upriver. I wouldn't consider it much of a treat to sit in one of your ratty little staterooms. Your bosses are making too much money for their own good. They're greedy, Neall."

"Hello, Lil Shannon," said the clerk. "Still, what other way could you get to Lewiston?"

"I can walk or I can ride," retorted the woman. "I can do both better than your stuffed Portland capitalists, my friend."

She was a woman with a rose-complexioned face, smiling and a little bold, and dressed on the high side of taste. She was his own age, Pierce judged, and knew as much of the world as he did. She turned her head with a rather swift gesture and met his attention. Her eyes were hazel and ready to be amused and he saw that she was accustomed to meeting the glances of men. She looked at him with a moment's steady interest; he bent his head slightly and left the office. The ticket line had lengthened and now stretched halfway back to the corner of the Umatilla House; and a man in line said: "That Lil Shannon in there?"

Pierce returned to the barroom of the Umatilla House and pressed through the thick crowd. All the talk about him concerned the mining camps of Burnt River, the Blue Mountains and the Owyhee, and Elk City and Florence; the smell of gold was in the smoke and whisky reek of the room. He got to the bar and bought a drink. He stood idle and solitary with the crowd moving around him and had hot beef and beans and bread off the steam table and he bought a cigar and got it properly burning, meanwhile watching the gold scales on the bar tip to the dust poured out of miners' pokes.

"Nothing down Powder River. Elk City's playin' out. There's a new strike on over beyond the Grasshopper diggin's, in Alder Gulch."

"Where's that, Joe?"

"Up the Clearwater, beyond the Bitterroots, other side of Bannack."

He heard this talk but paid little attention to it, for his mind went back to Portland to review the scene aboard the *Panama Chief*. The Captain had meant to kill him and the Captain's voice had betrayed a tone of pleasure. He remembered the sound of the belaying pin on the Captain's skull and the way the Captain's mouth sprung wide open, and all during that time the smell of land had rolled over the water, rich and thick and racy with the freedom he had to have. There had been a black streak in the Captain.

Somebody said "You're in my way," and drove a shoulder point hard against his arm. The cigar, lightly held between his teeth, flew from his mouth and hot ashes sifted back to his face. He made a complete turn and came about and saw a man's square, sun-black face stare up from beneath the flat brim of a hat. He looked straight into a pair of mud-gray eyes and noticed temper move in spongelike contractions across this man's full-centered lips.

He waited a moment. He said, almost gentle with his words: "An accident?"

"You can do your sleeping somewhere else, can't you?" said the man.

Men crowded behind Pierce. He pushed his shoulders backward to relieve that pressure and he pulled up both arms and batted the man with his open left palm and hit him on the chest with his right fist. The man went backward into the crowd, into the arms of a tall fellow wearing a mustache and goatee. The tall one clenched and showed his big white teeth in a smile as he caught the falling man. He said, wickedly easy with his words: "There's your meat, Rube, go after him."

Rube struggled out of the arms of the tall one. He was short and broad and sweat rushed a thin glistening film over his sun-blackened cheeks. He was speaking to himself as he moved forward; and he lifted the point of one shoulder, as though to cock his fist. Pierce shoved himself clear of the bar. He hit this muscular, slow Rube in the belly and drove the wind out of him. He waited until Rube's head dropped and thereafter caught him fully on the temple. Rube went down to the floor.

Pierce said: "I don't like to be crowded. Keep your hands out of your pocket." Then he looked up to the tall fellow with the goatee who still smiled. He said nothing but he watched that smile as wickedness honed it thin. The tall one had a fresh, light skin and a set of agate eyes in which brightness danced; and small wrinkles deepened at the corners of his temples, and he seemed to be laughing deep in his chest.

Rube rolled and stood up. He shook his head and he looked at the tall fellow with the goatee. "What'll I do, George?"

"Why," said the tall George, "nothing more along that line, I guess." He inclined his head at Pierce. "You're handy with your fighting, brother. If I wasn't full of supper I'd take you on for a set."

"Why?" said Pierce.

"Just for fun," answered the tall one. "I

44

think I could do you in." His smile was constant and winter-chilly. Light kept dancing oddly on the gray-green surfaces of his eyes. He had a streak in him, Pierce saw — a pure wild streak which registered at the down-slanted corners of his lips.

"Suit yourself," said Pierce. "I'm going upriver."

"My name is Ives," said the man, "George Ives" — and he waited, as though the name might remind Pierce of something. When he saw it did not, he added: "I'll talk with you on the boat."

"If you bring a fight," said Pierce, "bring a good reason with it."

"Fighting's reason enough," said George Ives. "Just the fun of it, friend."

"Not the way I fight," answered Pierce. "There's no fun in it."

"All right," murmured Ives, and touched his short, dull partner on the shoulder. These two left the barroom.

Pierce returned to the bar and bought a fresh cigar, and took time to light it; and strolled to the lobby. The night turned better though he did not know why; he felt clean and at ease.

He crossed the lobby to the stairs, noting that Rube and Ives had disappeared. At the foot of the stairs, he found a redheaded young man idly waiting for him. The redhead smiled. "Ketchum and Ives usually stick together.

Those names don't mean anything to you? Well, if you go to Lewiston, don't consider this deal closed." He was high and robust and indolent, he was a character who seemed delighted simply to be alive and a spectator to the odd maneuverings of the world. "One other thing," he added, "close up your guard when you scrap. A trained pug would have knocked your head off whilst you were pullin' that punch forty miles up from your socks." He strolled away, whistling between his teeth.

Pierce climbed the stairs and went down a hall to Number Four and knocked; and entered the room on hearing Diana Castle's voice. She stood at the room's window and had apparently been looking into the street. When she came around he saw loneliness on her face. She gave him a glance that he had come to expect from her, long and thoughtful and deeply interested, as though she tried to reassure her faith in him. For his part, he was ill at ease.

"I have the tickets. The boat leaves at five-thirty." He moved around the room, noting the narrow bed and the four walls, and growing more irritated with himself. "I'll stand out in the hall. When you're in bed — and the light's out — I'll come in and sleep on the floor."

She said: "You don't like it, though."

"No," he agreed instantly. "I don't. I keep thinking of where you came from and of what you're throwing away. I keep thinking of your dad." He turned full at her and he walked forward, and he did a thing so wholly unlike him that he had his own great marvel at it. Her soft fragrance slid through the armor of his self-sufficiency and he reached out and lifted her chin with his hand. He saw a quick flare of fear answer him and dropped his hand at once, once more embarrassed and irritated. "When a good man comes to you, what will you tell him about Madame Bessie's house, and this room tonight?"

"A good man would understand, wouldn't he?"

"There is no man that good."

"What have I done wrong?"

It was — and he struggled with the thought and could find no simple answer — the rebellion which made her break old ties and old standards and surrender security and gamble with man's respect. It was the willingness to do this that made the wrong. But he could not properly say it, and so stood still, shaking his head. Diana Castle said it for him with her brief, quick words.

"It is a man's world. You lay down the rules. You make our places for us, in which we are supposed to stay. You have the fun and then you come home to us and we are your audience, properly grateful for the secondhand warming of what the outside world looks like. Don't you suppose a woman can be hungry for the ugly and raw and dangerous part of living — the real part? You're not afraid of discomfort or misery, you don't feel that the mean and evil things through which you pass leave a stain on you. Why should they leave a stain on me?"

He said "I do not know," and left the room. He stood outside until he heard her call, and went back into the room. The light was out and the night's thin wind blew through the opened window. She had put a blanket on the floor for him. He rolled himself into it and lay long awake, hearing the soft rise and fall of her breathing and unable to make up his mind about her. "Good night, Jeff," she said.

They ate in the dining room of the Umatilla House at four, with daylight gray at the windows and soon after were in the small train which ran fifteen miles around the unnavigable rapids to the landing at Celilo where the upper river boat *Tenino* waited. Going aboard, Pierce and Diana Castle stood on the cabin deck and watched the crowd distribute itself. Lil Shannon walked aft with her free and easy manner; she bracketed Pierce and Diana with a glance and moved in a rustle of silks toward the lady's parlor. In a moment Will Temperton came forward with a little girl of about ten. He lifted his hat at once to Diana and bowed when Pierce said: "My wife, Mr. Temperton."

48

Will Temperton had a grave, soft voice and he made a ceremony of introducing his daughter. "Lily Beth, may I present Mrs. Pierce. And Mr. Pierce. The cabin is at your disposal, of course." He led them aft along the narrow passageway between rail and deck structure until he reached the proper stateroom and opened the door.

Diana said: "Lily Beth, do you mind too much?"

Lily Beth lifted a guarded glance. "I don't mind," she said passively. Will Temperton watched his daughter with a degree of helplessness. The man, Pierce thought, was somehow at once outside all this, powerless to step in. But Diana Castle's voice came pleasantly into the strain of the silence. "Perhaps I could help you with your hair and your clothes. Men don't know a great deal about those things."

"Yes," said Lily Beth. "Yes, thank you."

These two went into the stateroom and Pierce turned to notice that Temperton appeared immeasurably relieved. "Your wife," said Temperton, "is kind."

"Some things a man can't do," suggested Pierce.

"Yes," said Temperton. Then he added with an irritable frankness: "It is a fiction that a man has less affection for his daughter than his mother. A damned fiction trumped up by —" He checked himself, gave Pierce a curt bow and went down the deck, disappearing into the saloon.

There was some wrangling at the landing and Pierce bent over the rail to find a middle-sized freckled individual of his own age arguing calmly with the purser who blocked his forward progress on the gangplank.

"The boat is full up. You must wait until Thursday."

"No," said the man, "that is too late. I mean to take this boat. It don't look full up to me."

"You're questioning my word, sir?" said the purser.

"Why not at all," replied the freckle-faced one. "Accordin' to your lights the boat is full. Accordin' to mine it ain't. I see space where a man could stand."

"No, sir," said the purser. "Step ashore."

But the freckle-faced one stuck to his position. "A boat's never full. Why, I could sit on top of that wagon. Room for six people on it."

"Step ashore," insisted the purser. "You are delaying departure."

"Another passenger is another fifteen dollars, ain't it? Your company is in business to make money, I'd guess. What would the agent in Portland think of a purser that didn't look to the company interests?"

The Captain put his head through the pilot-house window high on the ship and let forth a blast of language. "By God, Mr. Wynkoop, haul up that windy debate! Let him on or knock him overboard."

The young man stood fast, resisting both refusal and a quarrel. He was single-minded on the subject. He would not grow angry and he would not back up and so he stood doggedly still and cheerfully eyed the purser. He pointed a finger at the ship's upper deck. "Lots of space up there. Just look around and see for yourself."

The purser meanwhile had reached his own conclusions and now shrugged his shoulders and retired to the boat, the young man following him aboard. Deckhands hauled in the gangplank, the Captain vented a whistle blast into the brightening morning and the *Tenino* sheered out to midstream.

Pierce took position under the pilothouse wall. Sunlight moved low from the east and the day grew moderately warm. Left and right the black walls of the Cascade Range sank into dun-colored grasslands; and far ahead the silver surface of the river moved between the emptiness of a sagebrush plain. Here and there on the shore line an Indian camp occasionally lay. Blue haze slowly threaded the horizons. Near midmorning the *Tenino* rounded a bend to sight a cavalry detachment moving along a ridge, the shapes of men and horses silvered by a rising, sun-shot dust. At noon Diana Castle joined him. "It is time to eat — and now we're free." Then she gave him a quick look. "But you wouldn't understand that because you have always been free." They moved aft toward the dining room. She looked up to him as if to see how he received her remark, and changed the subject. "Lily Beth is a nice child. But some kind of trouble has locked her tongue. She looks at me as though she dared not be herself."

After noon meal they moved to the forward end of the cabin deck and watched the river turn through shallow rapids and straighten again to straight calm channels. The pulse of the engine was a hard, constant heartbeat through the ship. Far-distant hills showed blue behind the haze. "Over there," said Diana, "is Idaho, and the mines. Will you be prospecting?"

"I expect. I put in a year in the California mother-lode country."

"I don't seem able to picture you bending beside a creek with a pan. Your star is a troubled one. You have little faith in the world and almost no trust in any person." She looked up to him. "People are all better than you think."

"Not where you are heading for," he said.

She said: "I guess I owe you an explanation. It was the third man, Jeff."

"Mr. Wyatt?"

"Mr. Wyatt, who someday will be a very

52

powerful man. In his own way he is harder than you, for he wouldn't lend himself to the weakness of picking a strange woman off the street as you did. He would have said: 'Move on, girl, or I'll have you run in.' " But she immediately added in a distant voice: "Of course he would first have looked to see if she was pretty. Had she been quite pretty —"

Temperton and Lily Beth rounded the forward wall of the cabin deck. Temperton would have continued on with Lily Beth, but she paused of her own motion and stood at the rail beside Diana. It was only a small gesture yet Pierce noted a veiled expression of defeat come to Temperton. He said in his grave voice: "You'd like to stay with Mrs. Pierce, Lily Beth?"

"Yes."

Temperton moved away and in a moment Pierce strolled aft and ducked into the saloon for a cigar. The bar was crowded three-deep and smoke boiled from wall to wall and all the gaming tables were surrounded. Pierce got his cigar, meanwhile noticing both Ketchum and George Ives in another corner of the saloon; and through a temporary gap in the crowd he discovered Temperton at one of the tables. When he saw that grave face and that immaculate figure thus engaged he knew at once the man's occupation. Temperton was a gambler.

He stepped out of the saloon's reek and fell in step with a giant of a young lad who smiled on him and seemed anxious to talk. "I hear there's plenty of gold," said the young fellow. "I never mined before. Some particular way of going about it, I suppose."

"There's a matter of luck in it," said Pierce. "If you know nothing about it, day labor work will make you rich a good deal faster."

"Anna said that," agreed the young man. "She said I wasn't the fellow to be lucky. I was the one, she said, to take a sure job. I guess she hated to see me leave Buffalo."

"Who's Anna?"

"The girl I'm going back to marry when I make my stake. I'm Nick Tibault."

"Don't stay away from Anna too long," said Pierce, and drifted on. A crowd stood on the afterdeck, watching a very old man methodically put three shots into a piece of driftwood near the shore. The redhead lay on the deck, soaking up sunlight, and grinned as Pierce arrived. Pierce squatted on his heels and swapped talk for half an hour or more while the paddles churned out a steady roar and the boat ceaselessly swung with the channel, like a hunting dog scenting out a trail. The redhead had an amused flow of conversation, a wry and skeptical view of life. His name, it developed, was Ollie Rounds. Other than that bit of information, he revealed nothing of himself. His words made a screen.

The afternoon wore on and sunset flung a bitter brilliance along the water. At supper Pierce met Diana and ate with her, and stood awhile in the twilight. Temperton presently arrived and Lily Beth and Pierce left her and found a place to sleep behind the bulwark of the pilothouse. He did not see her again until late dusk the following day when, with the journey almost through, they took place at the forward railing of the upper deck and watched lonely settlers' lights wink along the shore.

"What will you do?" he asked.

"I don't know. But you're through with me when we step ashore. It was luck to find you. I won't forget. What are your plans? Or maybe I shouldn't ask. That's the rule, isn't it, on the frontier? Never ask questions."

"I don't know."

There was the briefest of twilights, so that one moment it was half dark and one moment thereafter full dark. He heard her soft laugh. "Well, we're footloose. You will not starve. You will always find something and so will I."

"You can pick your ticket. Woman are scarce in this country. Whenever you speak there'll be a dozen men to jump."

She said: "I wish you wouldn't be harsh." She gave him a steady look through the darkness. "Why should it matter to you at all?"

"No," he said, "it shouldn't matter at all. Everybody's got a life to live. Root hog or die. Take care of yourself and watch the other fellow to see he doesn't trick you. That's about all of it. I wish you luck."

"No," she said, "you really don't. You think I have thrown everything over. You have your idea of what a good woman should be and you dislike me for spoiling the idea."

Far upriver a cluster of lights broke the black. He was thinking of her with a disappointment that astonished him. It was feeling that had no proper place in him. She should mean nothing to him, yet she did.

She faced him and touched his arm. "I didn't tell you about George Wyatt. I was to have married him. That's why I ran away. Do you understand now?"

"You could have refused him easily enough, couldn't you?"

"I guess you don't understand. My father wished it, and all the relatives wished it. It would have joined two families and two firms. I liked him, but not enough. And still, I wondered if it wouldn't be sensible to put all strange things out of my head and be what everybody wanted me to be. It was very easy to be agreeable, Jeff. That's what frightened me. It was easier to marry him and be a pleasant lady than to run out in the rain and wait by Madame Bessie's house for help to come along." She fell silent, watching the outline of his face in the river dark. She held his arm, making him look at her; and he felt the swirl and rush of her feelings, the tempest which was having its way with her. "When a woman does the agreeable thing, half-heartedly for the sake of propriety and comfort, she is no better than Madame Bessie," she said. "There's such a thing as feeling that the years are going by, leaving you lost behind. I have never watched a boat go upriver without thinking I should be on it. And so I got on the boat. That's all."

"No," he said, "not all. What will you do?"

She dropped her hand and turned from him; and her hand made a little dismissing gesture and her voice was cooler than the night, and far away. "We're almost in." She turned from the rail and as he followed he had the sense that he had failed her.

They moved to the main deck and stood by as the *Tenino* blew for Lewiston and drifted half-speed to the landing. Rows of lights lay along a bluff and tar barrels burned at the landing and people came down Lewiston's main street to stand in groups; and voices carried across the water from ship to land and from land to ship, and bells jingled in the *Tenino's* engine room. The boat jarred softly against the landing piles.

"Where's gold?"

"New one over the Bitterroots! Alder Gulch! You got a long way to go, brother!"

The gangplank bridged the gap to shore. Pushed by the crowd, Pierce and Diana Castle crossed the landing and moved up an inclined road, passing touts who cried out the names of saloons and dance halls.

"The Luna House should be somewhere near," said Diana.

They went along the glitter and racket of Lewiston's long irregular street between tents and boarded buildings and rough log huts. This town was lusty, its saloons standing door to door as far as they might see. A sharp wind blew out of the Bitterroots eastward and the boat passengers, stung by the thought of gold, rushed ahead. Pierce and Diana passed a dance hall at whose doorway women stood and beckoned trade, and arrived presently before the Luna House, which was a square two-story building without paint. She stopped here and gave him a smile which, real and generous as it was, still held its shadow.

He said: "Here's your purse."

"You're broke, Jeff. Take what you need."

"I'll get along." He was troubled by another thought. "Those people on the boat will know you as Mrs. Pierce. I don't see how you'll get around that."

"They'll soon be gone to one place or another. It won't matter."

"We're in a different country. News travels from camp to camp. Wherever you go somebody will recognize you and wonder — and maybe make some guesses about your being with me."

She shrugged her shoulders. "It was something we had to do."

"So-long," he said.

One quick crease came to her forehead. She bent nearer to look at him. "Will I ever see you again? Will you be around here?"

"I don't know," he answered. "But I wish you all the luck. I really do."

Temperton and Lily Beth arrived. Lily Beth said with pleased relief, "Are you going to stay here?"

"Yes," said Diana. But she had her eyes still on Pierce as he stepped away and raised his hat and said again: "So-long."

She lifted her shoulders and made a gesture with her hands and gave him a swift-vanishing smile. Pierce moved down the street, solid against the dance of shadow and saloon light. Diana came about and put her hand on Lily Beth's arm. "Time for bed, isn't it?" She had forgotten about Temperton at the moment and didn't notice the manner in which he looked at her, then to the departing Pierce, and back to her.

Pierce slept in the hayloft of a livery barn and had breakfast in a tent restaurant on Lewiston's rambling main street. Later he bought a razor and a cake of soap, returned to the livery to shave, and presently faced the day.

Like all boom camps, this one had been hurriedly thrown together of cheap lumber, canvas and logs. Fully three quarters of the town consisted of saloons and dance halls; the rest of it was made up of stores, miners' supply houses, livery barns, restaurants, these being surrounded by irregular rows of tents and cabins. At this hour the tide of traffic was at a peak, wagons rolling into Lewiston with supplies and freight teams moving out toward the mines along the Salmon and Clearwater.

"This town," said the stable hostler, "used to take in a lot of money supplying the mines. It will be three-quarters empty by fall. Everybody's going on to the Grasshopper and Alder Gulch diggin's in Montana. That's where the boom is now."

"How d'you get there?"

"Most of the crowd's goin' the north route by way of the Coeur d'Alene and the St. Regis, through Hell Gate, down the Deer Lodge to the Beaverhead."

"How long a trip?"

"With a good horse maybe twelve days." Then the hostler said: "I can set you up with an outfit for a hundred dollars."

Lil Shannon stepped from the Luna House and stopped when she came abreast Pierce. She gave him a smile. "You're staying here?"

"Don't know."

"Never stick to a downgrade camp." She was not so much bold as straightforward.

There was no doubt of her trade, but still she was an attractive woman, energetic and brisk and self-confident. She had brown hair and soft hazel eyes and a frank manner of looking at a man. "You're no farmer. You've been in places like this before."

"Yes."

She seemed very careful in her appraisal of him; she held her interested smile. "Takes money for an outfit. Got a stake?"

"No."

"Alder Gulch is your place, Jeff. I'll stake you."

He had no idea where she learned his name but her use of it warmed him. "No," he said, "but you're all right."

"Yes, I'm all right," she said and shrugged her shoulders. "I'm leaving for Alder Gulch today." She dropped her eyes and studied the walk, and suddenly added: "Ketchum's not to be trusted, but Ives is the one to watch. You've left your wife rather alone, haven't you?" When he failed to speak she murmured "Good luck," and moved on.

He idled along the street and looked back toward the Luna in the half-expectation of seeing Diana Castle. More wagons rolled out of Lewiston. A single rider came tearing into the street and dropped from his horse in front of a building that had a small stage office sign extending from it. Ollie Rounds stood half asleep in front of the Gem saloon; and

61

grinned amiably.

At noon Jeff ate and, being restless, toured the town again. Over on the back side he saw men unloading lumber from a long line of freighters and was hailed as he strolled by. "You want a job? Pay's five dollars."

Pierce shucked his coat and moved to a wagon. A length of lumber slid down from the wagon and somebody said "I'll take the other end," and he looked around and saw before him the blond-headed young man who had argued his way aboard the *Tenino*. "Name's Ben Scoggins," said he. "You're Pierce. I heard about your run-in with Ives and Ketchum." They moved back and forth between wagon and lumber pile, gently sweating under the sun. Other wagons came up to be loaded, and moved away on the long trip to the mines. Half-through the afternoon Scoggins spoke again, as though there had been no gap in the talk. "None of these miners keep what they get. It is the trader that makes the money. That's what I got my eye on — tradin'. But there ain't no use wastin' time. Five dollars is five dollars. I can do my lookin' for the main chance at night. Ain't thrifty to be idle."

The boss came around at six to pay off. Pierce returned to wash up at the livery barn, had his supper and sauntered along the street. Night dropped and lights moved out of saloon and dance hall, and glowed yellow through tent sides; and the outbound tide of men suddenly seemed to reverse itself and come back in doubled volume, filling Lewiston brimful. Coming past the Luna House, he saw Diana Castle on the porch.

He stopped at once and showed his pleasure. She watched him without speaking for a moment and it occurred to him that loneliness had its way with her. She had been listening to the full-rounded echoes of the street with a thoughtful expression and now as her glance turned to him he noticed the softening of expression. Her smile, delayed as it was, turned her pleasant and pretty.

"What have you been doing, Jeff?"

"Getting information. Also did a half a day's work. Everybody, it seems, is headed for Alder Gulch."

"Are you going?"

"Better see what's here first."

He hunted in his pocket for a cigar and took time lighting it; and out of impulse he held up a hand to her. She came down the steps at once and they turned toward the river, slowly walking. "Anything happen for you?" he asked.

"No — not yet."

At the landing men worked at the *Tenino's* heavy cargo by the light of tar flares and wind came in from the eastern hills, brisk-cold. They swung aside, following a road away from town, silent as they walked. The fragrance of her clothes came powerfully to him, and he felt the swing of her body and even the warm tone of her personality. The road followed up a slight grade so that presently they came to a place from which they saw Lewiston lying a little below them, all its lights winking in the night.

"Why, Jeff," she said. "You're lonely."

"Yes," he said, "I suppose I am."

Her voice was gentle for him. "You always seemed very composed and self-sufficient to me."

"Always have been a lone wolf," he reflected. "I never see a lighted house at night but what I think of the people inside. They've got everything."

She spoke in a low, tentative voice: "Would you be thinking of some woman somewhere?"

"I left home when I was twelve. A woman has been something I never knew about. I'm speaking of your kind of a woman. Your kind has been to me something like the light of a star a long, long way off."

She caught her breath. "Then that is why you distrust me. The star fell and when it came near you it wasn't what you thought. You built a woman into something that never was. You are disillusioned."

He shook his head and turned down the hill with her, the softness gone; and the moment's undercurrent of nearness was gone. At the hotel he lifted his hat. "Luck," he said. She only nodded, and watched him go down toward the glowing heart of town. In a moment he entered a tent saloon. Turning, she discovered Will Temperton waiting. He lifted his hat. "May I have a word?" he asked.

She knew, of course, that he was a gambler; for his was a type of man that showed its professional signals always — the neatness, the soft, steel-like courtesy, the gentle and dead tone, the undercurrent of complete fatalism. He was one of those.

"I would," he murmured, "say nothing to offend you. If I am wrong I must ask your complete pardon. I would not presume to make any comment on your affairs except that I have a daughter and I need some help."

"You have a lovely daughter, Mr. Temperton."

"She has no mother. And I believe you've observed that there are times when I cannot help her. Not so much in the matter of dress. In other things. In being able to make her see that I would do anything on this earth for her. I can't tell her. It must be done another way." He hesitated before adding the next phrase. "She must know that I love her and would give my life for her. I do not mean that idly."

"I know."

"I believe you do. But she needs a woman to draw her out and to take the place of a mother for at least a while. She's too much alone. Probably you know my trade."

"Yes."

He was long still, struggling with his choice of words, and with his own feelings. "It is the only trade I know," he said at last. "Now you know why I take the liberty of being frank. The gentleman is not your husband is he?"

"No," she said.

"Thank you for not taking offense. I had to know. Lily Beth and I are starting for Alder Gulch tomorrow. I have arranged for the carriage and pack. I should like you to go along as her companion. It is worth two hundred dollars a month to me, or any other sum you'd care to set. As her companion. I mean nothing else by the offer."

"Is her mother dead, Mr. Temperton?"

He delayed his answer and seemed hard put. "No," he said at last. "She is not dead."

She had her quick start of feeling for the girl, and for the woman who had lost Lily Beth. This was what came to her and clung; and afterwards she discovered that she watched the big tent saloon into which Pierce had gone. "You were nice to offer this chance, but I can't accept it."

She expected him to argue. He did not. He took her decision much as he took the turn of an unfavorable card. When the card fell there was never a back-turning of it, no question and no argument. "I'm sorry," he said, and turned into the Luna House.

IV: "Take Me with You"

THE FOLLOWING night Pierce stepped into the Gem with two days' pay in his pocket and found elbow-room at the hundred-foot bar. Ten barkeeps sweated at their work and housemen scurried and ducked through the restless crowd to serve the packed poker tables, the roulette wheel, the faro layouts, the blackjack games. Inside this huge tent was a gold mine greater than any gold mine to be found in the back hills; for out of those hills men came with their dust, hungry and lonesome and eager to spend. As the shrewd Ben Scoggins had said, the money was in trading and not in digging.

Pierce got his drink, meanwhile noting here and there some of his companions on the boat. Rounds patronized a blackjack table, casually testing his luck. Ketchum stood near the doorway and stared at the crowd with his dead, wicked eyes. Ives, Pierce observed, was at the far end of the bar with a group of men he seemed to know.

He paid for his drink and slowly ruffled his remaining nine silver dollars between his fingers, now considering the cost of an outfit. A month's work at the lumberyard would turn the trick, but a month was a long time and the tide of the gold rush was in full swing. If a man stepped out of the tide he was in the shallows and all his luck went bad. Everything was luck unless, as Ben Scoggins intended, a man got into trade. Pierce thought about that too, but not for long. He was no trader. He had freighted on the long Santa Fe trail, he had tended stage station up the Platte, he had ridden Pony Express out of Julesburg, he had taken his year of action in the war and, being wounded, had drifted to the California gold-fields. He had been many things, but never a trader.

He moved to the blackjack table where Ollie Rounds was, laid his nine silver dollars before him and signaled the dealer for cards. He looked at his cards and said: "Stand on these." The dealer went around the circle and looked at his own hand, and debated and took a card. He broke himself and paid off, doubling Pierce's stake. "Play eighteen dollars," said Pierce.

Ollie Rounds said: "Luck."

The cards came around again. Pierce studied his pair and stood pat. Somebody stirred the crowd behind him and pressure pushed Pierce against the blackjack table. The dealer said: "Pay twenty."

"Pay me," said Pierce and turned to have a look at the cause of the confusion. George Ives had made a hole in the crowd with his shoulders and George Ives's face was ruddy red and his green eyes danced. "Friend," he said, "I just remembered we had a conversation."

The blackjack dealer cut in, speaking to Pierce. "What're you playing?"

Pierce turned to Ollie. "Play my stack. Play it straight through." He turned from the table again, watching the crowd give George Ives room. This Ives, Pierce considered, cut a figure in his clothes. He had a tremendous diamond ring and when he lifted his hand to adjust the flowing black tie at his throat, the gem flashed like an engine's headlight. But if he was a fop he also had a straight-grained nerve. He wanted trouble; he laughed at the thought of trouble and now stood inviting it.

"I guess we did," admitted Pierce. "You bring a good reason?"

"A fight's a fight," said Ives. "I think I can do you in."

The crowd had backed against the tent walls, sensing violence. The dealer said, "I'll pay eighteen," and Ollie Rounds answered, "Pay here then."

Pierce saw Ketchum posed like a sullen dog near the door, and then his glance returned to Ives's full-blooded face, to the man's high smile and to the dancing deviltry of his eyes. "All right," said Pierce, "here's your fun," and caught him across the mouth with a short, smashing blow.

Ives, making his stand for the crowd's benefit, had not been quite prepared. He fell backward and down, striking the packed dirt floor with his head; he rolled like a cat and leaped up and his smile came broad and brilliant through a sudden-bleeding cut in his lips. He hallooed a great shout and dropped his head a little and ran in.

He was a faster man than Pierce; he had his skill and his complete assurance. He struck Pierce twice on the head as Pierce slid sidewise and his eyes, now small and cool, measured Pierce and he struck again, catching Pierce on the neck. Pierce lifted his forearm to block these swift light blows, but they broke through his defense and cut and stung and all this while George Ives danced away and circled and jumped forward and his light eyes were half closed and very bright, and filling with cool pleasure.

Pierce stood on his heels, neither retreating nor advancing; he pivoted to face his constantly swinging, never-still opponent. His hat had dropped and his head was a motionless target and his big hands lifted and lowered to screen himself. He waited out that feinting, shifting, dancing attack and as he

70

waited he watched George Ives's lip corners pull in and his nostrils begin to spring wider from need of air. Ives darted forward, his feet making a sandpaper sound on the packed dirt floor and he caught Pierce under the belt and followed it with two rapid jabs to face and temple.

Back in the crowd a voice called: "Cut him to ribbons, George! Stand off and slice him down!" The blackjack player's voice came through the half-sound of the saloon: "Pay eighteen," and after that Ollie Rounds answered: "Pay here — and ride the stack." Rube Ketchum, still by the door, let his big shoulders fall until he was in half a crouch, watching Pierce with his empty, morose eyes.

And at that moment George Ives ceased to smile. He came to a full stop, with his breath racking in and out of his chest and he flung up his head and cried, "Damn you — come on! What are you —"

This was the moment for which Pierce waited and now with George Ives stopped he jumped forward, struck him a single, sweeping blow on the cheekbone and stunned the man in his tracks. Ives brought up his arms to cover himself. Pierce tore them down. He moved on step by step, beating Ives backward. He made a second jump and seized Ives at the chest and he lifted Ives from his feet and threw him against the tent wall. Ives stumbled and fought for balance, half bent over. Pierce caught him again and at these close quarters he pounded at Ives's face with his left hand until he saw light turn gray in the man's eyes; and he lifted him from his feet and flung him to the hard dirt floor — and stepped back.

Ives was hurt. He lay on his side without wind. His leg kept pushing forward in a kind of steady jerk and he put his free hand to his face and held it. Pierce murmured: "I told you there was no fun in this business."

Ollie Rounds cried out: "Stand still, Rube!"

Pierce now remembered the doglike Ketchum and wheeled and found Ketchum frozen in his crouch, one hand gripping the gun at his belt. Ollie Rounds had stopped that draw before completion; he had turned from the blackjack table to fling the muzzle of his revolver dead down on Ketchum. "Stand still, Rube," he repeated.

Ives came up from the floor and braced himself on spread legs. He scrubbed sweat and dirt and blood from his face with a slow pull of his palm. He lifted his chin and found Pierce. The smile was gone and the assurance was gone, so that for a moment he was dull and voiceless and not in command of himself.

The blackjack dealer said: "How about this stack?"

"Cash in," Pierce said. "We've had fun enough." He never let his eyes leave George

Ives, and now watched remembrance come to the man. The dash and daring, Pierce observed, was a thin cover stretched over Ives's character; for what he saw now — coming out through the breaks of that cover — was a ruined pride and a cruel, conscience-less greed to repair it. Yet Ives was a dissembling man; now he searched for his smile and found one ragged streak of it, and said: "I thought I might do you in, friend. You're better than I figured. But you're slow. Next time —"

"What next time?" asked Pierce.

"Always a next time," said George Ives and made a sharp turn on his heel and left the saloon. Ketchum followed like an obedient dog.

Ollie Rounds murmured, "Here's your velvet," and slid the blackjack stake into Pierce's pocket. He caught Pierce by the arm and his tone got rougher. "Come on — come on," and he moved with Pierce to the saloon's door. Out in the street Pierce stopped and felt the weight of his pocket. "What's there?"

"I ran it through the deal four times straight. Five hundred dollars. Let's get out of this. I don't like it."

They moved over the street, hearing the hum and boil of talk rise again in the Gem. Ketchum and Ives had vanished and Ollie Rounds seemed in a greater and greater haste. At the stable wherein Pierce had made his lodging, Rounds retreated into the runway's darkness and called Pierce after him. "Where's your gun?"

"Haven't got one."

"Man — man," grumbled Ollie Rounds, "what's the matter with you? Take mine. I'll get another."

"Ollie," said Pierce, "thanks."

But Ollie Rounds was already on his way to the rear entrance of the stable and his voice came back with its overriding urgency. "Think fast. They'll be back." With that final warning he disappeared.

Pierce lifted the gun given to him; he sighted it against the stable's single lantern to check its loads. The hostler, smelling trouble, had drawn away from him and the hostler called from the blackness of a stall. "I don't want a fight in here. Move on, friend. Move on."

Pierce advanced to the edge of the archway, thus commanding a view of the street. Men trafficked steadily in and out of the Gem and the other saloons and dance halls sitting side by side; and freighters rolled out of town, and more men came in from the hills to leave their dust on Lewiston's bars. His teeth ached from the beating he had taken around the face and his scarred knuckles steadily throbbed. Another upriver boat had landed and the passengers marched up from the landing and barkers ran out of the saloons and began to call, and a solitary figure paused in front of the Luna House briefly and afterwards walked forward. He was for a little while in the shadows but even then the manner of his trudging gait and the swing of his bulky shoulders arrested Pierce's interest; a moment later he crossed a beam of store light and turned over to the Gem and at that instant Pierce identified him. This was Mister Sitgreaves, plodding doggedly upon his errand of retribution.

Pierce had been holding the gun in his hand. Now he tucked it inside his belt and as soon as Sitgreaves entered the saloon Pierce left the stable and walked to the Luna House. He got Diana's room number from the clerk, climbed the stairs and knocked at her door.

The first thing he noticed, when she opened the door, was the quick look of fear that came to her face; and the first thing she said was, "What's wrong, Jeff? What happened?"

"Nothing," he said, and wondered at the impulse which had brought him here. "I thought I'd say good-by. I'm leaving for Alder Gulch."

She wore a long woollen robe which she had evidently purchased since her arrival; and her hair had been done high on her head for the night. She faced him, holding the lapels of the robe together and for a brief moment she showed him a lost and lonely expression. "I thought you meant to stay."

"No," he said. Then he smiled. "I met you

in the middle of the night. Now I'm saying good-by in the middle of the night." When he smiled the bitter-alum of his spirit vanished and left him cheerful. He had, she thought quickly, two complete sides to him, one on which the world had laid its marks of distrust and hardness, and one which remained buoyant and free. It made her say with some vehemence: "Why did you bother to come here at all?"

"Maybe," he said, "just to say thanks." Then, he gave her a keen glance. "Or maybe not. I don't really know."

She lowered her eyes. Her hair blackly glistened under the lamplight, her skin was fair and smooth and rose-colored; she had a woman's good and wide and clean-edged lips. She lifted her head and then he saw the flare of the same alert spirit which had been with her in Madame Bessie's. The same half-hidden sense of enjoyment was there. "There's nothing here for me, Jeff. Take me with you."

"Why?"

She made expressive turns with her two hands. "Everybody's going on to Alder Gulch. I don't want to be caught in another back eddy as I was in Portland."

"It is a hard trip."

"I won't complain." She watched him and saw his smile go. The change that went through him was clear enough, turning her heart heavy. "I know," she softly added, "what you are thinking. I shall be alone with you again. I am making myself cheaper." She sighed and she shrugged her shoulders. "We must make the best of it. Take me."

"All right," he said. "Meet me in the lobby in half an hour. I'll get an outfit together."

"You'll need my purse again."

"I had a little luck at blackjack," he said. He turned down the hall at once, crossed the street and ducked into the livery barn. Forty-five minutes afterwards he brought a hastily acquired outfit — a horse for each of them and a third for a pack animal — into a dark alley near the Luna House. She was on the hotel's porch waiting and came at once to him. He gave her a hand to the sidesaddle of her horse and immediately turned northwest in the direction of Walla Walla. He said: "This will be a rough trip. I want to push along fast."

"I don't mind."

"Here we go for Alder Gulch."

They camped that night in a stage station on the Old Fort Walla Walla road and next day reached the junction of the Palouse and turned northeast along a route heavily marked by travel. Two days later they were at the Spokane and here swung east, curling around the Coeur d'Alene Lake. A driving day's ride brought them into the Coeur d'Alene Mission. So far they had been in open, rolling land, and so far they had found shelter in toll-ferry houses or lone horse camps and rough taverns sprung up on the trail. Beyond the mission lay the rough and timbered heights of the Bitterroots into which the trail plunged and lifted and dodged from canyon to canyon. They forded creeks swollen by spring rain and slipped through deep mud-mire. Five days from Lewiston they arrived at the summit of the Bitterroots and came beside the St. Regis River, which moved east into a mountain valley skirted by high hills. They camped here in a slashing rain, covered by dark pines weeping dismally on them. Diana cooked supper over a fire which Pierce nursed into a roaring blaze; they made their beds on the sodden ground, wrapped in the tarps Pierce had thought to buy in Lewiston.

A great rain wind whirled over the mountains and cried and crashed through the trees. The fire soon died. The river moved through its rocky glen with a battering roar. Pierce watched the near-by shape of Diana beneath her tarp, wondering if she slept. Then he heard her say: —

"You haven't told me why you left Lewiston in such a hurry."

"I saw Sitgreaves come into town. He was the Captain's brother."

She was a yard away from him and she turned beneath the tarp so that he saw her face as a pale image in the tempestuous night. "You're not afraid. Why did you run?"

He lay still and carefully brought up those reasons which had been so clear to him in Lewiston. On sight of Sitgreaves he had known he could do one of two things — he could run or he could kill the man; and he had at once known he would run.

"Those two men were drivers. That's the way they ran the ship. But that's the way all ships are operated. According to their lights they were good officers. They figured they had to be brutal or else lose control of the crew. That's the system at sea. The Captain had to settle me or watch his whole crew go overside, for the rest of the men were the same as I was, prisoners shanghaied aboard. He missed me with his shot and I hit him. It might have been the other way around just as easily. I had luck and he didn't. I don't blame the skipper. I feel sorry for what happened to him. There isn't any mercy in the world."

Wind howled and slashed through the pines and the river beat up its cannonading roar; and the world's raw force sang its terrible hallelujah through the dark.

"This mate Sitgreaves was the same. He saw his brother die. He liked his brother and so he told himself he'd come after me. You see what's in the man's mind? He thinks right and justice are on his side. He's not a crook.

If he were I would have shot him out of his saddle in Lewiston. His conscience is clear and his law is clear to him — tooth for tooth, claw for claw. He's the avenging angel of the Lord — and it seems so right to him he'll wear himself out to do what he's got to do. I can see his point. Well, I had to shoot him or run. I ran. I do not want him on my conscience."

"What a strange mixture of things I see and hear in you," she murmured.

"Are you warm?"

"Listen to the wind tell us how great it is to be alive. Never be content with little things. The world is wide and all things are wonderful and somewhere, for every living soul, there is adventure to make his life sweet and his days good."

"The wind," he said, "is laying down the only law. The weak shall perish, just and unjust alike. Christian charity is a golden dream. The meek and mild will rule when the sun is shining and there are no wars. But when men grow flabby, and the fear of death makes them flinch back, and if the love of comfort holds them indoors, they die. You are hearing trumpets blowing, Diana. We are to arise and march. It doesn't make any difference where we're going. Nobody knows. It is the doer who alone counts, the fellow who sweats and is not afraid. The others do not count. Are you warm, Diana?"

"Yes. What is that sound?"

"A big gray lobo wolf answering the wind."

They followed the St. Regis, through little valleys and between great dark gorges. They passed Hellgate and Cantonment Wright and pursued the crooked turnings of the Hellgate River. Peaks showed white high above them in the early summer's sun and creeks whirled past them, foam-white between great boulder banks. They traveled rapidly by a steady stream of traffic moving toward the new gold strike, past wagon trains and solitary riders, past lumbering lines of supply outfits, past graves fresh-cut in the yellow clay soil; down long mountain grades thick with mud and through little valleys turning green and between the lanes of pine and early spring flowers red and yellow and white. The smell of everything around them was thin and wild, and everything was new and empty and vast. At the mouth of the Deer Lodge they swung south, here coming upon three women who traveled with a freight outfit. One of the women was Lil Shannon. She gave them a wave of her hand as they ran on. Ten days from Lewiston they labored over a rough spur of the Rockies and saw the country undulate before them in long, heavy and barren stringers. "Over there," said Pierce, "is Alder Gulch." That night they stopped in a miner's settlement and a miner's squaw wife took Diana into a house while Pierce pitched camp beside a creek.

They were not far from journey's end now, and the sense of ending was with them again, bringing its uncertainty and its strangeness. During the evening Diana came out and joined Pierce over the campfire, to match his silence with her own. When he did speak up it was to ask a question he had asked her before.

"What will you do?"

She shrugged it aside, not thinking of it. All along the route they had dropped little pieces of their individual stories so that now they knew each other better. It was of this that Diana spoke.

"How did you ever come to leave home, Jeff? You never told me."

"Six of us in the family. Four boys and two girls. My father died and my mother moved to Boston to get work. There never was enough work. One day she called my oldest brother into the house and handed him a dollar. That was about all the money we had. She just said, 'You'll have to go out and make your way. I can't keep you.' He was fifteen at the time. I remember she kissed him and pushed him out and closed the door. We never saw him again. Work was scarce and all of us were starving most of the time. My mother had nothing else she could do. When my next oldest brother was fourteen she sent him away. It went like that until there were my two sisters and myself left. One day when I was twelve I came home from school and found her waiting for me at the door. She had tied my clothes in a bundle. She had a loaf of bread and some apples in a sack. There wasn't any dollar. She just said, 'It is your turn.' She had kissed my other brothers when they left. She didn't kiss me. I was the youngest boy. She didn't even take my hand. She just said, 'Good-by.' I went down the road about two hundred yards. When I looked back I saw her in the doorway. That was the hardest moment in my life, nothing like it before or since. I wanted to cry, but she wasn't crying — she had been through so much she couldn't cry any more — and so I couldn't cry. I waved at her. She didn't wave back. She just closed the door and I went down the road."

He bent forward to poke up the fire and she saw the flame of the fire in his eyes, the bitterness on his face, the bare and depthless hurt leaping through him. "I got a job as a breaker boy in a mine, and one thing and another, drifting from place to place. Just before the war broke out I came back from St. Louis to find her. I had written a few times but the letters never got to her. She had been moving around from one shack to another. Well, I went back. She was dead. My sisters were married. Never heard from my brothers." He dropped a piece of brush into the fire and added, "It took me ten years to understand why she didn't kiss me when she pushed me out of the house. She couldn't stand to do it. It would have made things that much harder. I have since never been able to feel the troubles of other people very much. When I think of her everything else looks pretty small."

She had said nothing. Turning, he saw that she had tears in her eyes, that she had her fingers tightly together and tried to keep from making a sound. He put a hand on her shoulder. "Shouldn't have mentioned it. It is my life, not yours."

She stood up. She pressed the tears from her eyes with the end of a finger. He rose, again speaking. "Never mind. I have gotten along, and so will you. Just remember that the hand of man is raised against the hand of man wherever you go. It will save you a lot of misery."

"I wish you didn't think that," she said. "Everything else about you is good. But you will always be like that until someday you'll see that people are kinder than you think. How lonely you are!"

He smiled in a fashion that was for him rather gentle and apologetic, as though he realized what he was and could not help it and wished it otherwise. And his smile was sorry for her tears. "Never let a man make you cry, Diana."

"I can't be like that. I must trust people. I can never lock myself away from them. What is the use of living if you have nothing or nobody to live for?"

She remained before him, watching his face in the close and deeply personal way she had; and the warm light of her eyes grew and her face changed in a manner he could not describe, but suddenly she was a shape and a substance before him and a fragrance and a melody all around him, so that the loneliness that always lived in him grew insupportable. The wall he held up against the world went down; the standards he held concerning women dropped away. She was before him and there was nothing between them — no barrier of his own making and none that he felt from her. He moved ahead and put his long arms around her and, watching her lips lift, he saw that she was smiling; and so he kissed her.

There was never any completion to a kiss, never the full giving of those things in him and never the whole receiving of that mystery which lay in a woman. He pulled back, angered at himself and on the point of apologizing. But the apology faded when he saw her smile die. She was fully open to him and silently saying it. In her a great tide moved and washed away her reserve, so that she faced him and read confidently what was in him and waited without embarrassment for him to read what was in her. She touched him with her hand and said, "Jeff," and she was waiting; and that hidden sense of excitement moved into view, as though this moment was a high point of her life for which she had so long prayed.

He dropped his head, he shook his head. He stepped clear and at once the fineness of the moment went away and his earliest doubt of her came back. For a little while she had carried him beyond anything he had experienced; now that was gone and his stubborn and familiar standards moved forward. By these he judged her.

"We have been together too long," he said. "The fault was mine."

She was stone still and then the change of her expression shocked him. She looked as though he had hit her across the face. She was cold and stunned, the great fine blaze of light dying from her eyes and leaving her dull. She caught her breath and turned away, half running back to the miner's cabin.

He kicked out the fire and walked over its coals until the heat scorched his boots. He was in the sharp-winded darkness, let down and bitter. She had offered too much to a man she had known only ten days; looking at him she had made no reservations.

They were on the trail at daybreak, saying nothing. They camped that night on the Beaverhead and the next day reached the

Stinkingwater at the mouth of Alder Gulch. This was the fourteenth and last day. Turning up the Gulch they passed stage stations, filed through a rocky narrow chasm choked by teams and riders and men afoot, and came upon a settlement. The road straggled upgrade with the Gulch, along whose edges were the potholes of prospectors one upon another. Camps clung to the edge of the Gulch, strung together like beads. They came to Nevada City, followed the road over a hill and fell into Virginia City, its streets and cross-streets ephemerally marked out by tents and brush wickiups and a few board houses; they made their way to the center of town and here halted.

Pierce lifted his hat. "This is it," he said.

"Thank you, Jeff."

"If there is anything you wish me to do —"

They were two strangers face to face across an unbridged canyon; and even as she thanked him her expressive hazel eyes were cool and showed him a reserve that seemed unchangeable. "No," she said. "There is nothing more."

He bowed, replaced his hat, and moved away through the crowd. Hammers flatted steadily against the day and voices lifted and fell, and wagons made a ceaseless parade in and out of town. Alder Creek sparkled under a fresh sun and four thousand prospectors stood along it with their sluices and pans and long toms and gutted the hillside where once an old river's channel had dropped its gold treasure. Somewhere a gun went off, making a nasal complaint but drawing no notice whatever. This was Virginia City in Montana, June of 1863. Near by the Ruby Mountains and the Tobacco Roots lifted burly shoulders to the sky and civilization and law were a thousand miles away, and men of all kinds and qualities poured as a steady stream from the corners of America. Here Diana Castle and Jeff Pierce now found themselves. He turned a corner and saw a saloon's sign on a wall: JACK TANNER'S. Music from a hurdy-gurdy house adjoining came out with the shouts of customers and the calculated laughter of the dance-hall girls.

V: Evil Prompts a Man

BARNEY MORRIS came into The Pantheon during the shank of the evening and placed himself at the bar. Barney, once a merchant in Ohio, was a chunky man whose ruby face was framed in fatherly muttonchop whiskers. Barney was one of the redoubtables of the Gulch, early-arrived on the scene and the possessor of a claim straddling Alder Creek half a mile above discovery.

The Pantheon stood on Wallace Street, newly thrown together from alder logs and brush and mud. A bar skirted the edge of a dance floor on which miners broke the day's work by whirling their favorite girls at a dollar a throw. On a raised platform at the far end of the room the fiddles and guitars pitched into a quadrille with the announcer sing-songing the figures through his nose.

Barney weighed out his dollar's dust on the bar scales and got his ticket. The music came to a dead halt, the announcer cried,

"Promenade!" and the ladies led their gentlemen promptly toward the refreshments which, at fifty cents a glass, ended every dance set. The miners took their whisky straight while the ladies, to whom this was a routine part of the night's business, drank ginger beer and moved back to the floor to await the next partner and the next set. Barney at once sought out Lil Shannon, gave her his ticket and squared himself away like a wrestler.

"You've been away," said Barney. "I've missed you."

"I took a trip to Portland," said Lil. "How's things?"

"Fair," said Barney.

"You've got a fortune out of that claim, Barney. Don't tell me."

But Barney was close-mouthed about his affairs and although Lil Shannon was an old friend he only grinned. Lil said: "Written to your wife lately?"

"Sure. She sent me a tintype of Bill the other day. Tall as I am now."

"Barney," said Lil, now completely serious, "you've made your stake. Don't stay here too long or the toughs will knock you over the head some night."

"Going home," said Barney, "in a couple months. Been away from Ohio two years. Kind of feel the need of my people."

The announcer yelled: "Gentlemen, claim

your partners!" The music moved into a waltz time and Barney, grim as death about this business, seized Lil Shannon and whirled her around, stamping his boots at every second swing. The room grew warm as all these black-burned men, stained with the yellow clay of the diggings, shaggy-haired and short-tempered, wheeled and collided and wheeled. The ladies were all accustomed to twenty dances a night and deftly maneuvered beyond the heavy feet of their partners. Lil Shannon laughed at Barney's dead-set expression and the steady motion of his lips as he counted the waltz rhythm. She wore a red gown laced with gold and her cheeks were rose and her brown eyes sparkled; and, turning around and around, she saw Jeff Pierce standing as an onlooker near the door.

"Barney," she said. "See the tall man with the poker face? His name is Pierce and he's new. I came up the river on the same boat with him. He had a quarrel with Ketchum and Ives at the Umatilla House."

"That pair came in yesterday. All the roughs are comin' in. This will be a mean camp, Lil. Your tall man's got nerve."

"Bump into him tomorrow and help him locate a claim," suggested Lil. "If he waits another week there won't be a yard of unstaked ground left."

"What you helping greenhorns for?"

"When I like a man," said Lil, "I like

him a lot."

"That's right. You're a big nugget in the creek, Lil."

"He knocked Rube down. That makes him all right."

The music quit and the announcer yelled: "Promenade!" Barney escorted Lil to the bar, paid for the drinks, and made his answer. "I'll do it for you."

"And you pack up and go back east. Everybody knows you got a heavy stake. It is getting tough for a man to ride from here to Bannack without being held up."

"Don't let any man make a soft touch out of you, Lil," said Barney.

"When I like somebody," said Lil, "I'm all for him." Pierce, she discovered, had gone, whereupon she turned to the dance floor and smiled at a small, young prospector who marched toward her with his ticket. A second miner moved in at the same time and brushed the small one aside with a straight-armed jab. "I'll dance with Lil," he said. The small man caught his balance and swung with a white, wicked smile. The big man had even then turned his shoulder to the little one. The little man brought up an arm and smashed it across the back of the big man's neck and dropped him to the floor. He gave his ticket to Lil and softly said: "Mine, I think."

"You're pretty fast," said Lil.

The young man said: "A runt like me learns

that first off. Fast or dead.''

Having spent a year in the California diggings, Pierce took time to study this new camp, and on the second day he left Virginia City and walked up the Gulch in the direction of Summit Camp. The trail followed the creek's edge, around piles of gravel and shaft holes and tents and brush shacks. All along this way men crouched with their pans, slowly dipping and slowly rocking. Back from the creek other men had staked the dry bars, here shoveling up the soil in buckets and carrying it to the water; farther up the hill, men scraped away topsoil to reach gold-bearing gravel deposited by some earlier riverbed. On every hand were to be seen the various contrivances for extracting gold from rock and dirt — the pan, the rocker, the sluice box with its riffles, the long tom. At one tent a string of washing hung on a line; before a brush hut somebody had tacked up his particular whimsy: "Mountain Home." A lone man walked down the Gulch, selling single sheets of month-old paper at a dollar a sheet.

Half a mile from Virginia City, Pierce came before a signboard containing the rules of the district, and stopped to read: —

The officers of this district shall be President, Recorder, Judge and Sheriff.

The center of the stream shall be the line.

Every person may hold, by pre-emption or purchase, two creek, bar hill and lode claims, and no more, but no person can pre-empt more than one kind.

Creek claims shall be fifty feet on the creek, extending across the creek from base to base, including all old beds of stream.

Gulch claims shall be 100 feet in length, on the gulch, and extend one foot over on each side.

Lode claims shall be 100 feet on the lode and twenty-five feet each side.

He was in this attitude when a voice turned him about, and a muscular, middle-aged man with a ruby face stood by: "You're the one that knocked Rube Ketchum down?"

"Yes."

"All this creek's staked, clear up to Bald Knob. There's a little canyon next to my claim, though, that ain't been claimed. Everybody rushes by, lookin' for gold to pop out like sunshine."

Pierce said: "You make a living locating claims for greenhorns?"

"Why to hell with you. I'm Barney Morris and I'm doin' you a turn. You knocked Rube

Ketchum down."

Pierce smiled at that. "Thanks," he said, and walked away from the creek with Barney Morris. A hundred yards onward the Gulch wall opened into a small dry draw. Morris said: "That's it."

"No water."

"You lug your pay dirt down to the creek. If it shows good color you can bring a flume down from the head of the creek."

The draw lay narrow between yellow-gray walls with a few dead alders standing fire-blackened on the low side. Pierce said: "Looks like a canyon I ran across down near Hangtown. I found a skeleton in that one."

"None here yet," said Barney Morris. "This is a young camp." He pointed to his own stakes at the edge of the canyon's mouth. "Start from here. You get a hundred feet. You go up both slopes to one foot over each ridge." He was aware of Pierce's thoughtful study, and so said: "You're a disbelieving young man. You don't know about this."

"Something for nothing is a bad bargain," said Pierce.

"You braced Rube Ketchum. That counts."

"Thanks again. I'll stake it."

"One more thing," added Barney. "Keep your mouth shut about what you got in your dust pouch. Always play poor."

Pierce paced a hundred feet up the draw. He built a pile of rocks at this point, climbed the side of the draw and made another rock pile under which he put a slip of paper with his name. After that he established the other corners of the claim and scanned the general lay of the ground without much excitement. Gravel was beneath a shallow layer of soil; and that gravel had to be taken bucket by bucket to the creek for panning. He would put some kind of shelter at the head of the draw but he would dig his first test hole at the foot of it. What he needed was a shovel and ax, a pick and a pan and a supply of grub.

Then, always aware of the sudden accidents and treacheries of life, he looked again at the spot he had picked for his cabin and observed that it was fully exposed to a man who might lie on the canyon ridge with a gun. This kind of thought always came clear and quick to him, born of his own particularly hard struggle for survival. He shrugged this reflection aside and returned to Virginia City, his first chore being to register his claim.

Afterwards he had a meal in a tent restaurant and moved to a store for his supplies. Everything in this camp had come by freight team through difficult country, from distant Salt Lake, or from faraway Fort Benton, or from Lewiston, which was a thirty-day haul. A shovel and ax, a pick, a pan, a lantern and a gallon of kerosene, and enough staple food for a week cost him sixty-five dollars. He paid fifty cents for three small apples, slung his supplies over a shoulder and lugged them down to a stable where he kept his horses.

There was no let-up in the steady stream of men pouring over the small hill into Virginia. Ox-teams and freight strings choked the half-formed streets and goods lay piled everywhere and carpenters flung together boards and two-by-fours and lifted building fronts in the space of an hour. A string of cattle, herded in from across the mountains, milled in half stampede through the congested, cursing traffic, and the owner of the tent restaurant ran out to the street with a rifle, to shout at a passing herder: "A hundred dollars for the first cow that runs in front of me."

The herder wheeled around. "Sold," he said. The restaurant man pulled up his rifle and took sight on a leggy beast careering around the corner of the Pantheon; he dropped it at his feet with one shot.

Pierce moved on, eating the last of his three apples, and met Ollie Rounds in front of Tanner's saloon. The redhead had a cheerful smile for him. "Wondered what happened to you. What are you doing?"

"Up the creek on a claim."

Ollie Rounds was amused. "You work too fast. Stop once in a while, my friend, and just loaf."

"Luck," said Jeff Pierce, and moved back to Wallace in time to see Diana Castle cross to the tent restaurant. The sun had dropped beyond the hills and the mountain country's quick twilight rolled blue and thin through the Gulch. When he came near the restaurant she discovered him and stopped. She had, Pierce thought, a pleased expression, as though all this was what she had hoped to find. She gave him a moment's attention, turning serious. "Have you had luck?" she asked.

"Yes," he said. "I staked a claim."

She nodded and entered the restaurant. Pierce got his supplies from the stable and returned up the Gulch.

The tent restaurant was nothing but a series of planks set on wooden horses, with drygoods boxes for chairs. One man served and one other man, sweating and cranky, worked over a stove at the rear. The meal was beans and bacon and bread and coffee, and the price was a dollar. Dessert was stewed prunes dipped out of a stone crock. Being hungry, Diana ate without complaint. There was never enough of anything in a camp like this. These men, hungry from work with gold in their pouches, took anything and everything offered, but there was never enough.

Rising from the table she remembered what

her father had once said: "Back East, where everything is settled and hardened into a pattern, people have forgotten how to be resourceful. Out here that's the main thing — to keep a sharp eye for a chance, and to seize that chance at once."

On impulse she turned to the rear of the tent and stood by the cook. "Why don't you make pies? Men like pie."

"Because," said the cook, never ceasing his rapid moving between stove and serving table, "I ain't got eight arms. I never was much good on pie anyhow."

"You've got flour and dried fruits."

He said: "Can you make pies?"

Her father's remark seemed right in her ear, freshly spoken, She said: "I'll come here in the morning after the breakfast rush. I'll make your pies for a dollar apiece."

"Stove's not big enough. I cook all day."

"I'll get another stove and put it outside the tent."

He said: "That's a bargain. You do it."

She left the restaurant happier than she had been for days. This was something she could put her hands to and this was a part answer to the question Jeff Pierce had repeatedly asked her: "What will you do?" She would do this. She would do anything that was within her ability to do. There was a place in this camp for a woman as well as for a man. For a straight woman. Going down the street, now a black lane through which the lights of saloon and dance hall and store made yellow flickering stripes, she smiled to herself and felt the goodness of the curt night air. Turning the corner of Wallace she came against Will Temperton. "Where's Lily Beth?"

"In bed. We made a long drive to get here today and she's tired. We're camped outside of town." He gave her a thoughtful appraisal. "You seem contented."

"I have found something to do. Tomorrow I begin making pies for the restaurant."

"You are pleased with that?"

"I'm pleased with anything I can do."

He nodded and seemed to understand. "I had thought to find better quarters. A tent is not much good for a young girl. The town is crowded."

She said: "I have a log house near the foot of the hill. I simply talked a miner out of it. If you propose to stay here let me have Lily Beth for a while."

"You have changed your mind?"

"Yes," she said. "But it will not be quite the same as you suggested. I want nothing for this. We'll see how Lily Beth and I make out together. Perhaps I can teach her to make pies." She was smiling at the thought, and again the deep sense of pleasure showed in her eyes. Temperton watched her with his grave, restrained glance. "She would like it a good deal," he said. "I'll bring her to you in the morning." He lifted his hat and added: "I must find some way of making this right with you."

Ollie Rounds stepped into The Pantheon, paused to locate the prettiest woman and bought his ticket. When the new set began he moved to the floor and claimed Lil Shannon. Most of these miners danced with a kind of grim fury but this man, smiling with his detached amusement, took her fashionably through the waltz. Somewhere he had seen better company than this. But, although she recognized background and breeding, she made no remark concerning it, for in this camp were a thousand men whose pasts were made up of sin and error and broken ties from which they fled and of which they wanted no reminding. It was the first thing a woman in a dance hall learned.

He said: "I might tell you how greatly you are wasting your talents here, but I think I won't."

"Why not?" asked Lil Shannon.

"There's too much sober advice in the world. I was brought up on duty and steady inculcations of usefulness and virtue. So now I find the world well lost for frivolity. I have no desire to leave monuments behind me. A fine day to live in, a meal to enjoy, a little drink and the pleasure of a pretty woman. What else is to be asked for?"

He was an engaging man, she conceded to herself, but these ready talkers and these smiling men hid much; mostly they hid from themselves. When the dance ended he escorted her to the bar and paid for drinks. "That's a handsome dress," he said. "If I were owner of a well-filled poke I'd scatter dust on it. It would make a pretty glow."

"Don't let it trouble you. I have made fifty cents from the dance. We're even."

He gave her a sudden intent look. "You don't like me, do you?"

She was a diplomat. She smiled at him and turned away. "I thought you didn't believe in being serious."

He left the dance hall and stood awhile with one shoulder against the wall of Jack Tanner's saloon. He lighted a cigar and savored its fragrance, at the same time realizing she hadn't liked him at all. She had seen through him, as he so constantly saw through himself. He moved the cigar between his teeth, summoning back his air of detached amusement, and turned into Tanner's. He ordered up a drink, remembering that he was close to the end of his money; and he watched the game tables and plunged a hand into his pocket and found a five-dollar gold-piece. He found a spot at the blackjack table and put his money into play. The big, lean man had turned this trick at Lewiston; maybe he too could turn it. He took his two cards and scanned them. He said: "Hit," and watched a king fall, which broke his hand. He shrugged his shoulders as he stepped away. Luck was a crazy thing which a man had to endure without comment.

Rube Ketchum came into the saloon and paused against a wall and at once Ollie Rounds pressed himself inconspicuously into the crowd and laid his glance on the man. Rube was clearly on the hunt and presently Rube's roving eyes settled on a small miner half drunk at the end of the bar. The miner was at the moment shaking dust out of his pouch to the bar scales; and when he had done that he rolled through the crowd and left Tanner's.

Ollie rounds slipped out of the saloon, knowing that Ketchum would soon be following the miner to waylay and slug him. He saw the miner turn from Wallace Street and fade into a part of town scattered with tents. Rounds quickened his stride, crossed Wallace's dust and skirted the tent restaurant's back side. Now running on his toes, he made a quick circle of the nearest tents and paused. Rube Ketchum would be soon coming up, and time got short. He touched the small gun in his pocket, but he did not draw it; and he placed himself close to the edge of a tent, hearing the miner thresh uncertainly forward. The man was talking to himself in a reasoning way, he was saying:

"Now Tom, turn here and you're all right."

As he passed the corner of the tent, Ollie Rounds stepped behind him, threw a forearm around his throat and flung a knee against his back. The miner made a short cry and began to twist, but by then Ollie had pulled the poke from the miner's pocket. He gave the man a long shove and whipped about, racing between the tents and at last coming behind a stable on Van Buren Street.

Here he stopped until his breathing had settled. He pulled his coat together and stepped into Van Buren Street, entering the nearest saloon. He took his drink quickly, and as he raised his head he saw himself in the back bar mirror, and at once turned his head away.

VI: Test of Strength

PIERCE CUT alders from the top of the draw and rolled them downhill to make his hut walls. He laid brush over the walls, layer on layer interlaced, and stretched a tarp across the brush for roof. He made a bunk frame with a pole bottom, using grass and sage stems for a mattress, and tacked an empty box on the wall for his groceries, adding a door to it to keep the packrats away.

This was the work of one long day, first dawn to late dark. Sitting in front of the cabin after supper, he faced the Gulch with its lamp and lantern light aglitter and aglow from Virginia City to the farther bend near Summit. Sound came out of the town like the steady simmer of a boiler fire and even by night the tide of travel never completely stopped. Wagons went by, and single travelers; and there were men calling out the names of other men. The mountain air, soft by day, now grew keen as wind drifted down from the Tobacco Roots.

Next day he moved to the bottom of his claim and dug aside a small section of top earth. He filled a bucket with coarser subsoil and moved to the creek. Squatting in the water, he swung and spilled the gravel from the edges of his pan, working the residue down to black sand. In that first pan he had one pea-sized nugget and a scatter of colors. Barney Morris came over and helped pan the rest of the bucket. "About a dollar," Barney said. "When you get a little deeper you'll find it runs better."

"I'm going up the side of the ridge and cut in," Pierce said. "Looks like the river might have banged up against the rocks and laid down a deposit."

"Might have been," agreed Barney Morris. "You'll find pockets in this country some-times. Maybe a patch a foot square just as yellow as the bottom side of a hound."

Pierce dug his holes in a line across the gulch and up the side of the hill. He made little dumps beside each hole and worked the dumps one at a time and that day made four dollars. After dark he went into town, bought a gold pouch, a wheel for a barrow and a twenty-foot plank. He worked until midnight to rig up a wheelbarrow. One wheelbarrow of dirt was the same as eight buckets and saved him that many trips back and forth to the creek.

The next day he wheeled his load to the creek and panned throughout the morning. Men came by in continual file, a freighter passed with a load of lumber for Summit Camp. He struck a good streak and made eight dollars in three pans, and remembered that this came from a hole halfway up the gulch wall. The rest of the barrow didn't hold much. It went like that, fat streaks and lean streaks. In the middle of the afternoon a horseman pounded through the Gulch on the dead gallop, shouting out his news: —

"Dillingham's dead! They caught Hayes Lyons and Buck Stinson and Charley Forbes! They're going to be tried right away! Go on down there!" He batted his hat across the horse's ears and rushed on.

It produced a general rush in the gulch. Miners left their rockers and long toms and sluice boxes, and headed at once for town. Barney Morris came by Pierce, who kept at his panning. Pierce said: "Who's Dillingham?"

"One of Sheriff Plummer's deputies," said Barney Morris. "And a square lad, too."

"Who're these other three fellows?"

"Charley Forbes is a loafer. Hayes Lyons is a damned scoundrel. Buck Stinson is one of Plummer's four deputy sheriffs, and a crook. You going down?"

"No," said Pierce. "Didn't Plummer know Stinson was a crook when he made him deputy?"

"Why," said Morris, "I suppose he did. But it is kind of hard to get a man to carry a star around here. Except for young Dillingham, none of the honest ones cared to risk it. So I guess Plummer appointed these hard eggs — the other deputies, Gallegher and Ned Ray, are crooked too — on the idea it was the best he could get."

He moved away with the crowd. Pierce resumed his work and was for the rest of the afternoon almost alone in the Gulch. He had finished his supper when the miners returned from Virginia City. He sat in front of his shack, watching cook fires spring up and shine on the creek. There was, he thought, less talk than usual among the men. Barney Morris came out of the darkness to squat and make his report.

"Young Dillingham was in the recorder's tent helping Doc Steele write out some mining records. Doc Steele's President of the District. Forbes and Stinson and Hayes Lyons rode over from Bannack. They came up to the tent and Lyons hollered out they wanted to see Dillingham. Soon as he left the tent they opened up." Barney Morris scowled as he recollected it. "Then Jack Gallegher popped up from somewhere — he's one of Plummer's deputies, like I told you, and no damned good either — and took these three fellows into custody. I don't doubt he was on their side but he had to make a show to the Gulch like he was doin' his duty."

"What was it all about, Barney?"

"Dillingham was a square deputy, like I said. The other three — Gallegher and Stinson and Ray — ain't. They got him for some reason." He had a short pipe. He clenched it between his teeth and sucked vigorously on it; he slapped a heavy hand on his knee. "We'll go hang 'em for it. Trial started today. Doc Steele and Doc Bissell and Sam Rutar are judges. You be there tomorrow to vote on the right side. Those scoundrels have got a lot of friends."

"I'll be there," said Pierce. He was still thinking of Plummer, though, and made mention of it. "Strange that a sheriff would pin stars on fellows like that."

Barney Morris rose. "Far as I know, Plummer is an honest man, but if I was you, son, I don't believe I'd air my opinions much. This is a tough gulch and it may get tougher. You be there in the mornin'."

Pierce was. At nine o'clock he found himself in Virginia City, surrounded by a thousand men from the other towns strung along the Gulch — Summit and Virginia and Nevada and Central. They filled Main Street, they moved to the hillside above the street and sat like gallery fans on the rocky points. The three doctors, Steele, Bissell and Rutar, were on a dais made by a wagon hauled crosswise of the street. Stinson and Hayes Lyons were being tried together, and at present their advocate was harking his impassioned plea into the warm day. Barney Morris nudged Pierce. "Two sheets in the wind now. Used to be a lawyer somewhere in the East."

When the defense attorney rested, Ed Cutler, a blacksmith appointed prosecutor for the occasion, got up and spoke less than a minute. They were, he said, guilty beyond the shadow of any reasonable man's doubt. It was cool murder, nothing less. They should be convicted and they should be hung. That was all. Steele, spokesman for the judges, rose on the wagon seat and had some trouble speaking because of the sudden ripple of yelling and hard-called defiance from the friends of Stinson and Lyons. Guns flourished here and there. Steele waved his hands. "You've heard the testimony. You're the jury. What shall we do?"

The discontent of the accused men's partisans was swamped by a prolonged roar from the crowd. "Hang 'em!"

"Get the rope ready!"

"Where's Forbes — put him up for trial now!"

"Guilty!"

There was obviously no need of a more formal means of determining the verdict. Steele turned to the men nearest the wagon box. "Biedler, get a party to set up a gallows and to dig two graves. Keep these prisoners under guard. Bring up Charley Forbes for trial.''

Appointed deputies led Stinson and Hayes Lyons away. Stinson shouted his passionate curses at the crowd. Hayes Lyons was laughing. Barney Morris noted that and spoke of it. ''He don't figure we've got the nerve to go through with it. These toughs have gall.''

The defense attorney now rose to make a long plea for Charley Forbes, bearing down on the fact that Forbes had cried, ''Don't shoot,'' at the very moment the firing had started. It showed his will in the matter, the defense attorney said. As a point of fact, he went on, Charley Forbes hadn't fired. His gun, reclaimed by the court, had all its loads intact.

''Sure,'' grumbled Barney Morris. ''Some friend of Forbes sneaked in and reloaded it after the shootin'. An old stunt.''

But the crowd, having gone through a morning of drama, grew better-natured. The toughs and sympathizers in the street began to set up a cry for pity and fair play, against which Ed Cutler talked with less effect. Afterwards young Forbes stepped to the edge of the wagon box and made his own appeal. He had a good voice and he had a frank air. He spoke of his family, he admitted minor sins and was ready to admit his waywardness, but he denied the murder and spoke for mercy. When Doc Steele got up and said: "What's your verdict, gentlemen?" the crowd was clearly for acquittal and shouted it. Forbes lifted a hand at the crowd, slid down from the wagon and at once vanished. Within three minutes Jeff Pierce saw Forbes, mounted on a horse, swing into Daylight Grade and ride over the hill.

Meanwhile X. Biedler had returned with his work party, having erected a gallows and dug two graves. Doc Steele silenced the crowd with his hand and said in a deep, slow voice: "I sentence you, Hayes Lyons, and you, Buck Stinson, to be hanged," and descended from the wagon. He made his way into the crowd, visibly moved by the responsibility he had been through. The crowd was restive again, shifting and turning and unsettled. Men began to move through it, loudly calling for "Fair play," and for a new trial. One man broke a trail with his shoulders, swinging his gun in the air. "They won't hang Hayes and Buck while I've got breath!" Somewhere else a sudden commotion sprang up. Pierce stood up on a pile of lumber in time to see Rube Ketchum make a dive at a miner and swing with his fists. Surrounding men moved in, throwing Ketchum back. Ketchum drew his gun and swept a clean circle with it until he stood alone. "Don't touch me, anybody," he said. "Don't touch me. I'm a friend of those fellows. To hell with you yellow ditch diggers!''

"Rube," called an even voice. "Rube, put up the gun." Lifting his eyes, Pierce found a man lying flat on the scaffolding of an incompleted house with a rifle centered on Ketchum. "Rube," he repeated, "put it down and be civilized or I'll fumigate you."

A party of miners drove a team and wagon forward. Biedler and some others boosted the two sentenced men aboard and made a rank around them. "All right — all right," called Biedler, "clear the way. No use taking all day on this." The miners spread and the wagon pitched slowly down the slope toward the gallows constructed at the foot of the street.

Silence moved into the town, through which rose the steady beat of a hammer operated by some industrious man who ignored this high drama. Stinson grasped the side of the wagon, shutting his jaws together so tightly that the hard bone ridges turned white. Woman from the dance halls scrambled up the hillside for a fairer view and one man's voice called: "So-long boys. It's a damned shame!"

Hayes Lyons, who had laughed at them all, now let out a great, choked cry that went up through the silence like a strangled gasp, and suddenly a woman on the hillside began to scream. "Let them live! Don't hang the poor boys! Don't kill them!"

It set off a tremendous crying and moaning

among the women. Men began to grumble. A tall, lithe figure leaped to a wagon wheel and wrenched at it; he threw himself into the wagon and seized the reins, bringing the team to a halt. He waved a piece of paper at the crowd. "Let me read this letter Hayes wrote to his mother!"

"Go ahead!"

"Read it — read it!"

Watching this man closely — for it was George Ives — Pierce saw him show deep emotion as he lifted the letter, and cleared his throat: —

"Dearest Mother:

I am writing you on my last day on earth. I have been condemned to be hung for a shooting scrape here — something that God knows I repent with all my heart. I guess I went blind crazy. I know I am causing you the greatest grief of your life and if I have not broken your heart before this with my wild ways I expect this will break it now. Tell my sisters that I love them dearly. Tell my brothers to stay away from cards and liquor. I wish I had it to do over again so that I could follow your dear teachings . . ."

The dance-hall girls were crying in steady, increasing volume. One of them raced down the slope and fell and got up again and pushed through the crowd. She dropped in the dust by the wagon. "Hayes," she cried, "I'll give my life for you! Hayes —"

The crowd, slowly flooded by this cataract of tears, found a shamed and half-hearted voice. "Hell," said a man, "let 'em live."

"Give him a horse and let him go to his mother!"

"Let's have another trial!"

"No — no! Don't waste no more time. Let's take another vote."

"Another vote!"

Biedler stood grim and formidable on the wagon tongue. "You voted already!"

"Take another vote!"

Biedler tried to speak, but the gathering sentiment swept him away. All he could do was stand and stare. A man got up on the wagon and asked for silence. "All in favor of hanging, walk up the hill. All in favor of letting them go, walk down the road."

"What the hell's the use of walking up a hill?"

The cries of the women continued on, wild and passionate, and hard on the nerves. Men screwed up their faces at the sound of it; and men openly cried. Confusion increased around the wagon. George Ives still faced the crowd, gravely holding up his hands in appeal. A self-appointed committee drew another wagon beside the first and a spokesman stepped before the crowd. "Everybody that wants a hanging, go past the outside wagon to be counted! Those against will go past the inside wagon!"

The crowd found this a simple procedure and moved in mass toward the wagons. Barney Morris pushed his way toward the outside wagon and wigwagged at Pierce to follow. But Pierce stood fast. From his place on the lumber pile he saw the crowd swing heavily past the inside wagon and knew that these two toughs would be free. Men, having voted once, slipped through to be counted a second time. A few minutes later Jack Gallegher, Plummer's deputy in the Gulch, sprang up to a wagon seat and yelled: "They're free! Let 'em go!"

Lyons and Stinson jumped from the wagon and were immediately surrounded by their supporters. The woman who had groveled in the dust now laughingly arose and seized Stinson's arm and the dance-hall girls on the hill ceased their wailing and composedly marched toward town. The play was over. Pierce smiled one dark short smile and joined Barney Morris. George Ives made his way through the crowd, grinning to himself. He winked at Barney and said cheerfully, "We skinned that cat, old man," and afterwards he caught sight of Pierce and instantly the cheerfulness turned cold. The memory of a defeat came to this arrogant man and the memory stung him. He put his long stare on

Pierce; he said, "You're here," and abruptly he wheeled away to join Stinson and Hayes and Gallegher. These four now marched loosely toward Tanner's saloon, surrounded by their partisans. Meanwhile the crowd, surfeited with drama, slowly moved away.

Biedler came up to Pierce and Barney Morris. Biedler was a stocky Dutchman with a bulldog face and a capacity for black anger. He was full of it now, and savagely exclaimed: "They cried for a pair of scoundrels! I wonder if any of them remembered to cry for Dillingham?" He had a shotgun in his hand. He banged the butt of it on the ground and he pointed to the gallows at the foot of the street and ground out his observation. "There stands a monument to defeated justice."

Other men gradually joined this group. A tall fellow with a dense black beard arrived and Barney introduced him to Pierce. "This is A. J. Oliver, Jeff. This is Jeff Pierce."

"The gentleman," commented Oliver, "who knocked down Rube. I heard of that."

Presently W. B. Dance came forward with a man of lesser height. This one wore a short set of chin whiskers on a dark, dreaming, melancholy face; and he had a kind of silence that was as effective as speech. He stood by, carefully listening, and now and then when other men turned the talk his way he only nodded or shook his head. Pierce observed that the group seemed to value his presence.

In a little while this meeting broke apart and Pierce strolled through Wallace with Barney. Barney was in a thoughtful and depressed mood and from time to time shook his head. "An honest man can't expect much from now on. The toughs are in the saddle. They know it, too."

"It was a touching scene," Pierce dryly observed. "They're smart people, Barney, and it is the smart people who run the world."

"Too bad — too bad," said Barney.

Tanner's, when they passed it, was in full swing. Pierce murmured: "The victors are celebrating." Neither of them said anything more during the half-mile walk up-Gulch. Pierce went on to his cabin, cooked supper, and sat outside the doorway in the dark, enjoying a cigar. Riders traveled the Gulch and all the sounds of men drifted clear and full through the bland summer night's air. Long later, around ten o'clock, he heard the advancing scrape of a man's feet and he rose and stood back against the cabin wall until he identified Barney Morris. Barney said in a dropped voice: "Let's go inside, Jeff."

Jeff followed him into the cabin and closed the door. He lighted a lantern and turned on Barney, now observing Barney's extreme gravity. "Ketchum passed my cabin a little while ago," said Barney. "I know what that means. They think I've got money, and now they're bold. I've got to leave."

118

"Bunk here," said Jeff.

"If they're of a notion to get me, they'll do it sooner or later. No, I've got to leave." He took out his pipe and made a business of filling and lighting it. The match was steady in his hand but he was, nevertheless, in the grip of fear. It showed on him. "I'm a marked man, Jeff. I can't ride from here to Bannack without being held up. I can't get on a horse and pull out tonight, either. They're watching. I'll have to sneak off afoot. Maybe I can reach Bannack. Maybe I can get beyond Bannack. Then I'd fall in with some freight outfit on the way to Salt Lake and I'd be tolerably safe."

"Want help, Barney?"

"Yes," said Barney Morris, "I do. Whether I make it through or not, I want my dust to get through. The family can be comfortable on what I've dug out of this country. I'll give you a hundred dollars to carry it to Bannack for me. Nobody's watching you yet. You haven't been here long enough to have any money. So you can ride as you please. Take the dust to Bannack and leave it at Oliver's stage office. I'll start walking tonight. I'll pick the dust up at Bannack, if I have the luck to get there."

"All right, Barney. But I don't want your hundred dollars."

"Why, son, I thought you disbelieved in sentiment."

"I don't believe in anything very much, Barney. But you did me a favor."

"That's more sentiment than you figure," said Barney Morris. He moved to the lantern and turned the wick until the room was half dark. He reached into his coat pockets and hefted out six gold pokes and tossed them on Pierce's bunk. "That's my stake, Jeff. Forty pounds, more or less, of sweat and trouble — and not as much fun as I thought it would be. I been away from my family too long. Now listen to me. You tell Oliver's agent that if I don't show up in Bannack three days from now to send it on to Mary Morris, Centerville, Ohio."

"I'll think of you under your fig tree in Centerville," said Jeff.

"I like people around me," said Barney Morris. "I don't like to be alone. If I had it to do over again I'd never have left my family. The money ain't worth it. Well —"

"Luck," said Jeff.

The older man nodded. He watched Pierce a moment, hiding his sentiment, then turned back to his own tent. He lighted his lantern in his tent and hunted up a pencil and paper and composed two letters. One was for his wife, which he sealed and put in his pocket. The other was a will, upon which he spent considerable time. Afterwards he gathered his belongings, though he took nothing that could not be comfortably carried in his pockets.

He wished, as he trudged down the Gulch, that he knew more about Pierce. Out in a country like this a man depended almost entirely upon himself, and so took little trouble to study others; therefore when a man really needed help he had to make a quick guess and trust in faith. It always came back to a matter of faith. No man was sufficient unto himself, but out here nobody knew that. The strong were proud and didn't understand. It was the weak and the needy who understood. It was too bad he could not pass on to Jeff Pierce his own wisdom in the matter; for the young man was sound and needed only something to soften his hardness.

He struck the back side of Virginia, circled to the camp to Doc Steele's tent and scratched on it. The judge's light was burning, and the judge called out: "Come in."

"Sorry to trouble you," said Barney. "Here's my will. If I show up missing the next few months this is what I want done with my claim."

The Doctor looked grave. "What's up, Barney?"

He had known Doc Steele as long as he had known any man in the Gulch but he could not break his attitude of secrecy, and now only smiled. "Just a matter of forethought. The toughs feel mighty strong. Those two fellows ought to have been hung."

"Yes," said Steele, "they should have been."

"Good night, Doc," said Barney. He left the tent, turned between the rows of brush wickiups and tents along the margin of town, and so arrived at the road which climbed Daylight Grade. Later at the top of the grade he stopped to take his bearings. Central City was a quarter mile forward, through which this road ran, but he struck into the hills to avoid the town and at last left the Gulch entirely. As he climbed the rough slopes he had certain inexpressibly regretful thoughts. He was an old, played-out man longing for his people, whom he might never again see. The sense of adventure had gone sour, the game had turned bitter.

There was a man in Virginia City known as Clubfoot George Lane, a shoemaker who set up a bench in whatever niche the town afforded and did his work and took his rather low spot in the community without comment; and this man, nighthawking through the town, saw Barney Morris go into Doc Steele's tent and later come out. Clubfoot followed until the latter faded beyond Daylight Grade, then went limping toward Tanner's saloon as rapidly as he could. He found Ketchum and passed on his information; ten minutes later Ketchum, Steve Marshland and George Ives moved over Daylight to the crest, and rode the Gulch steadily downgrade toward the Stinkingwater. This was the route to Bannack, and no matter what detours Barney Morris made he would eventually have to come out of the hills beyond the Stinking-water or the Beaverhead.

VII: On the Bannack Road

AFTER EARLY breakfast, Pierce saddled his horse and turned down the Gulch with the six heavy gold pouches tight-rolled in a slicker lashed behind the saddle. A brilliant sun rose from behind the Tobacco Root Mountains, turning the land to first gray-gold; and early as it was the road held the steady-risen dust of travel. He passed horsemen and single men hiking, and strings of freighters drawing high-piled merchandise, and now and then a fancy woman driving a light rig through morning's cool. From Central onward the road was a continuous noisy street connecting all the towns as far as Junction, where Alder and Granite Creeks met. Beyond Junction the canyon grew narrow and rugged to Daly's Roadhouse on Ramshorn Creek. Here, fourteen miles from Virginia, the road passed from the Gulch into the Stinkingwater's small valley, ran past Cold Springs Ranch and reached Baker's Ranch. At Baker's he found

Ben Scoggins resting in the shade of a wagon and four-horse team.

"Why, now," said Scoggins, "I'm pleased to see you again. Where you at?"

"Up the Gulch, near Virginia."

"Virginia's where I'm going," said Scoggins, equably. "After you left I did some trading around. Got this wagon and these horses. Knew I could sell anything in this country. It was just a matter of what kind of goods I could make the best turn on. I got sardines."

"Whole wagonload?"

"Four thousand cans. Sort of a tasty article a hungry miner would buy any time. No waste space — you can crowd a lot of sardines in a wagon. I'll start up the Gulch and I'll just holler as I go. Dollar a can."

"Luck," said Pierce, preparing to go.

"I never bank much on luck," answered Ben Scoggins. He lifted his gray-blue eyes, his shrewd and humorous eyes. "Your wife — she's here?"

"Yes," said Pierce, and went on.

Beyond Baker's he forded the Stinkingwater and arrived at Dempsey's, which was a stage relay point. The road, nothing more than a pair of ruts in the hard earth, lifted from the Stinkingwater to low bluffs and ran westward over a series of barren undulating hills. North of him at a distance stood the McCarty Mountains, across which he had come with Diana Castle a few days before. Southward the Rubys lay high against a brilliant sky. The air was thin and rich with grass smell. Fourteen miles from Stinkingwater he skirted Copeland's Ranch on the Beaverhead, and continued to Stone's. Here he stopped and ate noon meal in the roadhouse bar, loafed a comfortable half-hour, and forded the Beaverhead. At three o'clock he came into Bill Bunton's ranch, another relay point for the stages. This was on the Rattlesnake; and Bunton, a long and slack man, came out of a corral to give Pierce a careful sizing-up.

"How's the color of Virginia?" asked Bunton. "I hear it is rich dirt."

"Fair, I guess," answered Pierce. "Just came in myself. This the road to Bannack?"

"Yeah," said Bunton. "Ten miles down that way." The man's eyes inquisitively rummaged Pierce, his horse, and his gear. "Business in Bannack?"

"Just looking around," offered Pierce and moved on. A quarter-mile down the road he swung in the saddle to observe that Bunton was still watching him.

The road, moving southwest, took the easy way through a bare dry country of shallow gulches and dry streambeds, through sage and short grass and scattered rock. Pierce struck a creek marked with prospect holes and gravel pile, and turned with it, so coming into

Bannack around five that evening. This town had been a year or more established and once had held a considerable population. Born overnight of a gold strike on Grasshopper Creek, it had recently surrendered its vitality to the newer camps in Alder Gulch.

A sign identified Oliver's stage office, but Pierce, not wishing to make his mission too obvious, drew up before Durand's saloon and went in for a drink. A hotel stood next door. Going to it — with eight thousand dollars standing at the curb on the back of his horse — he washed, had supper and came to the street to light and idly nourish a cigar while twilight arrived and the citizens of the town sat along the walks and Durand's saloon began to grow noisy. One gentleman, nicely dressed and with a round face marked by a well-kept mustache, came past him and looked at him, half sharp and half pleasant, and strolled on.

He finished his smoke and rode to the stage office, which still remained open. He unfastened the thongs holding the slicker, carried it inside and rolled the six heavy gold pouches on the counter before a clerk.

The clerk's reaction was somewhat odd. First glancing at the open doorway, he quickly hauled the gold pouches from the counter and carried them to a safe.

"I'll take a receipt," said Pierce. "That belongs to Barney Morris. He is to claim it as soon as it arrives. If he doesn't arrive within three days you're to ship it to Mary Morris, Centerville, Ohio. You got that?"

The clerk wrote out a receipt in a flourishing, upright hand. "Barney's on the way now?"

"Started last night."

The clerk gave Pierce the receipt. "You're leaving town soon?"

"I'll wait for Barney. He should be along."

"If I were you —" said the clerk, and closed his mouth upon the rest of his advice. Somebody strolled down the walk and turned in; and the neat, round-faced man who had earlier passed Pierce now came forward. He had black clothes and a white shirt and a string tie carefully put together, and he drew out a cigar and smiled on both men pleasantly. "Nice evening, Harry."

"That's right," said the clerk.

The man turned to Pierce. "I don't think I have met you. My name's Henry Plummer. I'm Sheriff of Bannack and Fairweather."

"Pierce," said Jeff, and offered his hand. The Sheriff's grip was light and quick. He found another cigar and presented it to Pierce. "I have been giving these out rather freely the last few days, having just been married. From Alder Gulch?"

"Yes," said Pierce.

"Hear you had trouble over there. Dillingham was a fine boy. Makes it difficult for me to know what to do about Stinson. One of my deputies, you know. Hard to believe he'd do a thing like that unless his hand was forced. Boys over there released him, so I guess they figured he had something on his side."

"Suppose so," agreed Pierce, adding nothing, offering nothing. The Sheriff's hazel eyes scanned Pierce with a light and searching attention. He was smiling and he was cordial. "If there's ever anything I can help you at, let me know," he said, and left the stage office.

The clerk took up his pad and fell to writing in the same steady, up-and-down hand. He seemed busy. Pierce lighted the Sheriff's gift cigar and looked down at that traveling pen. The clerk was writing, over and over: "Montana — Montana — Montana." Pierce pulled smoke into his lungs and blew it out. The pen made a steady scratching echo in the silent room; outer sounds moved in. The clerk looked up with a brief irritation. "Something else?"

"No," said Pierce, and left the office.

He was on the dark side of Bannack's street. He moved through these shadows, leaving a wake of cigar smoke behind. Durand's saloon, directly across the way, was an eruption of light and confusion. Men came steadily into town. The Sheriff was ahead of Pierce and now he crossed the street and came

129

back with every mark of indolence; he stopped at the saloon and looked through the doorway awhile and seemed to debate with himself, and at last went in. Pierce halted and leaned a shoulder to a wall. A woman and a small girl passed him and swung into a store; three riders entered town, rounded before Durand's, and dismounted. When they faced the light from the saloon's doorway, Pierce recognized Ketchum and Ives. He didn't know the third one.

He remembered that his horse was still standing by the stage office; and he had forgotten his slicker. He grunted to himself and moved back. When he stepped into the stage office the clerk pulled up his head and for that one slim interval Pierce saw fear unsteady the man. A wagon came clacking into the street. Pierce got the slicker and turned out with it; when he reached the sidewalk he noticed the wagon had stopped near by. Two men got off the seat and came to the tail gate and other men moved forward from the night. Somebody said: "What you got, George?"

"Dead man."

"Where'd you find him?"

"Four-five miles out in the brush, short-cutting over from the Rattlesnake."

The two lifted the dead man from the wagon and brought him to the walk. Pierce found himself on the outer edge of the crowd, and used his shoulders to push through; looking down, he saw Barney Morris lying there, a bullet hole passing through his head, temple to temple.

One of the men said: ''Better call Plummer.''

''Why,'' said one of the men who had brought Barney Morris in, ''a dead man's just a dead man. You call Plummer.''

Another figure pushed into the circle. ''Hell, that's Barney Morris. He used to work a claim next to mine, down Grasshopper.''

Plummer was at this moment coming out of Durand's saloon. Pierce withdrew from the crowd and stood at the sidewalk's edge with his head pulled down by his quick and angered thoughts. He moved to his horse, got to the saddle, and rode to the street's end, here pausing. Plummer had come into the circle. Pierce heard him say: ''That's Barney Morris, one of my best friends!'' The crowd grew. Looking beyond it, Pierce noticed Ketchum and Ives and the third man paused at the doorway of Durand's. He touched his spurs to the horse and went on out of Bannack at a trot. The horse was stiff with his day's work and had little run left in him and kept falling back to a walk, and had to be spurred. He passed Bunton's and near midnight came to the Beaverhead. Here he made a dry camp well away from the road.

Ives patronized Durand's bar with Steve Marshland and Ketchum until the crowd came back. Some miner said: "Old Barney had a lot of money and never spent any. He had a good claim on Alder. I heard once he had fifty thousand buried."

"Not a dime on him now."

Ives looked wryly at his empty glass and put it aside. He said to Marshland and Ketchum: "Come on." The three of them left the saloon and walked as far as the corner of the hotel. They turned down a side street, saying nothing. Half a dozen houses fronted this side street; beyond that was a corral and a shed and the slope of a bold hill. The three stopped at the shed and leaned against it. "This the place?" asked Marshland.

"Sure," said Ives.

Boots cracked against loose rocks on the other side of the shed and a shape circled the shed's corner, lightly advancing. The shape stood before them, medium and slim — and Henry Plummer's voice said: —

"All right?"

"No," said Ives. "He had nothing on him but a single eagle."

"He wouldn't leave the country without his dust."

"Maybe he sent it out by express."

"No," said Plummer. "Clubfoot's watched Barney all the time. Barney didn't send it that way." He remained still, doing his own calculating. "But there was a man in here tonight who stopped off at the stage office. He carried a slicker into the stage office. It appeared to be heavy. When I went in the slicker was open on the counter."

"Tall man?" said Ives.

"Name was Pierce. You know him?"

"Yes," said Ives, "I know him."

"It is probably in the stage office then," said Plummer calmly. "But we can't afford to touch it there. We'll wait and watch. I'll handle that. You boys go back to the Gulch."

"Where's Pierce now?" asked Ives.

"Haven't seen him around," said Plummer. He turned away. A few feet off, he paused to say, softly. "About Pierce —"

"I'll take care of him," said Ives.

Rising before daylight, Pierce made the long run into Virginia City by three o'clock. When he reached Wallace Street he saw Steele. The Doctor hailed him.

"Where's Barney? I saw him last night and he seemed in trouble."

"Killed on the Bannack Road last night."

The Doctor showed some amount of shock. "He knew it was coming. Come to my wickiup. I've got something for you."

Pierce left the horse and returned to Steele's tent. Steele got a huge Bible from a box and opened it, producing a single sheet of paper. "This is what Barney left with me last night," he said.

I, Barney Morris, sound of mind but uncertain of the future, am about to leave the Gulch and go to my home in Ohio. I ought to be in Bannack tomorrow night. If I am not I can be considered dead. In which event I empower the judge of Fairweather District to make the following disposition of my claim, Number Fourteen above Discovery. This claim is to be given to one Jeff Pierce, he to have it entirely, to work it fitly and in proper season; he to send half of what he pans out to my wife, Mary Morris, Centerville, Ohio. BARNEY MORRIS.

VIII: The Wild Bunch

THE FIRST shacks and tents in the Gulch began near the junction of Granite and Alder creek. As soon as Ben Scoggins reached this spot he stood up in the wagon and began to sing out: "Somethin' fancy to go with beans and bacon! Sardines straight from the Coast! Dollar a throw! Come and get it!"

As he had shrewdly judged, there was never enough of anything in a new camp. Men came out of the creek at him; they ran down the hillslopes. Tying down the reins to the brake handle — the horses moving and stopping and moving — Ben disbursed sardines from the tail gate all the way up from Junction settlement. He was sold out by the time he topped Daylight's ridge and looked down upon Virginia City. In his pocket and in his pouch he had four thousand dollars more or less in gold and coin and dust. This was the middle of the afternoon with sunlight making a pretty sight of Virginia and the upper Gulch. He was a blond young man standing in the wagon with his hat brim jiggling as the wagon took the grade, smiling a rawboned smile at a good and just world; and even in smiling, not forgetting to cast a competent glance at the possibilities around him. Coming into Wallace, — driving his outfit through the congestion of other wagons and lumber piles and loose horses, — he paused by the scaffolding of an incomplete structure. There was a man standing by with the attitude of business about him, whereupon Ben Scoggins, always with a mind to business, hailed him.

"Need any haulin' done?"

The man turned as though struck. "Yes," he said. "There's a whipsaw outfit working over near Bannack. What'll you charge to freight lumber here?"

"How far's Bannack?"

"Seventy miles."

"Two days each way. Four days a round trip." He gave the man a swift size-up. "Hundred and fifty dollars."

"Good God," said the man, then shrugged his shoulders. "Everybody's so damned crazy about digging they got no time for day work. All right."

"All right," said Ben Scoggins, and drove on. To himself he added: "Might as well be workin' while I'm lookin' and listenin'. Never hurts to keep busy."

He had turned into Wallace Street and now saw Diana Castle coming out of the tent restaurant. He lifted a strong whoop into the day. "Well, you're here!"

"Yes," said Diana, smiling because he smiled.

Scoggins reached under the wagon seat and pulled out four cans of sardines. "You got a birthday coming?"

"Next December," she said.

He said, "Happy birthday," and presented her with the sardines. "Where's the tall, hungry-looking fellow?"

"Up the Gulch on a claim."

He noticed she left off smiling when Pierce was mentioned. There was something out of order here; whereupon he covered up the awkwardness by going easily on to other things. "Nice day — nice year. Well, nice. See you again." He cut around Wallace into another street of tents, heading back toward Bannack. Near the edge of town he passed a blacksmith shop and got a call from a man there.

"Want to sell that outfit?"

"Whoa," said Ben Scoggins. "Whoa." He braked the wagon and settled on the seat. "I'll sell anything, any time. Buyin' and sellin's my trade. What you offerin'?"

"What you want?"

"No," said Scoggins, idle and innocent, "you set a figure."

Fifteen minutes later he had concluded a deal. By this time the open-air transaction had attracted half a dozen idle men, one of which was Ollie Rounds. Going inside the stable — which was a log house with a brush roof — to consummate the sale, young Scoggins gravely winked at Ollie Rounds. In a little while he came out of the stable. Rounds joined him and they walked on alone. "You're here, too," commented Scoggins. "Got a claim?"

"Never liked to shovel," said Ollie Rounds. "Every time I see you, you're dickering."

"The idea," said Ben Scoggins, "is to pass a dollar back and forth a lot of times. Each time, of course, gettin' a little bit of the dollar to stick. Business is mighty simple if a man remembers that. If he don't remember it, everything's complicated."

"Trouble with that idea," said Rounds, "is that if a piece sticks to everybody pretty soon the dollar is all gone."

"Ah," said Scoggins, "that's where you're wrong. A dollar is like a shovel or a machine. A man uses it to make something. Then he passes it on and the next man makes something. By the time it gets around the circle it has left a lot of new things behind it. And it is still a dollar. That is all you got to remember. But some folks don't have the knack of usin' a dollar to make things with."

Both of them laughed. "Bound to get rich,

ain't you?" said Ollie Rounds.

"Wouldn't wonder."

Ollie Rounds quit smiling. He gave Ben Scoggins a direct look. "Then don't pack your money in your hip pocket, Ben. This is a tough camp."

Scoggins searched and weighed Ollie with his candid glance. "You always got an ear out for that sort of thing, Ollie. I thank you for the warnin'. But," and he added this in a careful way, "it would be better for you not to take such an interest in the shady side. Someday it might sort of draw you down."

"Always liked to see what goes on beneath the surface — the things other people do not see."

"Sometimes," gently reflected Ben Scoggins, "it is better not to look in that direction." He went down the road and up over Daylight grade. Striking through the sinuous and lusty course of the Gulch, he reached Junction at twilight and, as he had expected, found a line of newcomers camped beside the creek. He picked out a wagon and found its owner. "Want to sell?" he asked.

At full dark he had made his deal. Possessed of a new wagon and team he continued down the Gulch, not really remembering he had no supper. The day had been good and profitable. Now he struck out for Bannack, his cheerful whistle making an uneven bouncing echo on the narrow rock walls of the lower Gulch.

Ollie Rounds returned to Tanner's saloon and stood at the bar to enjoy his before-supper drink. The big tent now began to fill and the poker tables were all operating. Marshland loitered near the door. Ketchum and George Ives sat in a game, and Will Temperton dealt at another; and it was on Temperton's unbreakable front that Ollie placed his interest. Everything struck that grave, steel-smooth face and slid aside without making impression. He was a sad man whose sadness, Ollie thought, came from his own defects of temper. Somewhere in Temperton, as in himself, there was a wire down, so that all his life was out of rhyme and badness and good-ness warred. Men were like this. Only once in a rare while did Rounds find someone in whom the purposes of living were clear and uncomplicated and sweet. Those men he envied because they had something he did not have, never would have.

Ketchum and Ives came to the bar for a drink. Ollie Rounds took his second whiskey and shook out dust from his gold pouch to pay for it; and left the saloon. He went down to the tent restaurant and had supper. Coming out, he saw Diana Castle leaving the back side of the restaurant with Lily Beth. Lily Beth had on an apron and there was a streak of flour in her hair; she looked tired but she looked contented. Ollie Rounds, who had a way with people, drew a smile from her and fell in step beside Diana.

"That was good apple pie I had tonight," he said.

"I made fifty-three today. Forty apple, ten apricot, three prune."

"Get a little tired of wrestling over that stove?"

"Why should I be tired?"

He smiled without his usual irony. "I guess it is the way you look at the world. Whenever I do something I keep asking myself, 'Why should I be doing this? What's the good of it?' And then I quit working." He gave her a quick glance. "Why are you working?"

"It's nice to be alive, Ollie. Nice to be free and able to make your own way. And it is wonderful to feel you're in the place where things are happening, and you're part of all that's happening."

"What's happening?" he said. "Just people going around and around."

"No, Ollie. Here are people who have rushed from the ends of the earth. They're working and cursing and fighting, swimming rivers and being lost in storms, and laughing, and being killed; and writing letters at night to their people back home. Some of them are lonely, sometimes they're afraid, sometimes ashamed of the things they do, but still they grit their teeth and take their punishment and go on. People who sit still in their houses grow stale and weak. These men, bad as some of them may be, are really alive. Why, you can hear the stamp of their feet all the way back to the Atlantic.''

He slowly shook his head. "Wish I could feel like that. And I hope you always feel like that.''

They had come to her log hut at the edge of the camp. Lily Beth reached out and took Diana's hand, and these two stood at the hut's doorway, grave and silent and together. Diana said: ''Now we've got to put the washtub on the stove. It is bath night.''

"Hear about Jeff?''

There was a lessening of the warmth of her eyes, a tightening at the edge of her mouth. She seemed to harden herself to what he might say. "No,'' she said, "what is it?''

"The road agents didn't find any money on Barney Morris because Jeff carried it through to Bannack. The road agents have got Jeff marked for that.''

She said in clipped words. "I'm sorry. He deserves to be let alone. He wants to be let alone.''

Ollie Rounds lifted his hat and moved back toward the sparkling, confused heart of camp. He slid through a line of freight wagons, cut around a blacksmith shop and reached the lower end of Van Buren Street. A pair of men stepped out of a space between tents, and one of them said: "Hold on, Rounds," and he jerked around and saw Ives and Ketchum before him.

Ives said, "Walk along with us, friend."

"Maybe — maybe not," Ollie Rounds answered. He was rooted in his tracks. His eyes turned blacker and his face grew thin; he held his stiff smile against them. "What for?"

"No harm," said Ives and stepped beside him. Ketchum was already at Ollie Rounds' other elbow; and the pressure of these two men moved him forward along the walk. They passed through the shuttered lights, they moved out of the heavy crowd. At the foot of Van Buren, in the shadows, Ives turned.

"You been flashing a poke in Tanner's, friend. You're no miner. I'd like to see that poke."

"No," answered Ollie Rounds, "I guess not."

George Ives said: "Don't be tough. You recall what happened to Barney Morris?"

"Go ahead," retorted Ollie Rounds. "Use your gun. You'll have a crowd on your neck."

"What crowd?" asked George Ives. "What crowd came when Dillingham fell? What crowd tried to stop Lyons and Stinson when they rode out of town? You're wrong. This town is ours and nobody touches us. Let's see that poke."

Ollie Rounds looked carefully at these men.

George Ives had an expression of lazy, idle interest on him; he was pleased with himself and he was amused at Rounds's resistance. But Rube Ketchum, savage and brutal to the core, without scruples or conscience, instinctively a hater of everything, showed greedy desire. Rounds recognized that glance and knew he was in great, immediate danger. He lifted the poke from his pocket and weighed it in his hand. His thoughts were swift and calculating; he balanced his life in his mind and suddenly made his choice and gave the poke to Ketchum. As he did so he took a slow, easy step backward. It went unnoticed. Ketchum dropped his head to look at the pouch, and George Ives turned half around, also to look.

"That's the pouch, George. The fellow had it in Tanner's other night."

Ives said, "How'd you come by this —" and turned, and quit speaking. Ollie Rounds had his gun lifted on both men.

Surprise and irritation went in ruffled waves across George Ives's face, and afterwards it smoothed carefully out. Ketchum's eyes flared wild instantly and he seemed to strain against his caution.

"I saw Rube watching him in the saloon," said Rounds. "When he went out, Rube started after him. I got there first. Hand the poke back."

Rube stretched his arm, half length, and his

body dropped perceptibly, in the attitude of tension. Rounds murmured: "Pull out of that, Rube. Nobody'd be sorry to see you dead. I'd be glad of the chance to drop you. I'm no easy miner. I haven't got a drop of pity in me and when it comes to rough-and-tumble I know as many tricks as you. Maybe" — and his voice had a dry, swinging tune — "I'd better do it now. I think I'm going to have to watch you. You damned cannibal."

"What's that?" said Ives, now interested.

"You don't know about Rube?" said Rounds. "The man got caught in a blizzard up on the Snake and ate his partner."

Ketchum's eyes glowed and grew dark, and glowed again. He was a black, burly man with no good in him. The smell of blood was about him, like the bad odor of a beast. His rage remained, furious and inhuman and inburning. He never spoke. It was Ives who said: —

"He means what he says, Rube."

Ketchum straightened and extended his arm full length with the poke. Rounds took the poke and put it in his pocket. "All right," he said. "All right."

"Now I'll say my piece," put in Ives, still the calm master of himself. "You've cut in on our game. You're an outsider."

"Always liked it that way," said Ollie Rounds.

"It won't work here," said Ives. "This

Gulch is for our crowd to work. A man that ain't in our crowd just can't operate."

"So far I'm doing well enough."

Ives held his attitude of amusement. "Listen, friend. There's forty men up and down this Gulch I can drop a word to. You don't know who they are and you can't watch 'em. When I say the word, you're dead before breakfast."

"You're the boss, then?" said Rounds.

"I'm the boss in this Gulch," answered Ives.

"All right," said Ollie Rounds.

George Ives gave Rounds a prolonged stare. "You're cool, friend. You might do well with us."

"I'd do well wherever I find myself," said Ollie Rounds.

"Yes, I think you might do well. Keep the poke. It is chicken feed."

"I'll keep it. I'll keep whatever I take."

"That's all right, too," said George Ives. "A man must look out for himself. But when we move as a bunch you'll do as you're told."

"I don't mind," said Ollie Rounds.

"Then it is settled," said George Ives. "There's a little meeting tonight down the Gulch. We'll all ride down."

"My horse is around on that side street," said Rounds, and turned with Ives. For a moment he had his back to Rube Ketchum, and a stark chill raced up his back, and he turned at one jump and saw Ketchum in the act of drawing. He had not yet put away his own gun, and now brought it down on Ketchum's head in a rapid side blow. Ketchum dropped into the dust, and rolled. Rounds took a full jump toward a building wall, and whirled again, laying the muzzle against George Ives. Ives hadn't moved, had made no gesture of offense.

These two exchanged long, steady stares until at last Ives spoke, showing his first anger. "What the hell are you about?"

"Watching my hole card, George."

"I said it was all right, didn't I?" flashed out Ives. "If I say it, I mean it. You don't have to watch me, or any of us. I will pass the word along."

"Him?" said Rounds, nodding at Ketchum.

"Rube," said Ives, as he would have spoken to a dog, "cut it out. You hear me — cut it out." He swung back to Ollie. "Now don't let me catch you pointing that thing on me any more. I'll meet you down Daylight."

Rounds turned through the tents and got his horse from the stable. He moved rapidly to the bottom of Daylight Gulch and he left the road and watched it closely until he saw Ives and Ketchum come along. When he was certain of them he moved out of the dark. Ives laughed softly at the maneuvering. "You're sure ticklish, friend."

The three of them rode to the summit of

Daylight, looking down upon the sinuous glitter of Alder's continuous lights. Ives said: "We'll split and ride on, one by one. Pete Daly's roadhouse is the place. Come right on — we're going to be late." Then he looked at Ketchum, who was a silent lump in the saddle. "Rube," he said patiently, "behave yourself." Then he rode away. Five minutes later Ketchum moved after him. A short time later Ollie Rounds followed.

He had been in the Gulch three days and in that time he had seen the constant tide of miners and camp followers roll up the course of Alder Creek and crowd along the dry walls. It went on without the least slackening, hour after hour, by day and by night. Going down the Gulch now, he pressed through this continuing wave of advancing men, on foot, on horse, by wagon and packtrain and freight outfit. From Daylight, on through Central, Nevada, Adobetown and Junction, there was scarcely a gap in the steady procession. The stores and saloons of the settlements were wide open and crowded, the sound of voices never faded, the lights of camp and tent and hillside fire burned endlessly on. In the soft wind and in the thin Montana air was a slugging pulse of excitement.

Past Junction he fell into the narrows of the Gulch. Now and then a fast-moving horse struck up sparks from the stony footing; and now and then some man's voice hailed him through the black. Fourteen miles from Virginia he came out of the Gulch at Ramshorn Creek and reached Daly's Roadhouse, a two-story building built of riven logs and chinked with mud mortar. Twenty or more horses stood in the shadows before the place; the door was closed and three men seemed to guard it. He came up to find Ives and Rube Ketchum waiting for him, and Ives introduced him to the third man. "This is Red Yeager. Everything's all right, Red. This is Ollie Rounds."

They stepped into a barroom which took up most of the lower floor and faced a considerable crowd. Some of them he recognized at once. Tanner — the saloon man from Virginia City — was in a corner. Clubfoot Lane was here, and Jack Gallegher who was Henry Plummer's Deputy Sheriff in Virginia. He identified Hayes Lyons and Buck Stinson, and he nodded at Steve Marshland. A few others he also knew by name, having had them pointed out to him in Tanner's saloon — Alec Carter and Bob Zachary, and Frank Parrish, and the surly one who was Boone Helm. There wasn't, he thought in idle amusement, an honest man in the crowd. In three days he had absorbed a good deal of camp gossip.

They seemed to have no fear of surprise or recognition. They had all the confidence in the world. George Ives moved around the room with Rounds, introducing him here and there. Ives, Rounds gathered, was one of the chiefs, for he had his unmistakable way with them. He was a slim man, clean-shaven in a group that went heavily bearded or mustached. He had quick eyes and he had a brain that was fertile, and he had a bold self-confidence.

Daly, the owner of the roadhouse, seemed not to be one of the crowd, for presently Ives told him to leave; and the Irishman went at once, as though relieved. Then Ives called: "All right — all right."

A back door had opened, and silence came to the crowd. Swinging about, Rounds discovered the Sheriff, Henry Plummer, at that door. The Sheriff came in, closed the door, and gave the room a short and thorough glance; and his eyes stopped on Ollie Rounds and stayed there, civil and speculative and very alert. Ives said: "It's all right, Henry. This is Ollie Rounds."

Plummer had apparently ridden over from Bannack in considerable haste. Dust was on his clothes and at the edges of his dark hair. He wore a fine black suit and white shirt; he had the manners of a gentleman and his voice was very smooth. He had a small, trimmed mustache and his face was round and on the soft side. Nothing about him revealed the mark of a desperado, and Rounds, never a man to be surprised at the turnings of life, found himself mildly surprised at Plummer.

Plummer said: "I can't stay long. I want you to listen to me."

George Ives tapped the bottom of a whiskey bottle on the table. "Order here. Bunton — Sam Bunton — shut up."

Sam Bunton was at the bar, both arms clinging to it; he was drunk and he was angry, and he slowly cursed the bare wall behind the room. Ives moved over to him. Ives dug a thumb in Bunton's ribs. "Shut up, Sam."

Bunton reared and swung. He said: "Where's my brother? He'll stand by me. Where's Bill?"

Bill Bunton came out of a corner, lank and sour and close-eyed. "Sam," he said, "cut it out or I'll break your damned neck."

"All right," said Sam Bunton, and stopped talking at once.

Plummer was cool and smooth in the middle of the room. He studied Sam Bunton and then gently said: "You get drunk too much, Sam. I want you out of this country inside of twenty-four hours. You hear me, Sam?"

"I've got a good claim up the Gulch, Henry. Why should I leave it?"

Plummer intended to speak again, but Ives spoke for him. Ives turned on Sam Bunton with a swift flash of violence. "You heard it. Twenty-four hours."

"Yes," said Sam Bunton. "All right, George."

The other Bunton — Bill — stepped away

from his brother. Plummer turned to face all these men. "Dance and Stuart will be starting a store in Virginia City pretty soon. It will be a place where most of the miners come at one time or another. Probably the express office will have space there, too. It will be a fine place to overhear what's going on, who's got money to be shipped out, who's flush and who's not. Clubfoot, as soon as that store is up you ask Dance for a little corner in it to put up your shoe shop. You can keep your ears open and hear a lot. By the way, I understand you're spending a lot of time in Tanner's saloon. Keep out of it. It pegs you."

"All right," said Clubfoot.

"I don't want you boys to gang up in one spot too much. It makes things too plain to the Gulch. Jack Gallegher will stay in Virginia City, of course. Ned Ray and Stinson will work out of Bannack. Bill Bunton sticks with his ranch on the Rattlesnake. Now we will split our crowd. Ives, Steve Marshland, Johnny Wagner, Alec Carter, Whiskey Bill Graves, and Rube Ketchum will headquarter in the Gulch." He pointed a finger at Rounds. "You will be there too. The rest of you men are roadsters, working between the Gulch and Bannack."

He watched these men with his calculating far-off thoughts. "The Gulch is rich. Men will be coming out of it with dust all summer, all year. Keep your ears open, all of you. No doubt some of these people will try to get their dust through by fooling us. It has been tried already. We have got to know what's going on. Any man that talks against us we must take care of at once. Little things make big things. Destroy the little things and that's the end of the big ones. One more thought. I won't be around the Gulch much. I'll spend my time in Bannack. You boys in the Gulch take your orders from George Ives."

He was obviously in a hurry. Now he came over to Ives and said a short word, and turned to Rounds. He offered his hand — a light and swift grip and a quick withdrawal — and he put the full power of his hazel eyes on Rounds. He said in his courteous way: "I hear you're all right." And then he dropped his light warning. "We all work together. And we don't back out. Glad to see you." He turned over the room and left Daly's, his horse soon drumming the road. Somebody called for Daly to come back and the bar grew busy and men filled the tables and began to play poker. Red Yeager, doorkeeper, came in. Rounds walked to the door with Ives, and stopped there. Ives pointed to the knot in his own neckpiece. "See that. It is a square knot. All the boys make that tie. It is a sign among us. If you should ever get in trouble you have only to say, 'I am Innocent.' That is a sign, too."

Rounds shrugged his shoulders. "Very

153

bold. Suppose I should talk? I'm a stranger to you."

"No," said George Ives, "you won't talk. We'd find it out. Nothing happens in the Gulch we don't find out. Anyhow, you're in this for what you can make, ain't you?" Then he slapped Rounds on the back and gave out a long ringing laugh. "Suppose you did talk. Who would believe you?"

"You remember I gave Pierce a hand in Lewiston. That makes no difference to you?"

He thought he saw the memory of that affair slice through Ives. But the man had a wonderful front and carried himself well. "I remember. But I don't mind. You play your game your way. You've got your tricks and your connections. So have I. That is the way it is done. You make a grandstand and it puts you solid. Nobody knows you're in this. That's what you want, isn't it?" He gave Ollie a steady, extremely close inspection. "You're thinking it is funny I trust you. I do not trust you. I trust nobody. But it doesn't matter. The more the merrier and you won't stray. I like smart people. I think you're smart." And now, coming closer to tap Ollie lightly on the chest with a finger, he significantly added: "You might be a friend of this Pierce, but first of all I've got you sized up as a crook. In a pinch you'll turn down Pierce for a profitable deal. It is all right, Ollie."

Somebody kept calling for Ives and he

turned away, again laughing. Rounds went out to his horse and moved homeward.

As he rode he turned over in his mind all that he had seen and heard, and marveled at it; and for a moment a thread of fear drew through him as he thought of his own position. There were times when, in common with all fatalists, he had his strange dark-lighted intimations of the future, and foresaw a grisly ending. This came now, and went away, and his natural carelessness made him once more confident. He began to whistle, and heard the echoes come wavering back from the narrow-placed walls of the canyon.

IX: The Jungle Beasts Growl

BY NIGHT the revels of Virginia City rolled up-Gulch in warm waves of sound; yet for two weeks Pierce never left the boundaries of his claims.

At times he was his own great puzzle, troubled by the lack of order in him and the lack of meaning in the world around him; and when these times came a black cape seemed to envelop him in blind bitter solitude, to make him feel as though he were the only living thing on the planet, with all the forces of the earth, impersonal and relentless, seeking to destroy him. It was a game of survival — one man against the gods. Survival was the one hard and fast law.

Now and then, in his unguarded moments, he caught the vague intimations of other patterns of life and when that happened he put his whole mind to the search, reaching out and out to capture those elusive things that might be. For a moment he heard the sound of them and caught the shadowed color of them; afterwards they vanished, to leave him more thoroughly alone with his dominating memory of the destruction of his mother and the scattering of his people by the brute savagery of the world.

It was this memory which made him hate the forces pushing against him and, hating them, resist and defy them. To survive.

He threw himself into his work single-mindedly, rising before light came to the Gulch and falling asleep long after night dropped down. This was the only way he knew by which to dissipate an energy which drove him so hard. Some of the prospectors along the wall of the gulch got together to build a flume which would carry water from the upper creek along the face of the Gulch shoulder and thereby do away with the hard job of packing pay dirt to the creek. He joined them and built the flume to his own side-canyon; he rigged up a sluice box, shoveling pay dirt into the sluice and turning water from flume to sluice. At the end of the week, when he cleaned out the riffles at the sluice box, he had five hundred and forty dollars of dust.

During the second week he moved over to work Barney Morris' claim. This was an obligation. The dead man's hand held him and the dead man's instructions bound him. Half of the gold from that claim went to him, and the other half to Mary Morris, Centerville,

Ohio. Sometimes at night, just before falling into dreamless sleep, he thought about Barney Morris' widow two thousand miles away who depended on a man she had never met — and at that moment the hint of a better reason for life touched him with its softness, and went away.

During the middle of the first week A. J. Oliver came up to see him. "That eight thousand dollars you brought into the Bannack office is still there. The toughs know about it, of course. They won't try to lift it out of the safe but the moment I start it to Salt Lake they'll stage a hold-up on the road."

"How'd they find out?"

Oliver gave him a gray side-glance. "They hear everything. It leaks out from places you wouldn't expect. You don't know with whom you're talking in this camp. I thought I'd wait until a good strong caravan of freighters started from Bannack and send the gold with them."

"Probably they're waiting for that," said Pierce. "Eight thousand is worth waiting for. I wouldn't do it, Oliver. I'd let it stay in the safe. About a month from now let's drop the news around that you've already smuggled it out. Might throw them off guard. Then we'll figure a way."

"You can't be the man to do it," said Oliver. "If you show up in Bannack the toughs will catch on."

"We'll do it through somebody else."

"All right," agreed Oliver. As he turned down the Gulch he stopped to add: "You know they've got you on the black list don't you?"

"Yes," said Jeff. "I know."

There were no secrets in the Gulch. News traveled from Summit to Junction with the wind, seeming to need no human carrier. Everybody knew the toughs had him on the list. But it was strange how this same news brought him friends. There was, it appeared, an underground wire for the honest ones. During the latter part of the first week Parris Pfouts, one of the new merchants in the Gulch, came up along the diggings. All he said in the beginning was, "You're Pierce, aren't you? I'm Parris Pfouts." Then he stood by, idle in the sun and not making much out of the visit; yet Pierce felt the survey of the man and the following judgment. Presently Pfouts added: "Barney Morris was a particular friend of mine. I hated to see him go. Any ideas on who did that?"

"Yes," said Pierce, "I know who did it." He kept on working. Pfouts remained indolent under the warming sun, not pressing the subject. He was, Pierce realized, wise enough to know that a direct question would be out of order. In this country men were close-mouthed before strangers, and so far he and Pfouts were still strangers. Pfouts simply said:

"There will come a time of reckoning."

"There was a time of reckoning," answered Pierce, "when you had Lyons and Stinson and Forbes cold with the goods. But the boys were washed out on a flood of tears. It is too late now. The toughs have the whip."

Pfouts said: "I have seen toughs before who had the whip. But they always used it too hard. And then they got wiped out."

"Not until this Gulch quits voting on tears. The strong and the smart always run things, Pfouts."

"I agree. The strong and the smart — and the honest."

"Maybe."

Pfouts smiled. "I heard you were considerable of a hard one. Don't believe in much, do you?"

"Not too much."

Pfouts moved upgrade to drop a word with Archie Caples on the adjoining claim; and later returned to Virginia City. This was on Thursday. On Friday, moving in much the same casual manner, Jim Williams appeared on a beautiful bay gelding and paused at the sluice box. Williams was near Pierce's age, a broad-chested and muscular young man with a dark and gentle face. His ragged mustache ran down around his mouth and fell into equally ragged chin whiskers and his eyes were a melancholy brown. He rested his arms on the saddle horn and, as Pfouts had done, took his time to estimate Pierce. "That flume," he observed, "saves a lot of work."

"Yes," said Pierce.

"I heard a piece of talk in town this morning," went on Jim Williams. "Ketchum opened his mouth in Tanner's and some brave words fell out. Your name was with the words. It is none of my business, of course."

"Thanks," said Pierce. He stopped his work and met Jim Williams' glance, and for a little while they frankly swapped inspections. This Williams was no talker. Pierce had met him before in Virginia City and had observed that he always kept in the background of a group, and yet he had also observed that Oliver and Pfouts and the substantial men of the district always liked to have Jim Williams' opinion. He was that kind of man, reserved and thoughtful; with an underlying sadness or pessimism strongly influencing his character. Pierce said: "Pfouts came up to drop a hint yesterday. He is too optimistic about law and order."

"There will be no law and order," said Jim Williams in a half-asleep manner, "until things get a good deal worse."

"The pack," said Pierce, "always follows the strong side."

"How many men does it take to make a strong side?" murmured Jim Williams.

"One man is enough," said Pierce. "One man against the whole damned world — if he's not afraid of dying."

Williams made a brief nod of his head and then he smiled. Pierce answered that smile and at that instant these two knew each other well, and trusted each other completely. Williams reined around and trotted down the Gulch.

Two days afterwards, near twilight, Pierce noticed Rube Ketchum move up the Gulch on the opposite side of the creek and pass by, neither looking toward him nor showing curiosity. Yet that lack of curiosity was itself a warning and after he had finished supper Pierce took his shotgun and blankets and climbed the ridge of the side-canyon and made camp in the brush. He repeated this the following nights. On Friday of the second week, again near dusk, Ollie Rounds and Ben Scoggins appeared before his small supper fire.

"We were having a drink in The Senate," said Scoggins cheerfully, "and we thought of you. Seemed natural to pay a visit. Ain't seen you for ten days or so."

Day after day with himself, dawn to dark, he had begun to turn sour. There was a limit to a man's loneliness, a time when cabin fever, or its Gulch equivalent, began to turn his nerves ragged and to canker his disposition. He was genuinely pleased to see them and threw an extra chunk of alder on the fire. Scoggins and Rounds dismounted and settled by the blaze. Rounds said: "You smoke these things," and offered Pierce a cigar. The three men lounged back and let the silence run. All up and down the Gulch firelights burned from claim to claim, and traffic went scratching and gritting along the gravel bars and voices kept calling. The hum of Virginia moved at them, the steady muted mixture of music and man-noise; and now and then a shot broke sharp-edged through and above this racket. Day's heat slowly lifted from the Gulch, replaced by coolness.

Pierce said: "I heard about that sardine venture, Ben. You're a damned Yankee trader. What's next?"

"Well," said Ben Scoggins, "I hauled lumber from Bannack for couple three days until I got my bearings. Met a fellow over by Bannack last week who was busted down with a load of flour he'd freighted in from Salt Lake. So I made a dicker and brought the flour up the Gulch."

"Sell it?"

Ben Scoggins laughed aloud. "Buyin' and sellin's my business. I sold out before I got to Central. There ain't enough of anything in this country."

Rounds pointed out a possibility: "Population around here doubles every week. If you'd held that flour a month, Ben, you'd gotten more for it."

Scoggins shook his head. "Always take a

profit when you see it. Keep turnin', keep goin'. The fellow that holds is a speculator, and speculators always go busted. Buy and sell.''

Pierce remarked: "You were in the flour business. Now you're out of it. What's next?''

"I bought a corner on Jackson Street. Puttin' up a store building. Sent to Salt Lake for a stock of general merchandise. Should be open by late July.''

Ollie Rounds, never a restful man, seized a stick and worried the coals of the fire around and around. "You have found your spot. Fifty years from now you'll be on Fourth of July platforms, talking about the old days of Alder Gulch.''

"No-o," said Scoggins, coolly making his forecast. "I will ride this wave until I see it about to break. Then I will sell and go. You never saw a mining camp live very long. All these fellows in the Gulch are travelers. They don't make a country. They don't stick. If you're bankin' on the future go to a country where men bring their families and take up land and start stringin' fence lines. Where they put up schools and go to tradin'. Traders make towns. Farmers make towns. Grist mills. Boats stoppin' at a landing make towns. This country ain't meant for big towns. It is grass and gold country. Gold will go. Grass will stay — and then the cattle will come.'' He looked at the other two men with his thoughtful eyes. "Maybe that's what I'll do. Take up land for a ranch."

Ollie Rounds grinned. "You leave that life to the tough fellows, like Jeff here. You stick to your last."

"A man can have his hankerings," said Ben Scoggins.

"Yes," said Ollie Rounds, and lost his humor, "a man can have his hankerings. But if he follows them they'll lead him to the swamps. Don't make pretty pictures, Ben. Let fools like me do that."

Pierce lifted his eyes to thoughtfully appraise Ollie Rounds. Horsemen slashed through the creek's gravel, bound toward Virginia City in haste. A hundred feet beyond this spot another fire burned large and bright, whereby Archie Caples did his laundry in a half-barrel, his knuckles drumming on the corrugated washboard. Virginia's music came clearer, and died away, and came again. Pierce said: "What are you doing, Ollie?"

"I never do more than I can help."

Pierce said: "Don't let the world make a sucker out of you, Ollie. It tries. That's the only game worth playing — to buck the big tiger trying to destroy all of us. Well, buck it. Don't let it push you along."

"Now, now," said Ollie Rounds, half surprised and half resentful, "no use giving me a lot of fatherly advice. Don't tell me to be useful and thrifty. That's Ben's game, not mine."

Ben Scoggins spoke in his amiable way: "Funny how three fellows like us — not the same kind of men in any respect — got thrown together. Does seem a long time ago, too, since we got on the *Tenino,* bound upriver."

"Willy-nilly," said Ollie Rounds. "The cards fall, nobody knows where. We're the cards. It is all one damned big joke on us."

"Don't rightly believe that," said Ben quietly. But, true to his manner, he swung the subject to keep the talk pleasant. "I have got no complaint. I have made ten thousand dollars in tradin' around."

Ollie blurted out an immediate warning. "Don't ever say it aloud."

Pierce's glance lifted again and struck across the flame. He watched Ollie Rounds with his lids half shut, with his face pulled together. Ben Scoggins saw this, looked at Ollie, and broke the silence. "Pretty night."

"All nights are pretty," said Ollie. "That's my belief — that's what I live for." He was once more his old casual self. He said to Pierce: "You can't work like a horse without getting ornery. How long since you've had a drink?" He reached into his pocket and pulled out a pint flask. "Ben and I thought this might be a good idea."

He passed it to Pierce, who removed the cap and held the bottle to the light. "Valley Tan," he said.

"Two dollars the bottle — cheapest thing in camp," said Ben Scoggins, "and the most plentiful."

"Surcease from sorrow," said Ollie.

Pierce watched the bottle turn amber and brown under the firelight. He had something to say, and framed it in his mind carefully, and said it. "It just occurs to me that both you boys, or either of you, may someday need help. I never offer my help, as a rule. But if you need help, just give a shout and I'll be with you." Then he said, "How," and took his drink.

A single horse came up the gulch and turned against Archie Caples' campfire. The rider got down and spoke in a short tone at Caples. Caples reared back on his heels. He looked up at the rider and shook his head; and then the rider moved at him and hit him across the face and knocked him against the gravel.

Ollie Rounds looked on, neither moving nor changing expression; it was a scene to him, nothing more. Ben Scoggins grumbled, "What the hell's that for?" and was genuinely troubled. It was Pierce who acted. Reaching behind him, he seized up his water bucket and flung the full contents on the fire, killing the flame at once. He was on his feet, and he said: "That's for me, Ben, not for him." Then, the water bucket still in his hand, he ran toward the creek.

"What the hell?" grumbled Ben, and lifted to his feet. Ollie Rounds's hand came out and seized Ben's leg. "Drop down, you fool!"

Ben kicked Rounds's hand away. "He's in trouble, ain't he?"

"You're big as a barn up there! Get down and crawl!"

The stranger at Archie Caples' fire slowly circled Caples as the other struggled up from the ground. Caples tried to turn and keep his eyes on the stranger, but the stranger side-stepped steadily and when Caples got to his feet the stranger jumped in again, hit Caples a great blow on the back of the neck with his forearm, and dropped him. Ben Scoggins growled in his throat and began to crawl ahead on his hands and knees, Ollie Rounds following behind. Rounds kept murmuring: "Watch it — watch it, Ben."

Pierce suddenly appeared up on the edge of the other campfire and threw a fresh bucket of water on it, immediately quenching the blaze. A gun yelled from the near-by Gulch wall and the bullet scutted on the gravel and sang away. Both Rounds and Scoggins, now running on, heard the sudden crush of Pierce's body against the stranger. The stranger let out a harking shout and the gravel reported the stamp of Pierce's feet as he rushed toward the Gulch wall, toward the unseen gun. Briefly he was a blur in the dark; afterwards he faded. Both Rounds and Scoggins moved after him, guided by the sound of his feet. Ben Scoggins called out, "Hey, Jeff!" And Ollie quietly cursed Ben for it. The gun on the ridge emitted its dry round voice into the dark, leaving a flickered bloom of light behind. Pierce fired at once in reply and then the hidden man's gun flared again from a different angle of the hill and steps rattled up the side of the ridge.

Pierce came back, his breath lifting and falling. He found Scoggins and Ollie Rounds and he said, "Let's see," and moved on to Archie Caples' water-damped fire. A few coals still glowed and by that light they saw Caples standing spraddle-legged and uncertain, both hands clasped around his head. "Fellow got away before my senses came back."

Miners were running in from all corners of the Gulch; and a lantern swung forward. Pierce stood lank in the growing light, water shining on his coat. "It wasn't for you, Archie. It was for me."

The oncoming lantern touched these four; and then Ollie Rounds turned and stepped back into the dark and waited until Ben Scoggins joined him. The two returned to their horses and started down-Gulch for Virginia City.

"A funny thing," said Scoggins.

"No — not funny. They won't let him alone."

"Who you talking about?" asked Ben Scoggins.

Ollie rounds made no answer to that. Later, on the edge of Virginia, he mentioned something else. "He knew what was up the minute the fellow hit Archie Caples. He knew it all — and he knew what to do. He's cut out for it. You and I are not. You stick to your trade and let Jeff handle the beasts in the jungle." At Wallace Street Ollie turned from Ben. He said again: "But they'll never leave him alone. Too much for one man, no matter how good he is."

That was Friday of the second week of his steady labor; on Saturday he worked steadily through the day, cooked his supper and sat back from his fire and slowly smoked his cigar; and as he smoked it the two weeks of unremitting work caught up with him and he felt the staleness in him, and the taste of the cigar grew unpalatable. This was always the penalty of solitariness. A man fed upon himself until his fat was gone and then he had to have another kind of nourishment. Rising, he killed the fire and struck for town.

Virginia, in two weeks, was a different camp. It crowded against the Gulch walls, it stretched up the Gulch and it spilled down the Gulch. Wagons and travelers moved forward from the Daylight Grade in full stream to choke the streets and to stir a dust that made fine yellow smoke against the light beams of store and saloon and dance hall. Cruising forward he came upon new streets which fourteen days before had not existed and, pushed to the edge of the walk by the crowd, he found himself facing a small single-story frame building across the way on which a newly painted sign said: "Diana Castle's Bakery." He threaded the tight-jammed wagon traffic to the bakery door and as he came to a pause before it he heard Diana's voice at his side. "How are you, Jeff?"

He didn't at this first moment turn to look at her. He kept his eyes on the shop's doorway, and he spoke in a tone as indifferent as her own: "This is it?"

"Yes. It is just finished. The stove was set up today. It was supposed to be for a restaurant down in Central but Ben Scoggins dickered the man out of it."

She went into the shop and came about. He stood fast, seeing the lovely shine of her hair against the lamplight and the roundness of her shoulder points and the straight line of her body. Her eyes were cool. She wasn't smiling and in a way she seemed still to be judging him and finding him wanting. But she said: "Come in."

He entered the shop and then did a thing which, when she came to think of it, was typical of him: he reached out and closed the door so that he would not be exposed to

171

sudden attack. That kind of suspicion and self-defense never left him; his life had been violent for so long that it was an unconscious reaction. He was very tall in the room and he had recently shaved and his face had a thick tan compounded of all his outdoor years and his eyes were dense blue and his cheekbones stood high and pronounced against his skin. He had on a pair of gray trousers and a blue double-breasted miner's shirt. Suddenly he reached up and removed his hat and he unexpectedly smiled, so that now the lean formidableness left him and he was a man she liked — and wished she could continue to like forever.

"Well," he said, "this is it?"

"Yes," she said. "I found my place."

"You're doing all this by yourself?"

"No. I have a baker to help me. You see my stove?"

It was a long, black restaurant range, scarred by its travels through this country, but she was obviously very proud of it. A coffeepot simmered on it, reminder of a hospitable gesture. She went to a cupboard and brought out a cup, and poured coffee for him; and got him a piece of pie. "You're thinner than when I saw you last."

He tried the pie. He said: "You're a good cook, Diana."

"I learned to cook when I was a little girl." Some thought came to him, its keen reaction

172

showing on his face; when she was aware of it she dropped her eyes, not sure of how she should feel toward this man who had so desperately hurt her. But a moment later she brought her eyes back to him and this was the way they stood over a long moment, no longer smiling, but reading each other until at last memory darkened her expression. She was thinking — as he was thinking — of the night he had kissed her; that moment became too real for her and she turned and moved away from him. At the far corner of the room she swung about.

"You're happy here?"

"Yes," she said. "I'm useful. I'm alive. I am doing something. But you're not particularly happy."

"Why shouldn't I be?"

She shook her head. "You never will be. You remember too many bitter things. You judge all people by the pain they might cause you or by the cruelty some of them used on you. You have no faith."

"Why should I have? I ask nobody for anything. I need nobody."

"That's it. Everything to you is a matter of not needing anybody, of hating to need anybody." She stepped toward him until the fragrance of her clothes and hair — the fragrance of a woman — enveloped him like warmth. "You won't change until someday you are very badly hurt and need help. But there won't be anybody you can turn to because you have closed everybody out. Then you'll know that there isn't any living soul who can travel alone. Then you'll find out you've got to trust people."

"And be sold out," he said.

She shrugged her shoulders and changed the subject. "I suppose you know I have taken Lily Beth for awhile. We have a cabin on Wallace Street."

"Where's her mother?"

"I haven't asked. But I suspect Mr. Temperton took Lily Beth away from her."

He moved restlessly around the room. She watched him, knowing him better than he knew himself. He was a man out of joint with himself, with great feeling and great wants imprisoned within the walls of his own black discipline. He was like a boiler with no outlet; one day the boiler would burst and he would destroy himself. The thought of it brought a trace of pity to her face, and then she was startled to hear him speak her name in an odd way. "Diana," he said, and looked as though he wished to crush her, or kiss her. He had his hands behind him and he was so near to her that she saw her own reflection in his eyes. She stood fast, remembering that she had once offered this man everything and that he had misjudged her, yet almost ready to forgive him for all the hurt he had caused her.

Somebody lightly tapped on the door, and

Will Temperton pushed it before him. He saw them and he said in his cool voice: "Sorry. Hadn't meant to intrude."

Pierce turned about. "No intrusion," he said as short and hard as he could speak the words.

Temperton inclined his head. He said. "I only wondered if there was anything you wished me to get for Lily Beth, Diana."

"No," said Diana. "There's nothing in town for her. We'll wait until Dance and Stuart's wagons come over from Salt Lake."

"Yes," said Temperton, "I suppose. Be sure and buy whatever you need." He gave Pierce the straight and sharp look of one who had his judgments but held them back; and turned out of the shop.

Pierce wheeled to Diana and then she saw everything had changed between them and her hope of goodness to come went away. It was in the new way he looked at her. He smiled a little, but it was a smile that came through the risen clouds of that old mistrust. For a moment he had forgotten; now he remembered and she was clearly aware of what he thought and what he felt about her. She waited for him to speak and then had her great shock. He took a step to her and closed her into his long arms and kissed her.

She held herself still until she knew from what terrible frame of mind he had acted; thereafter, more outraged than she had ever known herself to be, more deeply hurt and inexpressibly ashamed, she pushed him away. She lifted both hands and struck his chest and forced him across the room until his shoulders hit the door, and she flung her full anger at him: "Don't come back — don't ever come back!"

Had she been less angry she would have pitied him again for the self-hatred he showed at the moment. He said in a completely dead tone "I am sorry," and left the room.

He went along Wallace Street with his head lowered, a man furious at his own folly; he used his arms to push a way through the crowd. The Pantheon was across the street and he turned over and entered the dance hall. There was no vacant space at the bar but he made a place by driving his shoulder between a pair of men, sliding them aside. He put both arms on the bar and waited for the bottle to come; and he took his drink. The music stopped and partners promenaded and he heard the laughter of the girls beside him.

"What's wrong, Jeff?"

Lil stood by, smiling at him. She had a partner but she turned her back to the partner and watched Pierce with her wisdom. She had seen men before like him — inwardly burning and outwardly frozen — and because she had seen them she knew what power of breakage lay now in Pierce. Nothing but wildness came out of a man when he was in a mood like that. She put her hand over his glass and she let her soft laugh fall on him and she took his arm and pulled him from the bar. "Our dance, Jeff," she said. The floorman called, "Choose your partners for the waltz," and the music swung down on the first long beat. She led him away, turning and turning, and she was light in his arms, a soft weight near him but always moving away from him, with her face flushed by the heat of the hall and her hazel eyes searching him. "What's wrong?"

"Nothing," he said.

"Nothing," she said, "is everything. How long have you been up the creek working?"

"Two weeks."

"That's what's wrong."

"Why?" he said, and for the first time seemed to take interest in her.

She said: "If men could live alone do you suppose there would be women like me in places like this?"

"Why should you be here, Lil? I always wondered."

"Don't ask foolish questions."

"No," he said, "I won't." But her manner drew a grin from him. "You seem to know the kind of medicine a man needs."

"Yes," she said, "I do." She ceased to smile and some of the liveliness went out of her. She was smaller and heavier in his arms and her glance dropped. "Yes," she added in a short, sad way, "I suppose I do."

He led her to the bar after the dance. She watched him take his whisky and she watched its effect on him. "But don't drink too much, will you?"

"No," he said, "I won't," and watched her go away with another miner. The music started again. He helped himself to a final drink and paid for it; as he turned from the bar he discovered Rube Ketchum at the hall's doorway, looking in — looking at him.

Ketchum immediately turned back into the street. Pierce started toward the door and came against a man directly in his path. He pushed the man aside, walked straight through the dancing couples and shoved his way to the door. When he got outside he saw Ketchum at that moment passing into Tanner's, whereupon he left the walk, ducked around a six-horse team and reached Tanner's.

Lil, moving through a quadrille, had observed Pierce's quick pursuit of Ketchum and she instantly abandoned the set and her partner, ran out the back way and circled through a space between the dance hall and the Globe store. Here, with Tanner's directly across the way, she stopped and waited.

When in Virginia City, George Ives usually held out at Tanner's, invariably standing at the far end of the bar wherefrom he commanded a view of the crowd and the doors. Ketchum, hurrying into the saloon, spotted Ives and shoved through the crowd. "He's on my trail, George. He's coming."

Ives's mind was of the sort that seized upon chance like a trap. He said at once: "Go halfway down the bar. Just stand there. Don't look at him." He pushed Ketchum away with a hand and thereafter wheeled on Steve Marshland and George Parrish who were near him. "Move around the room." Then he looked through the crowd until he caught Jack Gallegher's attention, and nodded. Gallegher stepped back against the far wall.

Pierce came into Tanner's and immediately located Ketchum. The man was at the bar, drinking, but he faced the back bar mirror and so had a view of his rear. Pushing forward, Pierce found a spot near Ketchum and signaled for a bottle and glass and meanwhile took time to consider his surroundings. He located Ives and he spotted both Gallegher and Steve Marshland, but at the moment he though nothing of them. Ollie Rounds, he discovered, was bucking a faro game, and Temperton dealt at a middle table. Ben Scoggins was just then entering the saloon; he discovered Pierce and moved over.

He said, cheerfully: "Shook yourself loose from the diggin's, I notice."

A pair of men left the bar, so that now Pierce and Ketchum were side by side. Ollie turned to occupy the vacant space and showed a small surprise when Pierce cut in front of him, crowding against Ketchum. His shoulder rammed Ketchum's shoulder, whereupon Ketchum spread his legs and braced himself against the pressure. Still, he did not look directly at Pierce. He raised his whisky glass and when he did so Pierce gave him a full shove which spilled the liquor; that aggression forced Ketchum against the tight rank of men at the bar and someone down the line said irritably: "What the hell's the matter up there?"

Scoggins murmured: "What's up, Jeff?"

"Nothing," said Pierce. "Just pushing a ——," and he used one unmentionable phrase on Ketchum, "out of the way."

Ketchum slid beyond the reach of Pierce's shoulders. He held both arms on the bar and he continued to watch the big man through the back bar mirror with a cautious and wooden expression. This seemed strange to Ben Scoggins, but as he looked around the room and noticed Ives and certain other toughs now watching the play he thought he knew how things moved. He came near Pierce, murmuring: "You're in a pocket."

Ollie Rounds had turned from the faro game to observe, whereupon Ben Scoggins made a signal with his hand which Ollie acknowledged by the briefest dip of his head. Jack Gallegher now strolled over the room to

Ketchum's side. "How's things going, Rube?" he said. "Everything all right?"

Pierce idly turned and caught Ketchum in the ribs with the point of his elbow. Ketchum flinched and backed away, at last directly facing Pierce. "Cut it out," he said.

"When you come to see me," stated Pierce, "come during the day."

"What's that?" asked Ketchum.

Gallegher remained to the rear of Ketchum, silently backing up the dull, black-witted man. He watched Pierce quite closely but at times his glance lifted to the far end of the bar. Ben Scoggins turned his attention to see what lay there and when he discovered Ives at the bar's end he grew increasingly troubled. He put his glance on Gallegher and he stepped around Ketchum and stood beside Gallegher, at once drawing the Deputy's aroused stare. "What the hell you doing here?" he grunted.

"Nothing — nothing at all," murmured Ben. "But I've got a forty-four in my pocket."

"Take your dime out of this game and go back to your store. You'll get hurt."

Scoggins grinned at the Deputy; it was not a full grin and not an entirely easy one but it covered, he hoped, the cool and trembling excitement in him. He stuck to his position. Ollie Rounds, he noticed from the corner of his eyes, hadn't moved from the faro table. Ollie closely watched Pierce, and the crowd in the saloon was also watching. The quarrel by now was clear to everyone.

Ketchum meanwhile seemed to find an answer to his problem for he scowled at Pierce and said: "You go to hell, Pierce."

He had not quite finished before Pierce batted him across the face with his open palms. Ketchum bared his teeth, shut his eyes and lunged forward with both arms wide-flung like a wrestler's. Pierce seized one arm and wheeled close against Ketchum; he pulled Ketchum's arm over his shoulder and he ducked and gave a sharp twist. Ketchum yelled and came off his feet and plunged headlong out into the center floor, rolling against the edge of the crowd, and falling. Players at the near-by poker tables scrambled away, kicking their chairs aside. Ketchum started to rise and got as far as his knees when Pierce ran in, seized a poker table and smashed it into Ketchum, sending the man down again. The rim of the table struck Ketchum on the head and when he dropped he lay without motion.

Gallegher called: "Pierce, I've got to take your gun —"

Ben Scoggins, who had never moved away from the Deputy, now murmured: "Shut up and stay out of this." Gallegher swung on him, furious at the check. Ben's smile was a smaller and smaller crease on his freckled face but he kept a hand in his pocket, snugged against the forty-four he said he carried there, and he met Gallegher's blistering glance and held the Deputy out of the play.

It was all he could do and he feared it wasn't enough, for Steve Marshland moved across to the main door and stood by it, and Frank Parrish sifted through the crowd, and Ives called out: —

"Let him alone, Pierce."

Pierce said: "Don't send him after me again, George."

"Who sent him after you?" challenged Ives. "What would I do that for?"

Now Ben Scoggins saw how it was meant to be. Ives and Ives's friends had neatly pulled Pierce into Tanner's and presently the trap would close. Meanwhile Ollie Rounds stood alone by the abandoned faro rig, all other players having retreated to the wall, and Ollie listened and watched and showed no feeling. Ives's entrance into the scene had changed the atmosphere for the crowd, so that men began to drift toward Tanner's back door and leave the saloon; and Dutch John Wagner appeared from somewhere and took stand, narrowly watching Pierce. Ben Scoggins, feeling the increase of pressure, risked removing his glance from Gallegher long enough to cast a questioning look at Pierce, wondering if Pierce knew the thorough danger he faced. The big man continued to watch Ives with complete attention, seeming not to know he was under fire from Wagner, from Marshland, from Parrish.

Pierce said: "Don't lie, George."

Ollie Rounds, standing at the faro rig, abruptly reached down and lifted the cased cards and threw them on the floor. He kicked at them with his feet and he stepped across the room until he was behind Pierce, between Pierce and Parrish. He kept going until he had gotten beside Parrish. Here he stopped.

The crowd watched this, now fully silent while Ives and Pierce faced each other across the room. Sweat cracked through Ben Scoggins' skin and the muscles at the back of his neck began to ache. Ives laughed in a hard, short way; his fair skin turned florid and his eyes had bright dancing points in them. "You're calling me names, you damned counterfeit fourflusher. Come on, we'll see how thin your liver is —"

He made a gesture with his shoulder and Scoggins, now forgetting Gallegher, saw Dutch John Wagner stiffen and make his pull. Scoggins yelled: "Look aside, Jeff!" But Pierce had seen this and flung up his gun and fired and knocked Dutch John off his feet. The echo smashed the four walls of Tanner's; men here and there dropped flat on the floor. Pierce ran at Ives, flat-footed. Ives, never moving from the bar's end watched Pierce and ceased to smile, and never moved. Dutch John started to shout and thresh on the floor. "My shoulder's bleedin'! Where's Steele —

get Steele!" Nobody seemed to hear him. Pierce stopped within arm's reach of Ives. Scoggins, hard-pressed to keep up with the swift onrush of this scene, got to wondering why it was that Ives had not tried to draw, and why it was that Steve Marshland, unguarded at the door, had not entered the play. Again taking his attention from Jack Gallegher, he looked back at the door and saw Jim Williams standing in it, quiet and bulky and very watchful, and freezing Marshland out of action by his presence.

Scoggins heard Pierce say: "You still think this is fun, George? I told you to let me alone." Then he did something that made Scoggins wince. He lifted his gun so rapidly that Ives had no time for defense and he smashed the barrel down on Ives's head and dropped the man senseless to the floor. Immediately he whirled around to face Parrish and Marshland. He saw Gallegher, and called: "What did you start to say, Jack?"

"We've got no quarrel," Gallegher immediately answered.

"Get the hell out of my sight."

Gallegher wheeled in quick obedience toward the door. Scoggins now joined Pierce and Jim Williams turned, so that these three followed Gallegher out; they watched Gallegher fade into Van Buren. Williams said: "You pushed that hard, Jeff."

"Yes," said Pierce. Sound began to rise

185

from Tanner's and Dutch John Wagner shouted: "Get Steele, somebody —"

Williams murmured: "Ives will bear it in mind."

"I expect so," agreed Pierce. He said, to both of them: "Thanks," and turned down Wallace. He crossed the street, moving past The Pantheon, and he stopped dead when he saw Lil Shannon's shadow come out of the small alley; he was on wire edge and he would have drawn had not her voice checked him.

"Jeff — what did you do?"

"A fight," he said.

She caught his arm and pulled him down the alley. "There were half a dozen men in Tanner's who'd have shot you. You fool!" She held his arm, pulling him through the alley and between the tents at the lower quarter of town. She went across Van Buren with him, and drew him into her log house. She closed the door and moved around in the dark, softly repeating. "You were a fool, Jeff." A lamp took light under her hand and she faced him with her expressive eyes. The dance-hall dress hung from her shoulder points and lay rounded and tight across the fullness of her breasts, and breathing stirred them, and she spoke again in a voice that pulled at him and asked him for his eyes. "Jeff — Jeff."

This cabin had a board floor and a boarded wall. There was a dresser and a stove and a bed in it, and the small things that a woman would gather about her; and a trunk with the initials L. S. R. on it. Those, he guessed, had once been her initials. He sat on the edge of the bed and he bent over with both hands across his knees. The sound of Virginia, the march of feet and the murmur of voices and the groan of wagons, never ceased.

"We are all fools," he said. "The damned world is full of beasts. All the prayers for happiness, all the little hopes, all the things people believe — those are lies. What is the use of lying?"

She came to him. She sat beside him and she said again, so softly and humbly, "Jeff, is there anything I can do?"

"No. There's never anything one human being can do for another."

She murmured: "Isn't there anything in me at all that you like?" Then she put her hand around his shoulders and pulled him into her lap. She put her arms around him, she held him tightly to her.

"I wish," she murmured, "I wish . . ."

X: Ives Sets a Trap

VIRGINIA CITY, lying in one small fold of the thousandfold Montana hills, grew by day and glittered by night; the noise of its sluice boxes, the stamp and shuffle of its many thousand feet, made a reverberation throughout the land. To a restless America which ever cast a longing eye westward, this town was the new Mecca, so that the impatient ones, the dispossessed ones, the misfits and the daring, the seekers of swift riches and the men who forever sought greener valleys came by the slow routes from the East to crowd Virginia and Virginia's sisters scattered elbow to elbow along Alder. They came up the Missouri to Benton and across the wild Rocky passes, or from Lewiston through the Bitterroots, or over the Oregon Trail to Fort Hall and thence north. By these routes they came in headlong rush.

In July there were seven thousand people in Alder Gulch. By September there were twelve thousand, of all kinds and classes, of all purposes and trades; veterans from the Civil War and renegades from that war, Frontiersmen from the Platte and the Purgatoire, trappers out of Ogden's Hole, Maine men and Ohio men and Tennessee men, doctors who turned from medicine to mining and doctors who stayed by their profession, lawyers like Edgerton and Sanders and lawyers who, standing in Tanner's or the Pony or the Senate, recited Shakespeare and afterwards begged the price of another drink, black sheep fleeing from good families and youngsters in search of fortune whereby they might return East to their people, gamblers deserting older fields for this fairer one, desperadoes guided by an unerring scent, dancehall girls and ladies no longer ladies and good women standing above this flood like white lights in the black.

This was Virginia City, pocketed in the loneliness of the hills, encircled by Blackfoot and Ute and Bannack, dependent on wagon train and express messenger for every article of life, enclosed by high mountain ranges over which the thin mud roads precariously pitched and twisted, blocked by wild white streams in which many a man and many a team was lost.

By September the Gulch was staked out solidly and the steady stream of newly arrived were pushing into adjoining gulches and deeper into the Rocky Chain. A. J. Oliver and Peabody and Caldwell had their stage lines established from Virginia City through Bannack and on to Salt Lake. Bummer Dan McFadden, living on handouts, was one day ejected from a saloon. Aimlessly wandering, Bummer Dan struck a borrowed pick into a discarded claim and discovered the richest bar in the Gulch. Flour went up to seventy dollars a sack. In the hill cemetery slept a growing company of men violently come to death. Idaho Street appeared in town and the camp jumped Daylight Creek. The Virginia Hotel went up, and Pfouts and Russell's store, Dance and Stuart's store, the Planter's Hotel and the Peoples' Theatre. Wood replaced log and canvas here and there.

A man named Fields was killed back of Tanner's for nothing more valuable than a two-dollar nugget on his watch chain. Harry Morphy, a miner with a thousand-dollar stake, set out from Virginia City to Salt Lake and vanished entirely. Two roughs killed a third rough in broad daylight between Daly's and Dempsey's, under view of twenty people, and rode slowly away. Late summer's heat struck the Tobacco Root Mountains and poured into the Gulch and tempers grew hotter all along Alder, and the roughs more openly predatory, and Virginia City went into its full swing so that it had its man for breakfast every morning.

A tough stood up two miners at dusk on Daylight Grade and relieved them of a joint thirty dollars. "Gentlemen," said the tough, "next time I brace you, have more money in your possession or I will kill you."

A. J. Oliver came up the gulch one morning in the middle of September to talk to Pierce.

"I need a driver on tomorrow's run. Harry German's sick. You've handled the ribbons I understand."

"All right," said Pierce.

Oliver said: "Cap Boyd is booked to ride the stage. He's carrying $2,500 in dust. Nobody knows of it, but it might leak out. Freight outfit left Bannack two days ago for Salt Lake. I had intended sending Barney Morris' money by them but I got word that the Innocents were watching, so I didn't. That wagon train was held up last night."

Pierce said: "Then it won't be held up again. If I drive the stage through tomorrow I'll hit Bannack after dark. I'll eat supper. Now if I could have a horse waiting somewhere on the edge of town, and if I could get that money, I'd ride after the freight outfit, hand them the dust — and it would be safe enough."

Oliver said: "I'll go to Bannack tonight. Your horse will be waiting in a shed at the end of the street, that last shed on the road to Horse Prairie. I'll get Barney Morris' money and carry it to the shed. There's some two-by-four joists that hold the shed rafters together, and some planks thrown on top of the two-by-fours. You get into the shed and reach up and you'll find the bags in a leather cantina on the planks."

"All right."

Oliver said: "Joe Gallup is head man in that freight outfit. Give the money to him."

Oliver had remained outside the range of Pierce's fire and had kept his voice down. Now he looked around him, closely eyeing the shadows and long listening. "Stage pulls out from the hotel at five," he said and went away.

Pierce let his fire die and sat in the darkness, engaged in his practical thoughts; and in a short while he went over to Archie Caples' fire. "Archie," he said, "I'm weary of working and I'm going to take a trip in the Tobacco Roots. If I don't show up on the third day, maybe you'd work my claims."

"Sure," said Caples. But he grinned a little at Pierce, by which Pierce understood Caples' skepticism. In these hills and in this camp nothing was what it seemed to be. Caution was on them all. Pierce returned to his cabin in the side-canyon, dug his gold pouches out of a sack of beans, and moved down the Gulch. He slipped between Virginia's tent rows, skirted the black wall of The Pantheon and so came to Dance and Stuart's store. At this hour it was crowded, but he caught

W. B. Dance's eye and led him back toward the office. "Like to leave my dust in your safe," he said.

Dance took Pierce's poke, wrote Pierce's name on a slip of paper and stuffed it into the neck of the poke. The safe stood in a corner, its door ajar. When Dance pulled the door back Pierce saw the layers of other pouches on the safe's bottom. "Young fortune there," he said.

"That gives you the idea," said Dance wryly. "Someday we'll have to run the scoundrels out."

Pierce said: "Who's going to start that?"

"There's enough honest men to do it any time."

"Takes something better than honesty," Pierce answered. "The meek will never inherit Alder." He made his way back through the crowd, through the aisles of sacked goods and kerosene and canned peaches, past the shelves of shirts and trousers and supplies. Clubfoot George sat in one corner, stooped over his shoemaker's last. He looked at Pierce and showed his sharp curiosity. He said, "Evenin', Pierce," and got Pierce's nod.

Pierce had a drink at the Senate, and loitered a little while watching a poker game — and turned down Wallace Street. He met Ollie and stopped for a chat. He said, "I'm going to have a little fun tomorrow and drive stage," and moved on. The lights of Diana's bakery fanned through an open door. He saw her standing behind a counter and he stood at the edge of the walk, hard in thought, with the rankling memory of their last scene reviving, with some of its suspicion and its wonder coming back. Then, head down, he plowed his way through the crowd and returned up the Gulch.

Cap Boyd was a jolly man who, having made his stake in the gulch, now prepared to depart from the scenes of his adventure. He had imposed strict secrecy upon himself and upon his friends, well knowing that any man who rode the stage to Bannack with twenty-five hundred dollars of gold dust in his belt was powerful bait for the Innocents. But still he was a jolly man and accordingly gathered his few chosen friends around him in the Senate for a last round of drinks. That last round became an endless circle which, begun in the Senate, moved on to the Pony, thence to the Alcazar and at last near midnight ended in Tanner's. By that time the group of friends had grown into a young crowd and somewhere near the shank of the evening Gallegher joined him for the inevitable. "Just one more drink, boys, before I leave." Cap shook hands warmly with Gallegher and mentioned the sorrow he felt upon departing from the Gulch which had been so good to him; and the last thing he remembered was his friends supporting him through the doorway of the Virginia Hotel, all of them singing one of the less respectable versions of "John Brown."

Gallegher detached himself from Cap's party at Tanner's and sauntered to the back room, to be presently joined by Ives and Marshland. Clubfoot George later came in. Clubfoot said: "Pierce left his dust in Dance's safe."

Ives drew a long breath of smoke from his cigar. "That's a give-away, I think. Harry German's sick, so he won't be driving. I happen to know Oliver once asked Pierce to drive relief."

"Might be," said Gallegher. "I just found out Cap Boyd's going out on that stage. He's got his dust in a money belt. It'll be around his belly."

"Should be sizeable," said Ives, and began to make his plans. "Steve and I will ride down tonight. We'll be camped somewhere beyond the Beaverhead. In a draw, about halfway to Bunton's. We'll stop the stage there." But, being a careful man, and one who also liked to spike all chances, he improved upon the idea. "I'll have Bob Zachary go to Daly's Roadhouse. He'll get on there as a passenger and ride with the driver. When Steve and I show up from the gulch Zachary can throw a fit of being scared and put on a nice show for us. If the driver tries to draw, Zachary can nudge against him, pretending to be scared, and spoil his aim."

"Might be a crowd inside the coach to put up a fight," suggested Marshland.

"We need another man riding inside as passenger. I'll find somebody for that." He looked at Clubfoot. "You hear who else is booked on the stage?"

"Pfouts is going through. Don't know who else."

"Pfouts could be tough," said Ives. "But I think he's too old a hand to start a fight with the odds against him. If he does the other fellow we plant in the coach can act scared, too, and sort of talk Pfouts out of it. All right."

He returned to the main room, met Ollie Rounds, and walked to the street with him. "Steve and I are tackling the stage beyond the Beaverhead tomorrow. Need a man to go down to Adobetown tonight and go on as passenger when it comes through. If the passengers get tough, you're to play scared. Or to be practical about it and talk them out of shooting. Bob Zachary will get on at Daly's and ride beside the driver — doing same thing."

Ollie said, idly: "Don't want to leave Virginia tonight, George."

Ives, who was a lady's man, came to quick conclusions. He grinned. "Woman?"

Rounds smiled. "I never talk about the ladies, George."

"One of those ex-gentlemen, aren't you?"

Ollie quit smiling. "That's my business."

"Don't get sore," said Ives. He had lost the light on his cigar and now took time to ignite it. He moved on to Baker's stable and later reappeared, riding to Van Buren and disappearing. Ollie Rounds stood fast, still outwardly indifferent. Rube Ketchum was on the other side of the street — and Rube was watching him out of dull, never-trusting eyes. Presently Marshland and Gallegher came from the saloon. Both men spoke to him, Gallegher stopping. Gallegher said, "Good luck, Steve," and Marshland nodded and went away.

"You know what's up?" asked Gallagher.

"Yes."

Gallegher laughed, short and unamused, finding pleasure in the retribution to come, — "If Pierce is driving, he'll be a dead man by tomorrow night," — and strolled on.

Ollie Rounds lighted a cigar and, as he cupped the match to the cigar's point, he took this opportunity to scan the far walk, where Rube Ketchum had been. Rube was out of sight, but Rube would still be watching. The man had that constant suspicion, that never-forgetting streak of brutal patience. Rounds crushed the match between his fingers and he tipped his head and watched the black night sky. Nick Tibault came by and said, "Hello, Mr. Rounds," and stopped to look in at Tanner's.

"Go in and have some fun," suggested Ollie. "You work too hard."

Young Tibault shook his head. "Anna wouldn't like it," he said and turned from temptation.

Somewhere Rube Ketchum hid himself and watched with his small red-rimmed eyes. Rounds left his place by the saloon wall and moved along Wallace in pacing slowness. He came to Van Buren, teetered on the walk's edge for a full three minutes as a wholly idle man might, crossed over and returned on the opposite walk of the street, turning into Diana Castle's bakery.

Diana was at the moment waiting on a miner. Rounds waited until the miner had gone, and looked into the rear of the shop to be sure the baker was gone. "I'm in need of a couple doughnuts, Diana," he said.

"How would you like a cup of coffee to go with them?"

She had always liked him, he thought; she had never seen through him. "Just the doughnuts," he said. He brought out a half-dollar but Diana shook her head. "We came upriver together, Ollie. So this is on the house."

"Stick by your friends, don't you?"

"Yes."

He said quietly: "Jeff's driving Oliver's

198

stage to Bannack in the morning. It will be held up beyond the Beaverhead. They're laying for him particularly. I can't go to Jeff — I'm being spotted. But I'll find Ben Scoggins. I'll tell him to come here. Have him warn Jeff not to make that trip." He put the doughnuts into his pocket, noticing the flare of real fear in her eyes. As he went out he thought of this. There was something wrong between Diana and Jeff, and it was now odd to find that she had any feeling for the long-legged tough man up the Gulch.

It was near midnight then, with the crowd thinning out and the stores closing one by one. Rounds had meant to cut in behind Scoggins' store and take the rear door, but when he got to Idaho Street he saw Scoggins come out, lock up his store, and walk away. Rounds crossed the street and so moved up behind Scoggins. He murmured: "Go see Diana," and turned across the street, circling back to Tanner's. He put himself at the bar and took a pair of whiskies straight, afterwards joining a late game at Will Temperton's table.

Scoggins had a drink and a bite of lunch in the Senate and then went to Diana's, there waiting for her to close shop. The two walked along Wallace Street, toward her cabin. "Where's Lily Beth?"

"Sleeping."

"You know," he said, "the only time I ever

saw her smile was when she saw you. That little girl was scared of something."

"And starved for something. She's just a little girl. She has needed a lot of love."

"Wonder," he said, "what her mother was like. This fellow Temperton loves her, but he never seems to show it. Mighty strange."

"There are a lot of strange things in the world, Ben."

He was an observant young man and he had a big heart. Now he offered her a piece of advice. "Someday you'll have to give up Lily Beth. That will hurt. Don't get too fond of her."

They were at her cabin. She turned to him, saying: "You're rather wise. But how can you stop being fond of anyone?"

"I guess," he said, "that's right," and looked at her with a great deal of thought. "You get tied up, and that's it. Maybe in Lily Beth, maybe in someone else."

"Ben," she said, her voice going away from him, "don't make too many guesses."

"Ah," he said, and grinned. He was a big bland-tempered man with a shock of blond hair; nothing appeared to trouble him too much. He had a way of hanging on without seeming to hang on. He was a man with always a soft answer; but behind the soft answer was a bulldog tenacity. "What was it you were to tell me? Ollie was mighty secret about it."

"Tell Jeff not to drive the stage tomorrow. It is to be held up beyond the Beaverhead."

"Didn't know he was driving for Oliver," said Scoggins. He had a kind of a mind which took first things first, so that now it was the fact of Pierce's driving the stage which interested him. "Must have gotten weary of working like a horse and living like a hermit. Jeff can't do anything by halves. All of everything or nothing of nothing. So he digs until he's sick of it, then he's ready for a bust." He spoke this in his easy, idle way and meanwhile watched her with his shrewd eyes, interested in her expression. She saw it and gently rebuffed him. "Ben — you're not subtle."

"I can try to be, can't I?" he said. "Can't stop a man from wondering how tough it would be if he tried his own luck."

"It's Jeff we're talking about."

"Not much danger for a driver in a holdup, Diana. It is a kind of road agent rule — to let the driver alone." But now his mind, marching methodically from point to point, reached a more important fact. "But he isn't just a driver. The toughs have marked his number. They'll knock him over."

"Yes," said Diana, "that's it."

He gave her another of his close glances and he saw the way her thoughts leaped ahead to that possible scene of Jeff's destruction. She stood silently worried. He said: "It will do no good to warn him. I couldn't stop him from making the ride. You know that, don't you?"

"I know. He would listen to you. He would smile and thank you — and nothing in the world would stop him from going to Bannack."

"That's a streak in him. I wonder why?"

"Why," she said, "the thing he really hates is force. As far as Jeff is concerned the world is a brute trying to break him. It is a challenge he has to meet."

"Why should a man be so tough about it?"

"If you knew his past you'd understand."

Having patiently plodded his way through the problem, Scoggins now reached the last strange part of it. He stood with his chin dropped, a fair and easy and honest man exploring the dark alleys of human behavior. "Ever occur to you, Diana, that it is mighty funny how Ollie should know about this holdup?"

"I am afraid for Ollie," she said, and said nothing more. Lifting his head he caught her expression; and between the two was a common thought at this moment. They both had their suspicions and shared them, so that now they both knew that their suspicions were true. Ben's reaction was to say, "Be better if Jeff didn't know it was Ollie that told us. He likes Ollie. Hate to spoil that."

"We all like Ollie," said Diana. "That is

what makes it so sad."

"Maybe," said Scoggins, who was at bottom very kind, "I ought to talk to Ollie."

"Nothing you say would help. He's like Jeff in that respect. He'll make his own hell and his own heaven. I guess we all do, Ben."

"I guess," murmured Ben, "I'll just get my gun and ride down to Daly's tonight."

"Why, Ben?"

"I'll be a passenger on that stage in the mornin'," said Ben. As he said it the motion of excitement went over his face. He could, Diana realized, fight in his own way for the things he knew about; but this was a new game and he wasn't sure of himself. She admired his courage, and she had her own fears for him. But she offered no advice. Men lived by the light of their own consciences and though a woman had the power to sway and change them — to turn them reasonable when they were unreasonable, or to turn them mad when they were sane — it was not a wise thing to do. For afterwards a man would hate a woman for the change she had made in him. All she said was, "Be careful, Ben."

He liked the way she said it. He smiled at her and then the smile faded and he looked at her with a good deal of wistfulness. She was a beautiful and robust woman, with woman's soft depth and woman's spirit and woman's fire so clear to him. He wondered if these were revealed for him in the way of a signal, or if it was his own desires that made them so plain. He wasn't sure and, being unsure, he only said, "Good night, Diana," and turned about. Ten minutes later he was on the road to Daly's.

XI: Death at Bannack

AT FIVE in the morning Pierce stepped up to the coach seat and took the reins from the hostler. He had three passengers inside the coach, Parris Pfouts, a gambler by the name of Dustin bound for Salt Lake, and Ed Poe who ran a whipsaw mill outside of Bannack; and he had Cap Boyd on the seat beside him. After the large night of celebration Boyd was a shrunken and pallid man nursing a monstrous headache. The express agent tossed up the strongbox and the usual crowd collected and Jack Gallegher passed by. Pierce turned the coach and its four horses around on Wallace Street and remembered the way Gallegher stared at the strongbox.

The horses dropped into Daylight and labored up the hill to the summit. Pierce threw on the brakes for the descent into Central City, Cap Boyd groaning at every jar and lurch. "My God, Jeff, I am going to die before we reach Daly's and I'm glad of it."

The air was crystal clear and high-mountain thin and contained the sharp essence of the bare brown hills. The sun stood half below the line of the Tobacco Roots so that the Gulch itself remained gray-tan while brightness rushed across the upper sky. The coach ran through Central, wound and bounced along the ruts and the gravel beside the creek, stopped at Nevada for one passenger, and continued on.

Smoke lifted from the thousand breakfast fires of the Gulch. They passed Adobetown and forded Junction's shallow creek, at this point entering the narrow gorge wherein night's chill and night's last shadows remained. The horses kept a steady trot and half-run, the heavy coach-top swayed side to side and the wood panels rattled and chains clanked and steel hoofs struck sharp against the rocky undercrop of the road. Boyd gripped the seat with both hands, turned white and wan. "I can see you have driven before."

"This used to be my game."

"All drivers," groaned Boyd, "are crazy."

Fourteen miles from Virginia City the Gulch played out into the valley of the Stink-ingwater, crossed Ramshorn Creek and came upon Daly's, where two passengers waited — Bob Zachary and Ben Scoggins. "My horse," said Scoggins, "is lame and I guess I've got to pay good money to get to Bannack. When did you take up drivin', Jeff?"

"Relief for Harry German," said Pierce. But he was puzzled. Scoggins had a shotgun with him, which was unusual, and Scoggins watched him in a particular manner. Meanwhile Cap Boyd looked down on Zachary and showed trouble. He climbed from the coach to stamp his feet around the yard. He said: "I'm too damned sick to go any farther."

Bob Zachary was a young man with mustache and goatee. He had a wide mouth and a heavy chest. He stood by, eying Cap Boyd all this while and saying nothing. Boyd looked at Zachary and shook his head. "I'm laying over until the next coach," he said, and started for Daly's Roadhouse. But he pulled up and gave Daly's a sudden glance and reconsidered his decision. "No," he added, "might as well go on," and climbed inside the coach. Scoggins started for the near coachwheel, intending to sit beside Pierce, but Zachary was before him. "I'll ride up," he said, and jumped to the seat.

"All right," Scoggins said, "I don't care. By the way, Jeff, I've got a new shotgun. If you hear me blazin' away at jackrabbits think nothing of it. Want to try this thing out."

He got into the coach and closed the door and Pierce set the horses into a run, now skirting the Stinkingwater and meanwhile wondering why Scoggins, who had never to his knowledge cared much about guns, should be packing the weapon. It was out of the way and accordingly caught Pierce's full interest. He thought about it from Daly's to Cold Springs Ranch. One mile beyond Cold Springs Ranch he paused at Baker's and sat on the box while the relay man changed horses. He forded for Stinkingwater, came upon Dempsey's Ranch and halted for a passenger — a very long and loose-jointed man with a tobacco-stained beard and a pair of bright, close-set eyes. Cap Boyd groaned when the new man crowded into the coach.

The road climbed the yellow ruts from the Stinkingwater valley, arrived at the summit and undulated forward through long barren miles of rolling country. Southward the Rubys stood black; the McCarty Mountains were bold to the north. Day's sun burned down and the thin air fanned dryly against the skin; and the brake handle, when Pierce touched it, was uncomfortably hot. Scoggins, he thought, was not a man for extra conversation and Scoggins had gone out of his way to explain that he wanted to fire the gun from the coach. Scoggins was also sufficiently experienced with the half-tamed brand of horses in the country to know that a gunshot would bolt the team. It was a foolish thing to do; and Scoggins was not a fool.

Suspicion, never at any time fully asleep in him, now freely fed upon the small things that would not make a reasonable answer. The land before him pitched up and down in bare brown swells, and from his place on the seat he was able to look far out into the trough of those swells, wherein road agents might wait. The man beside him — this Bob Zachary whom he only casually knew — seemed nervous, and kept sliding on the seat, crowding into his, Pierce's side.

Pierce said: "Where's your horse?"

"Lame," said Zachary.

"Everybody's got a lame horse this morning. Get over on your own side of the seat."

Zachary moved over. After a while he said. "Well, the horse wasn't lame. Tell you the truth, I'm carrying a little money on me and I was afraid to ride through alone. The damned country is full of road agents." The sun was straight overhead but this Zachary pulled the brim of his hat over his eyes and half rose from his seat to scan the forward country. "What would you do if this thing was held up?"

"Haven't thought about it."

Zachary turned on him. "You wouldn't tough it out, would you?"

"Depends on how the play came up. I've done it before."

Zachary said: "Don't do it. You're up here broad as a barn. So am I."

They came to the rim of Beaverhead valley, at the bottom of which the silvered ribbon of river made its lazy loops. Pierce took the stage down in a rocketing run and stopped before Copeland's, halfway between Virginia City and Bannack. This being nooning place he threw the reins to the hostler, went in to eat and came out to squat under the sun while the hostler brought up fresh horses. He rested with his eyes half shut. Zachary came out and walked to the hostler. "Any trouble around here lately?"

"Guess not," said the hostler.

"Glad when I get to Bannack," said Zachary.

Pierce pulled his lids nearer together against the bright sun. Scoggins strolled along the yard, using his shotgun like a crutch. He stopped in the center of the yard and teetered on his heels and cast a short glance at Pierce. Pierce said: —

"If we're on a grade when you let go with that gun the horses will jump right over the rim."

"Won't be on a grade," said Ben. "Just somewhere between here and Bunton's." Then he added an afterthought: "Simply want to make a big noise."

Pierce lighted a cigar and bit his teeth into it. The long-legged passenger came from Copeland's house and moved to the stage. He stood by the door and he looked at Zachary until the latter shook his head and climbed to the top seat. Pierce dragged a deep draught of smoke into his lungs and expelled it. He said: "All in," and moved to the coach. Climbing up, he kicked off the brake and moved away from Copeland's, following the east bank of the Beaverhead. Twelve miles onward the road took a gravel ford over the river, left the valley and pointed west for Bannack across a dry and broken area. Suddenly Ben Scoggins' shotgun sent its hard noise into the hot day.

The horses sprang to a full run. Pierce wrestled them back to a trot, saying nothing, but Zachary let go with a genuine display of anger — "What's that damn fool doing?"

"Trying out his gun," said Pierce. Zachary was again crowded against him; he straightened his shoulders and gave Zachary a boost that almost flung the man off the coach. "Dammit, stay on your own side." He turned his head as he said it and caught the full flare of a temper that belonged in no timid man's system. Zachary at once turned his head away. "All right," he said, "I'm just nervous, I guess."

"Sure," agreed Pierce. He had a Colt in his holster and he had a carbine lying along the footboards; and he watched the broken land before him with a constant attention. They slammed into coulees, labored out of them, ran on and dropped again. Bunton's Ranch, sixty miles from Virginia City and ten out of Bannack, lay somewhere to the front and the afternoon was well on; the sun streamed from the low west against his eyes, making it difficult to sweep the distance. At this point he reached down, put the carbine between his knees, and spoke to Zachary.

"If we're jumped," he said, "I'll throw the reins to you. You keep those horses at a dead run."

"You're a damned fool if you do," said Zachary. "You want to live, don't you? So do I. You play peaceable and we won't lose anything but money. Look here, friend —"

"Keep those horses at a run of I'll lay you out with the barrel of this gun."

He saw, then, something for which he had long looked. Off to the right a pair of hat peaks showed from a deep coulee; and dust lifted from the coulee in signal of horses coming on the gallop. Ben Scoggins had also seen it, for the shotgun began to issue its spanging echoes into the hot and dusty air. Zachary yelled: "We're jumped! Pull in — pull in!" And at the same time he drove his shoulders hard into Pierce's flank and grabbed the reins.

The sound of the gun had bolted the horses again. Pierce surrendered the reins to Zachary and then he reached out with his hand and slapped Zachary twice across the face. He knocked off Zachary's hat and he brought the muzzle of the gun around. "Keep going or I'll kill you!"

The hat peaks rose up from the coulee and a pair of riders rushed headlong at the coach. Scoggins' gun flung its full charge at them and Pierce pulled up his gun, took aim from the pitching deck of the coach and began to spot his shots. He saw dust fly from the strike of the lead. Along the sights of the gun he made out the two men, both dark-dressed and with neckpieces lifted. One of the men had a hat with a brim that broke down in the rear; he noticed that as he fired.

Both men wheeled wide and pounded slantingly back toward the coulee. One shot reached them, his or Scoggins', and a horse floundered to its knees and sent its rider out of the saddle. The man struck the ground, rolled on and on and disappeared beneath the coulee's rim. The second rider reached the coulee and vanished in it; and afterwards his gun began to speak back at the coach. But his revolver was a poor weapon at the distance and the coach rushed ahead at full speed and in a little while got beyond range. The firing quit.

Pierce put down the gun and took the reins from Zachary. Zachary said in a short voice: "Might have gotten us killed."

That was all, but Pierce now had his man spotted. And he also knew that Scoggins had been forewarned of the holdup. He coaxed the team out of its run and, at a steadier trot, brought them into Bunton's for the last change of horses. It was six, with the sun ready to slide behind the Bitterroots. Bunton stood before his corral, no relief horses ready.

"Trouble?" he asked.

"No," said Pierce. "No trouble."

"We got jumped," said Zachary, "but we outran 'em." He descended and stared at Bunton a moment and shrugged his shoulders. The inside passengers got out. "Where's the horses?" asked Pierce.

"Didn't expect you so soon," said Bunton.

"What did you think might hold us back?" Pierce wanted to know.

Bunton turned to the corral without answering. Coming down from the seat, Pierce unhitched and slapped the weary horses away and waited for Bunton to harness up the new pairs. "You sure have made it tough on other drivers," Bunton commented. "Those road agents will knock 'em out of the box from now on."

"That's too bad," said Pierce.

"Yeah," said Bunton. "I'm workin' for Oliver's line and I hate to see anybody hurt."

Pierce said, "All in," and climbed to the seat, waiting for his passengers to get aboard. The long-legged man had disappeared into Bunton's shanty and Zachary shook his head. "I've had enough. I'll make it through after dark." Ben Scoggins suddenly got out of the coach and took place beside Pierce. He grinned down at Zachary. "Hard life, friend."

214

Pierce slapped the horses forward. Sunlight dropped between the Bitterroots and the sky turned red and twilight began to run over the flats. "You knew this was coming," said Pierce.

"I knew it," admitted Scoggins chuckling.

"Not saying where you heard it?"

"No, not saying. That Zachary was planted on you. So was Long John Franck."

"Who's Long John Franck?"

"The greasy one that stayed back at Bunton's with Zachary." Scoggins began to laugh. "Cap Boyd was feeling low until the fun started. This Long John began to yell for us not to fight back. He pushed up my arm and spoiled my aim. Cap quit being sick and got Long John around the throat and damned near choked him to death."

In full dark Pierce drove the stage before Bannack's hotel, tossed down the reins and stepped to the walk. Cap Boyd came out of the stage. "Come on," he said, "the drinks are on me. We'll have some fun —"

A cool voice said, "Trouble?" and Henry Plummer moved forward from the shadows of the hotel, slight and unimpressive and neat.

"No," said Pierce, "no trouble."

Cap Boyd said: "We were jumped but we got the drop on those fellows. They never got inside shootin' distance. We drove 'em right back to the Gulch and we knocked one of 'em off his horse."

Plummer's pleasant and courteous voice was only half interested. "That so? You're lucky. I have been expecting trouble. Been a lot of talk going around. These road agents are pretty cocky. How big a bunch tackled you?"

"Two," said Boyd. "And I think —"

Pierce said: "Let's get that drink," and jiggled Cap's elbow.

Henry Plummer said: "Any of them look familiar to you, Cap? Maybe I could get some idea. I'll have to break that stuff up."

"One was George Ives," said Cap positively. "I'd know him, mask or no mask."

"George Ives?" said Plummer with surprise. "I wouldn't have thought it of George. You're sure?" He came nearer Cap and his mild face remained unchanged. Still, his eyes were large and round on Cap Boyd — they were luminously intent.

"Let's get that drink," said Pierce.

"You damned right it was Ives," said Cap positively.

Plummer nodded. "You're lucky, Cap. Be careful where you walk. They might be sore and hunt you up. Going to Salt Lake?"

"In the morning," said Cap. Then caution came to him for the first time and he lowered his voice. "Say nothing about that, Henry."

"No," agreed Plummer, "I won't say a word," and strolled easy-footed into the dark.

Cap Boyd said, "Well, let's get at our

216

drinkin'." But he caught the expression on Pierce's face and he drew himself together and said, "What's wrong, Jeff?" Then doubt came to him, and a sense of fear damped his jolly spirits. "I guess I talk too much."

"Yes," said Pierce. "Ives will hear what you said."

"Plummer won't mention it."

"Ives will hear of it," repeated Pierce. "You'll have to get out of town, Cap."

The three of them entered the saloon and got their bottle and glasses and moved to the free lunch. Cap Boyd had lost his appetite entirely; he took three whiskies straight. "I have got to get a horse," said Cap. "But if I show up at the livery stable they'll catch on. Jeff, get me a horse."

"Who'll catch on?" asked Scoggins. "Who's in town you're afraid of, Cap?"

Cap shook his head. Pierce paid for the drinks and murmured, "Follow me," and walked to the hotel. He signed for a room and went up the stairs with the two men still following. They threaded a hall to its end and entered a back room. Pierce lighted a lamp and stepped to the room's open window and looked through it thoughtfully. He turned back. "Ben, go back to the saloon. Buy a bottle of whisky, a deck of cards and get some poker chips. Just drop the remark we're booked for an all-night game up here."

Scoggins didn't understand but he went

217

down the hall. Cap Boyd said: "Jeff, we're wasting time. Get me a horse. I'll start for Salt Lake tonight."

"Sure," said Pierce. He opened the room's door and scanned the hall; he stepped across the hall to the opposite room, and knocked softly on its door, receiving no answer. He opened the door, fading into the black. He was still inside this other room when Scoggins returned with the whisky and cards and poker chips. Scoggins said: "What's up?" Cap Boyd shook his head, and both men stood in the hall waiting.

Pierce came back. Cap said, "Open that bottle. I need a drink."

Scoggins said: "Give me an idea what this is all about, Jeff."

Pierce turned up the lamp wick and pulled down the window shade. He murmured, "Easy now," and led them into the second room. At the window he said, "Here we go," climbed through, and dropped from sight.

Scoggins and Cap Boyd came after him, made a twelve-foot drop through darkness, and found themselves in a narrow, black passageway between the hotel wall and an adjoining empty building.

"The horse idea is out," Pierce said. "No way of going to a stable without being spotted. If we stole a horse and got caught it would be a legitimate hanging."

The sound of rapid-traveling riders moved

in from the edge of town. Pierce led the way through back alleys, skirted several houses, crossed a dark rear road and at last came out upon the empty land south of Bannack. The three paused here. A dog crept through the shadows and began a steady barking. Pierce said: "Start walking for Salt Lake, Cap. Walk by night and hole up by day until you strike a freight outfit. You'll maybe starve for a couple days but don't drop into any of the relay stations until you're fifty miles from this place. Ben, you light out for Alder and don't show yourself until you reach your horse at Daly's."

"Where you going?" asked Scoggins.

"Something else." He trusted these men yet his sense of solitariness and his faith in himself would not let him share his plans. He put out his arm and took Cap's hand. "Good luck, Cap."

Starlight threw its frost-gleam down upon the blackness of the land. Cap Boyd's shape was small in the dark and his shoulders were round. He stood entirely silent a long while, thinking ahead and finding no pleasure in his thoughts. He said: "Always liked to have people around me — always liked to hear the boys laughin' with me. This is goin' to be all alone, Jeff."

"Sure," said Pierce, and his voice touched a note of sympathy and understanding that Ben Scoggins had not thought lived in this hard man. "You're thinking of a lot of camp-fires you sat around, with a lot of men to share the heat. You're thinking of the Senate and the crowd. But you're always alone when you take the road. Every man is. And every man, sooner or later, has to take it. Your friends fall away and the sun goes down and there's nothing but a black trail moving through a damned brutal world." He fell momentarily silent, and when he again spoke it was to share with Cap some of his own bitter rebellion, some of his keen hatred of the world's injustice. "Don't buckle up. To hell with anything that tries to stop you. You fight back. You duck and dodge and hide and you push on. When you get to Salt Lake you can laugh because you beat the game that tried to beat you. So-long, Cap."

"So-long," said Cap. For an instant he stood irresolutely before Pierce and Scoggins. Then he turned and moved west and disappeared in the dark.

Scoggins said: "My God, Jeff, you really believe that? Ain't there anything hopeful in your scheme of things?"

"Hope?" said Pierce. "Hope and warmth and a happy end for us all? Is that what you're talking about? A place where we can fall asleep and have no trouble? A place for music, and women laughing, and sunlight always coming over the hill?" He drew his long breath, and he said, "No, I guess not.

I'll see you later, Ben. Be careful."

"Sure," said Scoggins and then, unmindful of their touchy position, he laughed aloud. The stray dog kept up its steady barking; and somebody came to the door of the nearest house, a hundred yards away, and called at it. "I am a peaceful man," said Scoggins, "and here I am up to my ears in trouble and likin' it." Still chuckling, he moved away and was lost.

Pierce turned west on the heels of the vanished Cap Boyd. He circled the main hulk of Bannack, aiming toward the end of the main street as it straggled into the open lots and sheds at the margin of town. From this position he had a decent view of Bannack's heart and saw the crowd drifting in and out of the stores and the saloons. A rider came from the west, passing him. He skirted a barn and aimed at the shadow of a shed — the last one on this road — and moved to it. He went around the four sides, located the door and stepped in. He heard the fiddling steps of a horse before him and he murmured, "Easy — easy," and struck a match. The horse was a long-legged bay, saddled and standing on dropped reins. He spotted the two-by-four stringers and the planks loosely thrown across them. The light went out. In the succeeding darkness he moved his hand along the planks, found the cantina which contained Barney Morris' gold and brought it down. Five minutes later he left the barn and took to the road, pointed west.

Ives and Marshland rode into Bannack a half-hour after the stage arrived. It was Marshland's horse which had been shot in the holdup, whereupon he had ridden double with Ives as far as Bunton's, there picking up a fresh animal. Now, bruised by the fall, he made for the saloon for a drink and something to eat while Ives located Henry Plummer. Plummer stood in front of a store, in deep conversation with Sydney Edgerton, Federal Judge of the territory, and never looked at Ives as the latter passed by. It was Edgerton, a very resolute citizen, who gave Ives the benefit of his sharp glance. Ives moved on into the back part of town and placed himself beside a shed. It was a good ten minutes before Plummer came along.

"What went wrong?" asked Plummer.

"Something leaked out. They had the bulge on us."

Plummer said: "Pierce and Cap Boyd and that other fellow are at the hotel in a poker game. Cap Boyd named you to me on the street."

"Did he?" said Ives and fell into a soft and wicked cursing. "By God, I'll stop Cap's mouth." He turned back instantly, found Marshland in the saloon and drew him out. These two moved up the hotel stairs and crept soft-footed along the hall toward the strip of light flushing beneath the room's doorway. There was no sound from the room. Ives, the cooler and tougher of the two, stepped against the door and drew his gun — and flung himself into the empty room. A bottle, a pack of cards and a case of chips stood unused on the table. Ives whipped about at once. "We've been sold, Steve. Come on."

Plummer was then moving along the main street's walk. He saw Ives and Marshland reach their horses and trot out of town; and with instant perception he crossed the street, got behind the south row of buildings and ran to the rear end of the stable wherein he kept his horse. He went out the back way and circled town, coming upon Ives and Marshland half a mile along the road.

"They slipped out on us," said Ives.

"They had no horses," said Plummer. "Where would they go afoot?"

"They knew they had to get out on the quiet," said Ives. "That would be Pierce's idea."

"Cap wouldn't go back to the Gulch. My bet is he's on his way toward Salt Lake."

"Means nothing," said Ives.

Marshland said: "I keep smelling dust ahead of us."

"I didn't see anybody leave town within the last half-hour," said Plummer.

"Listen," said Marshland.

Marshland and Ives immediately retreated from the road. Plummer seized the bridle of his horse and backed away. Down the road, in the direction of Bannack, was a small ragged tattoo of sound, stopping and starting, and at last becoming the echo of a man on the run. The man's labored breathing came forward and presently the man's shadow appeared. When it arrived abreast of Plummer the Sheriff called: "Who's that?"

The man stopped and his frightened wind lunged out. He turned as though to run away, and then he said in a disgusted voice, "Oh, hell," and turned again. "You on the way to Horse Prairie?"

"Yes," said Plummer.

"Give me a leg on your horse," said the man. "I'm damned weary of walkin'."

"What makes you walk?" asked the Sheriff, and reached for his matches.

"Lost my horse in the brush. Threw me and ran."

Plummer scratched his sulphur and held it out; and by it he saw the weary, owl-like face of Cap Boyd. At the same time Cap Boyd saw him and a loosening wave of relief went over his face. He drew in his breath. "By God, Sheriff, I'm glad to see you. I —"

"All right, George," said Plummer.

Cap Boyd turned his head, for the first time noticing Ives and Marshland. Both men had their guns on him, and then Cap Boyd knew that he was dead. Knowing it he turned his face on Plummer, at last aware of Plummer's evil and condemning him with a single terrible glance in which fright and courage and hatred struggled. Ives and Marshland fired together. Their bullets shook Cap Boyd off his feet and tore through him. He fell with a small sound and was dead.

It was Plummer who stepped forward and knelt over Boyd. The match went out but he didn't take time to light another. He said: "Four pouches in his belt."

Marshland said: "Still wonder who's ahead of us."

Plummer went to his horse and climbed to the saddle. The three men remained silent until at last the Sheriff said: "It was Pierce who brought Barney Morris' money to Bannack in the first place. You suppose he could have got it tonight and gone on toward Salt Lake?"

"Let's follow."

"No," said Plummer. "I want to go back to Bannack and find out if the money's still in Oliver's safe."

Pierce caught up with the wagon team fifty miles out from Bannack, turned Barney Morris' money over to the wagon master and started back for Alder Gulch by a roundabout route through the hills. He arrived at Junction four days after his departure from the Gulch; and at this place met a miner who told him of Cap Boyd's death. When he reached Virginia City he looked up Oliver. Oliver told him something else: —

"That freight outfit was held up night before last. They killed the wagon master and they got Barney's dust."

"A clean sweep," said Pierce, and said nothing more. He stood before Oliver and let no expression, no emotion out of him.

"One other thing," said Oliver. "The toughs have made it a point to get you."

On Thursday afternoon, as was his invariable custom, Temperton called at the bakery for his daughter and took her on an idle walk through town. Sometimes they explored the Gulch, pausing to watch the rockers and long toms at work; and sometimes he hired a rig and drove Lily Beth down to Junction and back. At six they usually ate at the Virginia Hotel, after which he would return her to Diana, gravely lift his hat to them and depart for the evening at Tanner's.

They were a sober, silent pair. Now and then Temperton started a politely casual conversation and at these times Lily Beth would dutifully listen and add her brief word when the occasion called for it. Once in a while he would take her hand and they would swing along this way; but sooner or later, under some reasonable pretext or other, she would withdraw her arm. He never appeared to notice this; yet always at that point the talk would stop for an interval and he would walk with his eyes affixed to some object before him.

On this particular Thursday he took her to his room at the hotel. He said, "I have a small present for you," and got a small white pasteboard box from the bureau. She took it and thanked him but didn't open it until he suggested doing so. The inside of the box had a satin cover and nested against the satin was a rope of jade beads with a jade pendant.

"I sent to San Francisco for it," he said. "The green should go well with your new dress."

"Yes," she said. "It will look very nice. Thank you."

He looked at her intently. "Everything's all right here?" he wanted to know.

"Yes. I'm fine."

"Is there anything you wish me to do for you or for Miss Castle?"

"No," she said, "we're both fine."

The expression of defeat made its brief appearance on his face and quickly went away. He moved to the window, long watching the street below him; and he waited there a considerable while, hoping that his daughter might offer some straightforward and natural bit of talk that would break the wall between them. It had to come from her, for he had no way of dropping his own reserve, he had no knowledge at all of the mind or the heart of Lily Beth. But she was, as always, silently waiting for him; and so he turned and said: "I suppose we should go eat. It's getting on."

"Yes," said Lily Beth.

They ate at the Virginia Hotel and returned to the bakery. He stood a moment, noting that Lily Beth smiled when she was with Diana and smiled at no other time, and presently he lifted his hat to them and said "Good evening," and left the shop.

Diana had watched him and she had watched Lily Beth, and she knew the afternoon had gone no better than before. "Were you kind to your father, Lily Beth?" she asked.

"I remembered that you said I should talk to him," said Lily Beth, "and I tried. But there wasn't anything to say."

XII: The Black Hat

OVERNIGHT WINTER laid its whiteness on hillslope and bar. Water buckets froze to the bottom and barrels burst their staves and ice formed in the creek and the gravel in mine shafts turned stone-hard. Wind hauled around to the east, sweeping from the Tobacco Roots down the Gulch, cutting through clothes and sliding between the warped spaces of building and cabin.

This was the first warning of long winter to come, therefore the hardy ones sealed their cabins with old newspapers, banked dirt around flimsy tents and prepared for the long siege, while the discouraged ones and the lonely ones prepared for departure. The stages leaving Virginia City were filled and other miners, troubled by the road agents, began to organize large parties, whereby to make the outbound trip with some assurance of safety.

All prices jumped. Virginia's human driftwood, which ate Virginia's scraps and slept in the open, now began to crawl tentatively into the back end of livery barns. Cold weather shortened the work day, so that miners spent more time in the saloons and at the card tables and tempers heated and sudden quarrels raged up and the hill cemetery showed its fresh mounds of dirt. Each day the toughs grew bolder and a feeling of terror spread like a smell up and down the Gulch. Each night the creek gold poured over the bars of Tanner's, the Senate, the Pony and the other thirty saloons and dance halls and hurdy-gurdy joints.

Ollie Rounds left Tanner's in the twilight of one afternoon and stopped at the bakeshop to pass the time with Diana. He wore a heavy buffalo coat with a fur collar, which drew Diana's admiration. "Where'd you get it, Ollie?"

"Bought it from a fellow down on his luck."

"You're warm — and he's cold," she said.

"Don't be so kind." He was well-fed and momentarily at peace with himself and in this mood could be as attractive as any man. "If everybody in this world started out warm, with money and food and jobs, half of the world would be cold again inside of a year. Some are foolish, some lazy, some blind. And some are unlucky." He helped himself to one of her doughnuts. "Which is why I've never permitted ambition to eat out my heart.

Wanting little, I've never been much disappointed."

She gave him a critical study. "You have a good deal of talent. None of it you use. Is it because you're afraid of failure that you never have tried to get on?"

"I don't like to be cold, I don't like to fail and I don't like to be hurt."

"So," she murmured, "you'd rather not try anything." Then she grew angry with him. "Men were not meant to be like that. Men were meant to fight."

"But for what?" he asked and ceased to smile.

"To remain men with pride and self-respect. To work, because we must all work. To do something about the cruelty and meanness around us."

"Like Jeff," he idly commented. "He fights. Look what it has done to him."

"What," she asked swiftly, "has it done to him?"

"Made him unhappy. Made him a man surrounded by toughs who mean to kill him."

She said, thoughtful and deliberate, "I doubt if he asks happiness. I doubt if he asks for anything at all. I think he's proud to have the toughs hate him."

He regained his cheerful manner. "Let him take my share of the struggle. I'd still rather be warm." He passed out of the bakery into the steady sweep of cold wind. Darkness lay on the land and lights sparkled through Virginia City's window panes. He turned up Wallace Street and for a few minutes visited with Scoggins. After that he returned to a stable, got his horse and galloped down the Gulch. At Daly's Roadhouse he ate supper and stood at the bar, drinking steadily and alone, and went to bed. Rising at five, he moved on toward Bannack. A few miles beyond the Beaverhead he dipped into a coulee and found Ives and Buck Stinson and Rube Ketchum waiting.

This day was bitter-cold. Ketchum nursed his sullen temper and Stinson was irritable. These three had been talking about him, Ollie Rounds guessed; it was to be seen in the manner they watched him. Ives said: "A little bit late, Ollie."

"Daly's was warm," said Rounds. "Anyhow, we've got an hour."

"No," said Ives, who had been standing at the edge of the gulch, looking eastward, "it is coming now."

The four men turned their neckpieces up around their eyes. Ives said: "Buck and I will head in the horses. Rube will roust 'em out of the coach. Ollie, you take the other side of the coach. After everybody gets out you go inside and see that nothing's been hidden under the seats. Look into the luggage too."

"Anybody in particular coming through?" asked Stinson.

"Fellow by the name of Jack Hilton. Club-foot George says he's got couple thousand in dust." He put his bare head over the gulch rim and brought it back. "Buck and I'll go out first. You two stay back a few seconds, in case there's trouble. If so, you open up from here." He got on his horse and signaled Stinson. "All right," he said. The two rushed along the gulch toward the road and suddenly flung themselves at the coach. The rattle and slam of the coach was a clear sound; and over this sound lifted Ives' abrupt shout. "Pull up!"

The coach halted at once. There was no echo of trouble, whereupon Rounds and Ketchum rode from the gulch and galloped forward, Ketchum taking the coach's near side. Rounds circled to the off side. The driver sat still, holding tight reins on his horses and showing more irritation than fear. Ives said: "Everybody out. Get down from the box, Bill."

"What the hell?" grumbled the driver. "You want these horses to run away?"

Ives moved to the off leader and took grip on the rein. "Get down. No damned foolishness either."

The driver jumped to the ground and the passengers stepped from the coach one by one, prompted by Ketchum. Ollie Rounds came forward and now entered the coach to inspect it. He heard Ives say: "Get back up,

Billy, and throw down the box and the luggage." Rounds left the coach and kicked open the blanket rolls and the suitcases as the driver threw them; he found one filled poke in a bedding roll. Ives was now sharply speaking to the passengers lined up beyond the coach. "Stand tight. It is too damned cold to be fooling." Then, coming toward Ives, Ollie Rounds had his first sight of the six passengers standing with their hands lifted. One of them was Ben Scoggins.

He whirled at once and stepped behind the coach so that he would be out of sight. But Scoggins' glance had caught him. He stood fast, now hearing Ketchum growl: "Hilton, what'd you do with it?"

"What?" said Hilton.

"Cut that out," said Ketchum. "You're salted with dust. Where is it?"

"Think I'd bring dust on the stage?" said Hilton. "I'm no damned fool."

"Ain't you?" asked Ketchum. There was, suddenly, some sort of scuffle. Rounds stepped ahead so that he might see it and as he came around the horses he caught sight of Ketchum pacing backward from the row of passengers. Ketchum aimed deliberately at Hilton and fired twice, tearing life out of the man before he fell.

Ives shouted in a gritty voice. "Stop that, Rube! All right — get aboard!"

Hilton lay curled on the hard ground, dead.

The passengers, shocked silent, walked around Hilton and climbed inside the coach. But Scoggins remained where he had been, looking at the dead man, and presently his glance rose to Ives, and moved to Ketchum, to Stinson, and at last to Rounds. There wasn't much on his face, Rounds thought. But Scoggins' eyes were a pale, squeezed-out color and feeling violently came from them. Ben was giving himself away, Ollie thought; there was so much fury and hatred in the look that Ives or Stinson or Ketchum, seeing it, might shoot him down. He turned immediately, speaking to Ives. "Let's get out of here."

Scoggins was the last man in the coach. The driver had returned to his seat and called down, "I'm reaching for my tobacco," and slowly dug a hand into his pocket. He took a massive bite on the plug and settled himself.

"All right," said Ives. "Go on."

The driver released the brake. The coach rolled on, its panels clattering and its big wheels bumping the ruts. The driver shouted the horses into a steady run.

"Rube," said Ives. "What'd you do that for?"

Rube said in his surly monotone: "He didn't bring his money."

"Let's get out of here," repeated Rounds; and at his word the four men trotted eastward. Wind pushed steadily at them. Around noon they arrived at Daly's. Ives and Stinson and Ketchum stopped here but Rounds pushed up the Gulch. Somewhere beyond Daly's, cold as it was, he removed his buffalo coat and tossed it into the brush. When he reached Virginia City, chilled to the marrow, he went directly to Dance and Stuart's, there purchasing a new cloth coat. "Some son-of-a-gun held me up last night," he said to W. B. Dance, "took my money and my watch and my coat."

He went to his room in the Planter's Hotel, ordered a jug of hot water and shaved. As he shaved he met his own eyes in the mirror and he saw the signs of weakness at the corners of his mouth, so that at last the face in the mirror disgusted him. He finished his shave and lighted a cigar, and he began a steady pacing around the room. He'd had his neckpiece over his lower face but he remembered how intently Ben Scoggins had watched him. He remembered, too, the sound of Hilton's broken wind and the deadness on Hilton's face as he fell. Rounds stopped his pacing and stood still, knowing it would be better for him if he left the Gulch at once. There was always a time when a man's errors caught up, when some sign or signal gave him away. That warning came to him now as a premonition; and as he walked back to Tanner's the idea of escape was strongly in his mind. But after he drank three whiskies in a row the old carelessness and the old sense of futility took possession again and he shrugged his fears away. He moved to Temperton's table and joined the game.

Hilton was a man well known in Virginia City and the news of his death caused a strong reaction in the Gulch. Somebody, in the heart of the night, put a sign on Tanner's which read: "The men who killed Jack Hilton probably hang out here. Maybe, before long they will *hang out* somewhere else."

There were rumors as to the road agents. None of them were definitely known, yet the Gulch had its guesses concerning the fancy idleness of Virginia's men who toiled not and did no spinning; it had its evidence of careless words dropped by some of the toughs, and it had its suspicions. Twelve thousand men, all watching, reached a certain community thought regarding the identity of some of the toughs. And so it was that Gallegher fell under the cloud and knew it and grew defiant and contemptuous of it; and George Ives was suspected, and Rube Ketchum definitely pegged. There were others on whom a more nebulous suspicion was pinned as well — and Tanner's was generally regarded to be their rendezvous. Yet, knowing or suspecting, the Gulch did nothing. The miners did not cohere. Half-knowing their enemies and half-realizing their power over them, they were yet too unsure to strike or too indifferent. And meanwhile, as they stood indecisive, the toughs grew bolder and words were openly passed in Tanner's.

There was an undercurrent running, though, unknown to the toughs or to the bulk of the men in the Gulch. Parris Pfouts came up the Gulch and stopped one night to speak to Pierce. "A little rough," he said. "If we could just get a few good men together . . ."

"No," said Pierce. "Not yet."

"How long are we to stand around and watch this?"

"Till the Gulch forgets to cry for sinners," said Pierce.

"Some of us," said Pfouts, "are beyond crying. Seems to me you'd be glad to throw in. They're after you."

"I'll take care of that," said Pierce. "I wouldn't ask a committee to do it."

"You're not doing anything yet," pointed out Pfouts.

"No," said Pierce, "not yet." He gave Pfouts a long look. "Why should you care?"

"A man wants to see his neighborhood clean," said Pfouts. "People have got a right to live in peace."

Pierce pointed to the cook-fires along the Gulch, to the lights shining through tent walls and cabin windows. "They cry for sinners, or they're afraid, or they don't care. If they won't clean house, let them live in a dirty house."

"No," said Pfouts, quietly stubborn, "it is up to us to make them see. If they do not see and will not act then the good and just must act for them."

"The good and the just will get no thanks for it, Parris."

"Why," admitted Parris, "that is perfectly true. The good and the just always stand alone, in the beginning. They always suffer for it, in the beginning. But then, when they show the way, people follow. That is the obligation of the good and just."

"You believe in being your neighbor's keeper?"

"Of course," said Pfouts. "Don't you?"

"No," said Pierce bluntly. "I am my own keeper. Nobody cries for me, and I will cry for no other man."

Pfouts smiled a very gentle smile. "My boy, you are too hard. You do not know about weakness. Some men are strong. Some see the truth, some do not. The strong must lend their strength to the weak or there will be no justice, and those that see the truth must make the blind ones see it or there will be no truth."

Pierce stood fast, disbelieving and yet closely listening; not to the words so much as to the way Pfouts spoke them, with a ring and a conviction. Pfouts smiled and Pfouts seemed to understand.

"No man," said Pierce, "ever defended me in need. No law ever went out of its way to protect me. There's only one law I ever knew about, and I had to make it for myself. You know what that one is? Protect yourself and survive."

"But," said Pfouts, "you will not survive under that law. You may live to be a thousand, but under that law you will nevertheless die another way in short order, and the rest of your years will be no good." He got on his horse, looking down through the dark at Pierce. "Injustice usually makes men bitter. Now I will say something which seems to make no sense. You will have to be hurt again before you cease to be bitter. When a man gets hurt and grows weak he sees what weakness is like — and then he comes to have pity for others who are weak, instead of despising them as he formerly did. And when he is weak he discovers that he needs help — and then he knows that nobody can stand alone in this world."

He went down the Gulch toward Virginia City, disappearing soon in the shadows. Two days later, the hard and sharp wind remaining steady through the Gulch, Jim Williams came before Jeff's cabin. Weather had whipped his dark face red and increased the expression of melancholy on it. He wore a plaid muffler tight-wrapped around his neck.

"Scoggins said one of that road agent outfit

wore a buffalo coat."

"Lot of buffalo coats around," Pierce suggested.

"That's right." He was about to add something, but studied Pierce awhile and apparently forebore. Then he said: "From the descriptions, though, I think I know two of those fellows. It's Ives that wears a hat with a brim flopped down in back. The other one was Ketchum. No mask could cover his dog growl."

"Why didn't Ives think to change his hat?" said Pierce. "I guess they're getting pretty bold. They don't care much."

"No," said Jim Williams, "they don't care much."

This was supper hour again and fires burned along the Gulch floor, whipped bright by an unrelenting wind. Williams watched this sight. "Funny thing. They know — all those boys — what's wrong. And they know how to fix what's wrong."

"They're not ready yet," said Pierce.

"No," agreed Williams, "they're not ready yet." He gave Pierce his rather gentle smile, behind which the coolest kind of a temper lay. There was steel in him, there was darkness and wildness in him, covered by his softly melancholy manner. This was the quality which drew Pierce to the man; and in turn it was that quality which drew Williams to Pierce. They were both alike. Williams said,

"So-long," and drifted away.

Pierce cooked his supper and did up his dishes. He stoked the cabin stove and drew a burlap curtain across the window. The wind had risen and the cabin corners were shrilly singing. Somebody pounded on the door and Archie Caples announced himself and came in with George Noon and Mack Sturgis who had adjoining claims. Sturgis brought a bottle of Valley Tan, whereupon Pierce got out his tin cup. They had a drink, after which Caples said, "I'm bound for town. Got to pick up a hundred pounds of spuds." He pulled the collar of his coat around his ears and settled his hat solidly on his head. "We're going to be snowed in fast one of these days. You fellows better be forehanded and lay in plenty of grub, like me." He opened the door, slid quickly through, and slammed it behind him.

Noon said, "How about a poker game?"

Pierce dragged an army blanket off his bunk and spread it over the cabin's small table. He brought out a deck of cards and a pile of chips. Wash McMurtry knocked and came in. "Cold outside," he said and opened his heavy coat.

Noon said, "Have a drink, Wash," and pushed the bottle at him. There was only one chair in the cabin so that when they settled around the table Pierce sat on the bunk, Noon used the chair while McMurtry and Mack Sturgis used stovewood for seats. They fell to the game, idly talking.

Noon said: "Hard winter coming. Leaves dropped early, antelope came out of the high hills sooner than usual." Noon was an old-time mountain man who had trapped his beaver with Bridger and Carson and Sublette. He was here now, digging for gold, making the last stand of an aging man who had never known anything but the plains and hills and never wanted to know anything else. He had a long beard and untrimmed hair falling to his shoulders; he had a set of restless eyes and a hawk nose and he wore old-fashioned fringed buckskin still. "Have a drink, Jeff," he said. "Whut's life fer if not to have some fun?"

McMurtry said: "You'll get your fun. Camp's turning rotten."

"All camps," said George Noon, "get rotten. You crowd men together and they spoil. Natural way of man is to be alone a long time, then to come to settlement just to git the sulphur and hell outen him, then to go back and be alone again."

McMurtry looked at his cards and said, "Can't open. That's all right for a hermit like you. But I'm a town man. So're most of the rest of the Gulch folks. Not right to see crooks flourish and good men die off."

Noon gave him the benefit of an old Indian fighter's eyes — sharp and sun-faded and showing the ice and iron of a complete individualist. "Dyin's natural too. Whut difference does it make how a man dies? You fellers are all too tender."

McMurtry said: "Jeff's not tender."

"Why now," said Noon, "I wouldn't mind havin' him at my elbow in case we was jumped by twenty Rapahoes. But he's a town man, too. Ain't no town man really tough. In towns you got to live next to somebody. Then you got to think of that feller's rights. When you get to thinkin' of the other feller's rights you're tender. I don't think of nobody but me. My skin and my meat. Jeff looks tough, but in a pinch he'd risk his skin to get somebody else out of a hole. That ain't bein' tough. I have seen him get mad at somethin' somebody did to somebody else. If he was tough he wouldn't give a damn."

Pierce grinned. "You talk too much, George."

"That's whut camp does to a feller. I ought to be in the hills lookin' fer sign and listenin' to the owl hoot. When you hear an owl hoot in the hills chances are it ain't an owl but a Ute givin' signal. Sure I talk too much. I'm gettin' old and mighty soft. I should be dead."

He opened his mouth to continue speaking; and closed it. One sharp, short sound whipped along the wind. George Noon lifted his head, an old horse smelling fire. The sound came again, flatting through the rumble and racket of the night's rising storm. Pierce put down his cards. He reached out and dimmed the lamp's light and took his gun and belt from the bed. The other men had risen. Noon was at the door. "Not far off." A third shot broke on the heels of his words.

George Noon had opened the door. Pierce, moving rapidly over the room, went through it with the other men following. Cabin lights sparkled through the black and windy night and cabin doors came open to show their yellow squares. Men were calling and lanterns began to bob up and down. There was a light still burning in Archie Caples' cabin. Since Caples was a thrifty man and now had gone to Virginia City, this struck Pierce as odd. Ahead of him another man stirred, quite near Caples' cabin. Pierce called: "Archie — that you?"

There was no answer. The man faded into the dark and then Pierce caught the sudden crush of his boots against the frozen creek gravel. Pierce had been at a walk. Now he broke into a run, rounded Caples' cabin and saw the door open. He put both hands on the door's frame and looked in. What he saw made him turn about so swiftly that he struck the following George Noon head on. He pushed Noon aside and rushed downgrade, still hearing the scut-scut of the fleeing man. Cabins stood all the way along the creek, so that he had sight of the running man from time to time in the light beams, but dared not fire. He reached the creek's edge, hearing the splash of water ahead. The fugitive had crossed over, whereupon Pierce forded the creek and ran against the pitted, gravel-strewn edge of the Gulch. He heard the man fall and let out a yell a hundred feet before him. This was near another cabin; and now the owner of the cabin opened his door and came out and flung a call at Pierce.

"Hold up there!" he shouted. "Hold up or I'll blaze away!"

Pierce pulled in. "You damned fool!"

"Pierce? I thought somebody was fooling with my sluice."

The fugitive was now lost. Pierce swung and walked back to Caples' cabin and pushed through the gathering crowd of miners, into the small room. Archie Caples lay face down on the floor, dead in his own blood, both hands thrown ahead of him and both hands tight-clenched. George Noon and McMurtry were kneeling over Caples and McMurtry said: "He's got a shoelace in his left hand. Must of grabbed at the other fellow's foot as he dropped."

"Been a hell of a fight around here."

Everything in the cabin had been ripped loose or broken or torn apart. The stove stood undisturbed but its chimney had been knocked down, so that smoke rolled up through the place and made the crowding miners weep. Caples' blankets were on the floor and his bed tick had been opened and its straw scattered. The flour barrel had been emptied, the woodbox tipped over. Somebody had made a rapid search for Caples' hidden dust.

There was a voice outside, saying: "Let me in there, boys."

Over in one corner lay a black, dirty hat. Pierce, moving through the small room, saw it and was arrested by it. He stood over it, knowing that it was not Archie Caples' hat. He bent down and picked it up; and turned to see Jack Gallegher shouldering through the door. Gallegher stared at the dead Caples. "Another shootin'?"

George Noon said: "Damned fool question."

"Looks like a holdup," said Gallegher. "Anybody see the fellow?"

Eight men crowded in this small ten-by-twelve room and half a dozen more looked in at the doorway and a hundred men stood out in the dark. But nobody answered Gallegher. Everybody looked at Gallegher, distrusting him and offering him no information. Gallegher shrugged his shoulders. "Hell of a note," he said, and then noticed the hat in Pierce's hand. "You find that here?"

"That's right."

"Caples'?"

"Not Caples' hat."

"Then," said Gallegher, "I'll take it," and moved his arm confidently forward. "Maybe I can get an idea."

"I'll keep this hat," said Pierce.

He saw — and all of them saw — the streaky hardening of muscles on Gallegher's jaw. He stared at Pierce with his black and insolent and close-guarded eyes. Trouble went through the place like a bad smell, rank and stifling. Pierce met it better than halfway.

"I can find this fellow as quick as you can, Jack. Maybe quicker."

Gallegher shrugged his shoulders. "I don't care," he said, and left the cabin.

Noon said: "The hell he don't care. Know whose hat that is, Jeff?"

"No," said Pierce, "but I can find out."

George Noon grumbled. "It ain't none of your business."

"I liked Archie Caples."

Noon turned to McMurtry and Sturgis. "You see? He's tender."

XIII: The Captain's Ghost

THE CALL started in the Gulch on the morning following Archie Caples' death and by afternoon three hundred miners whose claims lay around Virginia City had gathered about a roaring fire near Archie's cabin.

There was no particular leadership to the crowd, for the habit of live and let live was very strong. But men grouped up and talked the matter over and the mass feeling was clearer than it had ever been. Those who had been indifferent were now shocked into violent anger, and many of those who had been afraid now found comfort in the general sentiment. Archie Caples had been well known and well liked, the killing had been brutal and near at hand. If lightning struck this close it was only a matter of time before it came still closer. That was the tone of the talk. Now and then some man, growing bolder, mentioned the one concrete way by which the Gulch could be cleansed.

A miner from Summit way first openly said it. "We'll get nowhere at all by talking. Everybody knows it, too. Get your men and hang 'em."

George Noon remained a skeptic. "Hang who?"

"We can pick some damned good candidates on short order," said the Summit man.

"Who'll kick the box from anunder 'em?" asked George Noon, and found no immediate takers. He said then: "Talkin's one thing, doin' is another. You boys are just lettin' off steam."

Pierce moved through the crowd, listening to the slow bubble and rumble of the various conversations; and saw the same defect George Noon had noted. Three hundred miners, if they wished, could sweep the Gulch clean from Summit to Junction. But these men were still individuals; they were not yet pulled together. Occasionally somebody stopped him to ask about the hat, whereupon he would answer: "Haven't found out about it yet," and move on.

Jim Williams arrived, carefully assaying the temper of the meeting but not adding any particular remark of his own. Parris Pfouts appeared with Neil Howie. John Lott, from Nevada City, came by, as did half a dozen other townsmen definitely on the right side of the fence. Gradually as the afternoon wore on sentiment began to weld the crowd; every-

250

thing had been talked over and convictions were pretty well arrived at. Somebody again asked Pierce about the hat.

"Haven't been to town yet to look into it," he answered.

The crowd waited for him to continue, and he observed that Williams and the townsmen waited. These townsmen, long biding their time, now felt the opportune moment had arrived. The miners were ready to act and needed only the voice of one man who would shape their sentiments, who would step out in front and take control. Understanding this, the townsmen waited for Pierce to do the logical thing. But he did not rise to the opportunity. He remained silent, not trusting this crowd which once had washed away its convictions in a flood of tears. What had to be done for Archie Caples, he would do himself.

Wash McMurtry said: "The stage has been braced three times in a week. A man with any money on him is a sure mark for a holdup or for a killing. We're fat cows for the toughs. Every once in a while when the toughs want meat, they just lead out another fat cow and slaughter it. What the hell's the matter with spunk? We could roll down this Gulch and tear every hurdy-gurdy joint to the ground in half an hour. We could run every tough out of town before dark came."

Someone deep in the crowd called: "Well,

let's do it."

McMurtry said at once: "Come right out here and say it louder. Then maybe we can do it."

The man stayed where he was. The crowd agreed with McMurtry, but it would not follow him. He lacked, somehow the magic of authority; and so the crowd, angry yet indecisive, waited for a surer voice and a better man to follow. Williams, coolly gauging all this, now spoke for the first time, presenting the opportunity once more to Pierce.

"What're you going to do, Jeff?"

"I'll find out about the hat," said Pierce. It was all he said, and he said it short and quick. The crowd was before him and around him; he was in the center of it. He had a feeling then that if he raised his arm and pointed it at Virginia City all these men would turn and go with him. The faith of men came out and touched him with its warmth. It was strange how that warmth, that faith and confidence, penetrated to those deep places in him which were lonely and empty. It unsettled him and brought up queer promptings and for a little while he was close to these men, and liked them, and had a moment's pride and a moment's quick response. But it was not enough. The old ways came back, the old hard belief in himself alone, the old thought of survival and solitary duties done

252

without favor and without help.

"What happens if you find whose hat it is?" asked Williams, still pressing the chance.

"I'll take care of Archie Caples," he said.

He noted the look of disappointment on Williams' face, and John Lott showed irritation, and Parris Pfouts regretfully shook his head. McMurtry once more tried his hand. "We know about Ives. We know about Ketchum. All we got to do —"

Jack Gallegher had arrived on the edge of the crowd and called for a way through. He rode into the circle and called out cheerfully: "Anything you fellows want me to do?"

McMurtry, who had been so brave, looked at Gallegher and met Gallegher's steady stare, and suddenly turned away into the crowd. That, Pierce thought, was the way this crowd was and would always be. Before Gallegher its bravery died. Knowing Gallegher for a tough these men were suddenly afraid for themselves and fell still.

"What's on the bill?" said Gallegher, still affable. "You boys want action?"

Pierce said: "Not from you, Jack."

Gallegher flashed back his quick answer. "You speakin' for everybody?" His show of easy friendliness dropped away. The crowd so clearly distrusted him that he felt it and understood it and was angered by it and recklessly abandoned the part he had been playing. "Pierce," he said, "you're a damned

253

troublemaker. You've run into me once before. I let it go. I'm gettin' tired of letting it go."

Maybe, Pierce thought, this man was working himself up to the point of shooting. Bitter as the day was, Gallegher wore no overcoat. He held his reins in his left hand, his right hand free to drop and seize the near-by butt of his gun. Pierce himself wore his big navy revolver beneath his overcoat and this bit of carelessness, he knew, Gallegher had instantly noted. This was the moment of advantage and Gallegher's eyes mirrored the forming thought, the gathering impulse. Pierce said, "I thought you were the man that was my friend," and took an idle step forward. He was at the horse's head. Gallegher, weighing each second of time, saw his chance grow narrower and made his decision and reached for his gun.

Pierce batted the horse across the head, unsettling the beast. At the same time he caught Gallegher by the arm and dragged him out of the saddle, seized the Deputy on the point of his shoulder, and flung him through the air. The Deputy hit the frozen gravel, let out a sharp yell, and tried to pull himself up. Pierce jumped at him, dropped both knees full on the Deputy's belly. He seized Gallegher's gun and threw it back under the feet of the crowd — and stood up and waited.

Gallegher lay breathless on the ground and

slowly kicked his feet into the gravel, pumping back his wind. The noise of his throat, like an empty vomiting, turned one man in the crowd sick, for he murmured, "This is none of my affair," and moved away. He was afraid as well and that fear caught on at once — the fear of Gallegher's vengeance and the vengeance of the toughs. The crowd began to drift until at last only half the miners remained.

Gallegher rose to his feet, ash-white and struggling so hard with the pain of his fall that he clenched his teeth into his lower lip. Pierce said: "I told you to let me alone, Jack. There's no fun in the way I fight."

Gallegher looked around and failed to see his gun. "All right," he said, made cautious by his helplessness, and went to his horse. He climbed to the saddle and bent over in it, and for a moment laced his hands across his belly. He got hold of the reins and lifted them. He gave Pierce a full-burning glance and murmured again, "All right," and rode off.

George Noon spoke up. "You did wrong. Should of killed him. Whut stopped you?"

Pierce said irritably, "I don't know." Williams and Lott and Pfouts and the other townsmen remained, and a few miners. But the bulk of the crowd had gone. He said to Williams: "There's your crowd. That's what they'll do."

"No," said Parris Pfouts, "they were ready

to go with you. It was just a word they waited for. You didn't say it."

"I'm not the keeper of their morals," answered Pierce. "I wave no flags and I lead no parades. I'll take care of Archie Caples."

"Alone?" said John Lott. "You're a little too proud of your ability."

Pierce shot an affronted glance at John Lott. "I will let you merchants make speeches concerning law and order. Why didn't you make your pretty speech here? I don't ask your opinion as to what I can or cannot do."

Lott was a redoubtable citizen and his feathers went ruffling up. "I'll pass judgment as I please."

Pierce bluntly said: "You're another talker. I don't like talkers."

Lott would have shot back his instant challenge had not Jim Williams made a gesture at him. "Never mind, John," he said. "This hand's been played."

Parris Pfouts added his reasonable voice. "All Lott meant was that Gallegher will gather the toughs and come after you, Pierce. It is a challenge they can't let pass."

"Just talk," said Pierce, still unyielding. "There's too damned much talk."

"Not this time," said Pfouts, still soft of voice. "This time they've got to take you out or lose their authority. You're marked."

Jim Williams put a hand on Pierce's shoulder. "There must be no misunderstanding between us. We must stick together. You and Lott have no disagreement.''

He was a gentle-voiced, melancholy soul, a sharp judge ·of men; and he possessed a temper which when roused was a deadly thing. But he liked Pierce and now he was the peacemaker. Pierce shrugged his shoulders and smiled at Lott. ''Forget it, John,'' he said.

Lott nodded. ''Of course.''

Gray dusk began to settle along the Gulch. Pierce returned to his shack, cooked up supper and made a quick meal. It was full dark then. He stoked the stove, shrugged into his overcoat and turned down the lampwick. He shoved the revolver into an overcoat pocket, took the hat which he had found at Archie Caples', and left the shack. Wind bit at his ears and sliced along his cheeks. He put a foot in the water bucket and found the water again frozen solid.

Reaching Virginia City he went directly to Dance and Stuart's store. ''Dance,'' he said, ''has anybody been in here buying hats last night or today?''

Dance said: ''I'd have to ask the boys,'' and went along the counters of his store, questioning his clerks. Pierce meanwhile watched Clubfoot Lane work at his shoemaker's last in the corner of the store. Lane was a large man with his alternate moments of smiling and dark silence; this was the end of a day and now he worked in silence. He gave Pierce a single look, noticed the hat, and went on with his labors. Dance came back. "No," he said. "I guess everybody's got a hat."

Pierce went to Pfouts and Russell's, and from there to each of the mercantile stores. He found one place where a sale of a hat had been made. But it had been a hat for Nathaniel Langford, and there was no question of Langford at all. He came into Scoggins' and asked the same question.

"Let's see the hat," Scoggins asked. He took it and tried it on his head. "Yes," he said, "I sold a hat. Seven and a quarter size. That's what this is."

"Who was the man, Ben?"

Scoggins looked shrewd. "A small-time bum in Tanner's bought it. But it wasn't for him. I know that because he just ordered the hat and didn't try it on. Somebody sent him after it."

"What kind of a hat?"

"A black hat, stiff brim, dented on four sides, not creased down the middle." He said: "How you been?"

"All right."

"Look thinner than you was. Going to the ball?"

"What ball?"

"Why, hell," said Scoggins, "it's been talked about for a week. At the Virginia

258

Hotel tomorrow night. All the good folks in the Gulch will be there. All the nice ladies." Scoggins looked down at his hands, and added: "I'm taking Diana." Then he looked up to catch whatever might be on Pierce's face. Pierce, naturally a tall man, straightened and what Scoggins saw was a confused and surprised expression. A ruffle of feeling moved plainly through Pierce; a thought stirred in him, and left its uncertain track. But he covered it immediately and only added: "Good for you, Ben," and started from the store. He had reached the doorway when he called suddenly back, "That the hat, Ben?"

Scoggins came forward in time to see Rube Ketchum idly move along the wall of the Senate. Rube Ketchum was a huge, clumsy shape inside a heavy overcoat; a muffler covered his ears and he wore a new stiff-brimmed black hat.

"That's the hat," said Scoggins.

"I had the idea it would be," Pierce said dryly.

"What's next?"

"Nobody knows what's next, do they?" said Pierce, and left the store. He was thinking of Archie Caples and of Caples' big hands drumming the Sunday washboard. He was thinking as well of Barney Morris now five months dead on the hill and of Mary Morris somewhere in Ohio. He did not mean to be bound to these people. Their lives were not his lives; and still their lives had turned to tragedy because of a brute world. It was the brute world against which all his anger rose.

Ketchum had walked on around the corner of the Senate, apparently unaware of being watched; he bowed his head against the knife-thin wind. Pierce turned the Senate's corner and kept Ketchum's heavy and bulky shape before him. The street crowd was pretty small on this cold black night. The saloon doors, as he passed them, sent out steady currents of warmth. Ketchum, now at the corner of Van Buren, hooked around it.

The Virginia Hotel was at that corner; and coming forward Pierce saw a man ride out of the windy night and stop at the hotel's porch. The man got down, his back to Pierce, and he tied the reins to the ring post by the hotel, and for a short moment he faced the hotel and stared at it; afterwards the scrape of Pierce's feet drew his attention and he turned — and as he turned he showed the square and blocky-bearded face of Mister Sitgreaves.

Pierce had not forgotten about Sitgreaves. Sitgreaves was part of his past and his past always remained with him, like the slow-burning coals of an old fire. But he had not recently been thinking of Sitgreaves and this now was a shock that set him back. Sitgreaves' somber eyes grew round in recognition and he seemed to settle and take on weight. He had, Pierce thought, judged Sitgreaves properly in the beginning; this man was a bloodhound who would never give up until death came.

Pierce said: "Five months is a long time."

"Ah," said Sitgreaves, "I lost your trail. After Lewiston there was no trace — until I met a man who had seen you. But I went the wrong way. I went to Utah."

"The subject seems firm enough in your mind."

"Why," agreed Sitgreaves, "I am a firm man and my people have all been firm."

"Step around the corner to the Senate. We will keep warm at least."

"There is no object in talk," stated Sitgreaves. "No object at all."

"I have a gun in this pocket. Just step into the Senate."

Sitgreaves shrugged his shoulders, but obeyed. The two of them turned into the saloon's smoky warmth and moved at the bar. Pierce wiggled a finger for bottle and glasses. He waited for Sitgreaves to pour a drink, afterwards pouring his own.

"It is devilish cold weather," offered Sitgreaves. "The Bitterroot passes will be closed soon, I think. The drink will help. But," — he gave Pierce the full benefit of his black, zealous eyes, — "I cannot drink with you in any sense. I will not tie any sentiment of mine to any sentiment of yours. You understand?"

Pierce nodded and downed his drink. He stood by, watching Sitgreaves take a pair of whiskies straight. Sitgreaves pressed the back of a hand across the damp ends of his mustaches. "Bully," said Pierce, "I don't want to fight you."

"If that is the extent of this visit," said Sitgreaves, "let us end it. The affair is out of your hands. The both of us cannot live."

Pierce spoke in a reasoning way: "I was trapped aboard that ship, Bully. I did not come aboard a free man."

"True enough," agreed Sitgreaves. "Otherwise we would have had no crew out of San Francisco. It is a custom of the sea. It may not be a rightful custom." He dipped his head in a moment's contemplation. "I have thought somewhat of that lately. The sea is hard. Still, that changes nothing. You killed my brother."

"He tried to kill me."

"Of course. You were ordered not to jump ship. Let us admit you were shanghaied. But you were on board nevertheless, under the Captain's law. This is the only law on a ship. Makes no difference how you got there. You were there. There is just that one law."

"But this is land," Pierce pointed out. "And the law is different."

"So it is," agreed Sitgreaves. "I have thought of that too somewhat. I would not know if there is a law to bring you to book. But that does not matter greatly. I will take care of brother Neal."

"I expect you'll try," said Pierce.

Sitgreaves gave him a surprised glance. "I have no recourse. It is a long way back to Portland. I will not bother to find an officer in this camp to arrest you and take you back. Maybe it would be impossible to convict you in a land court if I got you back there. Landsmen do not understand. You see what that leaves me?" He spoke evenly and fairly, with a heatless conviction.

"That is your side of it," said Pierce. "Listen to mine. I have never lifted a hand at any man unless he lifted a hand at me. I let people alone. I wish to be let alone. Your brother tried to kill me. Now here you are. It is a little different with you. You feel you are right, and I give a man credit when he feels he is right. If you were a road agent I'd have no hesitation about you at all. But it is your brother you are thinking about, which I can understand. I would hate to draw a gun on you, Bully. Better think again."

"Is that all?" asked Sitgreaves politely.

"All right," said Pierce. "It must be your way."

"Yes," agreed Sitgreaves. "Let's not talk about it any more."

"I have got a few things to do," said Pierce. "I'd like not to have to think about you for a day or two. Is that agreeable?"

"I can make no bargain with you," announced Sitgreaves. "Understand me. I am a patient man, and a just one. My people have been patient and just. I have come a long way and I am not in a hurry. But I will make no bargain or truce with you." He nodded at the bulk of the gun in Pierce's overcoat pocket. "You have your opportunity now. You had better take it."

"No," said Pierce, "go on. Get out of my sight."

But Sitgreaves was not satisfied. "I can accept no favor from you. I do not accept this as a favor. I want you to know that. I will hunt you, fairly or any way. I will shoot you in whatever situation that seems best. You might see me when I fire. But you might not. My mind is clear on that point."

"You're a fool," said Pierce. "If I shot you now you'd be dead."

"No," said Sitgreaves, "you are wrong. If you shot at me now, you'd miss. Justice is entirely on my side and I cannot be hurt. I have no fear. The bullet is not in your possession which will kill me. But I have the bullet which will kill you."

He had the dark, long and in-brooding face of a Yankee witch-burner; an intense and colorless flame burned in him. He wore the armor of impregnable faith, double-buckled by righteousness. He was the judge and the

264

executioner and his own gods were clear before him. Pierce shook his head. "Go on, Bully. Go on." Standing at the bar, he watched Sitgreaves leave the saloon.

He poured himself a second whisky but he never drank it; for then he remembered Rube Ketchum and he turned and left the Senate at once. Sitgreaves was at the moment going around the corner of the hotel. In the other direction, toward Van Buren, Pierce saw Rube Ketchum in front of Jarman's big freight stables. He crossed the street diagonally, moving at Ketchum and at once drawing Ketchum's attention. Ketchum shifted, crossed the street and entered Van Buren. When Pierce reached the corner he saw Ketchum's heavy body pass in and out of the store lights.

Two hundred feet separated them. Pierce quickened his steps, bucked the hard wind and had closed half the distance by the time Ketchum reached Wallace Street. Coming around that corner Pierce found Ketchum stopped near Tanner's. Ketchum, knowing that he was followed, seemed at last to decide upon a stand. He had his back to Tanner's wall and he had his revolver lifted and pointed in the general direction of Van Buren Street — waiting a fair shot. As soon as he saw Pierce he steadied his aim and fired.

A team and wagon was at this moment coming down Wallace Street. The teamster stopped the horses, wrapped the reins around the brake handle and made a broad jump from the wagon and rushed toward the shelter of a wall. Two men near Tanner's retreated to an alley. Somebody inside Tanner's pushed open the swinging doors to study the scene, and vanished. The music in The Pantheon stopped. A man tried to lift the window of his second-story room in the Planter's Hotel, failed, and smashed the glass with his gun.

That first shot went wide and short of Pierce. He came forward, with his navy out of its coat pocket, until he was abreast the outshining lights of Diana Castle's Bakery, and he had a thought about her as he moved across the light, into the street's half darkness, there taking a short side-step and pausing. Rube Ketchum fired again over the long distance; and then, having missed twice, Ketchum's courage faltered and he started to turn at Tanner's door. This was the way Pierce's bullet caught him, tore into him and knocked him against Tanner's wall. Ketchum dropped his gun and his new hat fell off and went rolling with the wind. He put both hands flat against the wall and his knees touched it and he collapsed reluctantly to the walk. The teamster started for his wagon, got halfway to it, and wheeled back for shelter again. Jack Gallegher ran out of Tanner's with George Ives behind him. The crowd in The Pantheon moved to the street and women stood shivering in the cruel wind, hands crossed against their bare shoulders. Ives bent down and put a hand on Ketchum, and straightened to speak to Gallegher. Then both Gallegher and Ives looked toward Pierce.

Diana came to the door of her bakery at the sound of the firing and saw Ketchum fall. Pierce was not more than ten feet from her door, reared straight in the windy night, his revolver balanced, the expression on his face solemn and cool. It was hard for her to describe the effect it had on her. He was one single man standing thoroughly alone in the heart of a brutal town; and he knew it and even then she felt that he was looking into closing shadows and finding no future way for him, but that he no longer cared. He held fast, she thought, to the only thing that had ever meant anything to him, to his belief that the world was a savage thing seeking to destroy man, and that man's sole purpose was to fight back and survive. He stood there, defying all that the world might do to him, a man born to resist and to be alone. And yet this one quality crowded all gentleness out of him and made impossible the deep friendships a man needed. He knew that as well as she knew it. For, watching him with care and anxiety, she felt that for all his resistance and for all his courage, he was near the end of his rope. The joy of battle was gone for him, his horizons slowly closed down and he really no longer cared if he survived. He was tired and without hope and a little sick at heart over a life whose vigilance and distrust had slowly squeezed the fun out of him. And he had at last realized it, she thought. Somehow it was on his shoulders and in the very way he held the gun half lifted.

Gallegher stepped to the street's middle. Ives stood by the fallen Ketchum. Both men closely watched him, and Marshland moved from Tanner's, and Scoggins came around the corner of Wallace Street rapidly, and Ollie Rounds stepped from the Planter's and stopped dead in his tracks when he saw this scene. Diana noticed the way his face lost its easy calm, and for her it seemed to show terrible things in the half-shadows and half-light — the head-on clash of his loyalty with the other black secrets of his life. She had long had her suspicions about Ollie. She was entirely certain now. Ollie, looking on at a man he greatly liked, was held fast by the associations he had with Ives and Gallegher. He could not move.

Pierce called to Gallegher, to Ives. "There's your man. Send a better one next time."

"Pierce," said Gallegher, "throw down the gun. I've got to take you in."

"No," said Pierce, "I won't fall for it, Jack. You're a mongrel dog, eating scraps somebody else throws at you."

Terror squeezed Diana's heart, terror

chilled her. Pierce's voice gave Gallegher no quarter, he made it almost impossible for Gallegher to draw back. Here he paused and built his own fate word by word. Gallegher stood quite still, but his head turned and he looked at Ives and Marshland who stood together. Far down the street she saw Boone Helm, watching. It was Ives who said, calmly enough: —

"You're damned rough. What could you expect Gallegher to do after that talk?"

"Why," said Pierce, "to crawl away unless you backed him up."

Ives gave a short, reckless laugh. "You want me in on this?"

"Come in," said Pierce. "This time you've got no coulee to run for."

Ives laughed again, loud and sharp. He threw a small, careful gesture at Gallegher; he moved away from Tanner's door and away from Marshland and he called through the driving wind: "Never would turn any man's invitation down, Jeff."

Scoggins moved in until he was at Tanner's doorway, behind Marshland. Marshland turned and said something at Scoggins. Scoggins grinned and held his ground. George Ives kept waving Gallegher aside and as Gallegher retreated to the farther walk Ives paced forward until he stood in the street's middle, facing Pierce. He stopped here. He flung his head aside and saw Scoggins, and he frowned at Scoggins. "What the hell you want?" he asked. Then caution came back to him and he made a half-turn, and at once the bravado and nerve went out of him. Behind him, idle against the wall of Dance and Stuart's store, Jim Williams waited and listened. Near Williams was the stocky, indomitable X. Biedler.

Pierce said: "Well, George?"

Ives shook his head. "Not now, Jeff. Not now."

Diana drew a deep, relieved breath, and then stopped breathing. Pierce said in a long and taunting tone: "Brave man, George."

Ives shook his head and moved toward the saloon. Pierce suddenly laughed at him, and wheeled away. He saw Diana and he halted and seemed about to speak to her, the black humor now out of him and a kind of despair on his face. One distant voice spoke through the wind and a gun shouted and Pierce's body wavered as though hard hit by a weight and a look of wonder came to him. He pulled himself around, drawing his gun. Gallegher stood rooted. Marshland and Ives had not moved. It was none of these. Williams and Scoggins were turning rapidly to search the street and Rounds ran forward, pointing at an alley near Dance and Stuart's. "In there!" he yelled. Then the gun shouted again and Diana saw a little tongue of light leap from that alleyway.

Pierce doubled over but he didn't fall. He knelt and braced a hand against the ground, his other hand pushing into his right side. That hand turned red and his lips flattened against his teeth and the muscles of his jaws hardened against the pain he felt. Other people were on the far walk, afraid to move because of additional gunfire that might come. Ollie Rounds had done a strange thing. He had walked out into the street until his body was between Ives and Pierce. He put his back to Pierce, facing Ives; saying nothing and doing nothing, but forming that shield. Scoggins remained by Marshland. Jim Williams stood still by the Planter's. Parris Pfouts came from Wallace Street on the run and, joined by Biedler, moved toward that aperture which had held the unseen marksman.

So, for this moment, Pierce was alone on the street, going through his private hell while cold wind tried to shove him over. Diana was nearest him, but she didn't move. He turned his head toward her and then she remembered all the humiliation she had known at his hands, all the fineness he had swept aside, all the glory they had lost. She remembered it and knew its cause was that indescribable iron spirit in him which made him suspect and resist and treasure nothing but his own strength. And this made her say to him now: —

"If you needed help, Jeff, I'd be there. But you don't need help, do you? You don't believe in kindness or pity. You stand alone, and you fall alone — and there you are. That's what you have always said. How does it feel?" She didn't realize how her voice rose with long-pent-up feeling. Ollie Rounds swung and looked at her, and now ran toward Pierce. Scoggins came on from Tanner's. But before eigher of them reached Pierce, Lil Shannon rushed from The Pantheon, dropped on her knees and put her arms around him. Standing stone-still in the bakery doorway, Diana watched men come forward and lift Pierce and carry him into the dance hall.

XIV: Lil Asks Her Question

THE BULLET had struck Pierce in the pit of the stomach and, except for a bone button on his overcoat, would have torn its way through him. The heavy button had deflected the slug around his right side where, striking a rib, it had gouged out a chunk of flesh and nothing more. When they stripped off his shirt they found the slug, flattened by the impact, lodged against his trouser belt.

Doc Bissell, called into The Pantheon, improvised a bandage while Pierce stood stripped to the waist before a hundred men and women and was embarrassed enough to blush. He got hurriedly into his shirt. Lil helped him put on his coat and said: "You come with me."

"No, I'll go back home."

She got a bottle of whisky from the bar and took Pierce's arm. "I want to talk to you," she said, and led him across the dance-hall floor to a little rear room. She closed the door. She said, "Sit down," and put the bottle on the table. There was only the one chair, so she stood against the door. She said, "You need a drink, Jeff," and watched him tip the bottle. He had a wide chest, he had black eyebrows, he had the smoothest and most stubborn and, at this particular moment, the most inexpressive face a man could own. He ran a hand across his face, as though to wipe away the fog before him, and then he put his hands before him and looked at them. He glanced at her, troubled by a thought. "Did I yell when I dropped down?"

"No, Jeff."

"Somebody yelled. I felt a little mortified about that. Thought it was me. But what would I yell about?"

The fall had shaken his pride. What really mattered was the fact that he had been physically knocked off his feet and for a little while had lost his grasp on the world. He was going back through the scene now, painstakingly filling in the blank spots. "Two bullets were fired. That's right, isn't it? I went down. Scoggins and Ollie came up. And you were there." He stopped and seemed to be puzzled. "Wasn't somebody else there?"

She knew then what was in his mind. She said: "She was standing in the bakeshop doorway. But she didn't come to you."

He stared at the bottle. "What did you want to tell me, Lil?"

"I was the one that came to you. Not Diana."

"Thanks."

"Take another drink."

"I don't need that big a crutch to walk on."

She walked to his chair and stood behind him. She put her hands on his shoulders. She laid the warmth of her hands against his neck and pulled his head gently back until it rested against her. "I wish you'd get drunk enough to forget all the queer things in your head."

"Not enough whisky in town to make me forget very much, Lil."

"You're a man, the same as any other man. You've known women like me. Why don't you take me just as I am?"

"I like you too well."

Like? That's a thin word. Why do you have to put me up on a pedestal? I don't want to be there. Not with you. I never asked you to put me there." She moved around the table so that she might see him. She shrugged her shoulders and made a little gesture of defeat. She moved the tip of a finger swiftly across her eyes. Other women could afford tears but for her they were a luxury. Nobody wanted tears from her. "Men," she said, managing a smile, "take what they want from a woman, and beat her down to get it. That's the part of them always hunting. And yet when they have done that to a woman they hate her for what she has permitted them to do. Bad as they are, they have got a streak of goodness in them. I guess it never dies, not even in the worst of men."

"You're a wise girl, Lil."

"I wish," she said, still smiling, "I were not that wise." She gave him a keen look, this woman who knew men so thoroughly. "The kind of a woman you will want will not love you as you are now. It is strange how clear you are to me and how much a puzzle to everyone else. You don't want anyone to be sorry for you."

"No," he said, "I don't ask anybody for anything."

"You don't understand people. People want to be asked for things. They want to feel they're needed. Here I am. I would give you anything you asked of me, because I know you need me or a woman like me. It would do you good to get drunk and wake up and find yourself in a woman's arms. It would do you good to feel ashamed of that, and know that you're not as strong as you think. Nobody can live cold and friendless. Nobody can live alone."

He got up from the chair. He stood near her, smiling down. And then she said, answering his smile, "I am a little sad, Jeff. It would be so nice if I could have the one thing you want a woman to have. George Ives will kill you. Or if he doesn't succeed, one of the crowd will."

"They'll try," he agreed, and turned into the big dance hall. Rounds and Scoggins waited for him. The three went on into the street, finding John Williams there. Williams said: "You got an idea about that fellow who potted you?"

"It wasn't one of the old crowd, Jim." He moved down Wallace Street with Scoggins and Rounds. The bakeshop door was closed when they passed it. He gave the lighted window a swift glance and saw Diana inside, and turned his head away. He said: "You don't have to walk up the Gulch with me."

Rounds murmured: "I always take a stroll about this time. Reminds me of blossomtime in a little ivy-clad cottage at Concord."

"Massachusetts man?" asked Scoggins with a Yankee's interest.

"No," said Rounds, "there was no ivy around my home."

When they reached the cabin, Pierce fired up the stove and filled the coffeepot. Scoggins stretched full length on Pierce's bunk, well-pleased with himself. "That Marshland curls at the edges in any sort of trouble. Not tough at all. Ives is the tough lad but he didn't have a good hole card, so he folded."

"Just for that deal," countered Rounds. "He'll be in the next one."

Pierce found two tin cups and filled them, and kept the pot for himself. He hoisted the pot at Ollie and Ben. "Both you lads moved in on that scrap. I appreciate it."

"Why," said Scoggins, still amused at himself, "I'm damned if I wasn't surprised to find myself where I was. I must be getting good."

"Ollie," commented Pierce, "never stand out in the middle of nothing like that again. You made too big a target."

Scoggins looked at Ollie, his eyelids pulled half together, and Rounds met that glance and after awhile turned away, buttoning his coat. "See you later," he said, and left the cabin.

Pierce stood by the door with his back to Scoggins. "Ben," he said, "have you asked Diana to marry you?"

Scoggins squinted at the tin cup. He moved the cup in a slow circle, watching coffee creep up to its edge and spill over. He took one more drink and got up from the bunk. He placed the tin cup on the table. "No," he said, "not yet."

Pierce said, "Don't let anything hold you back," and turned from the door. He passed Scoggins without looking at him. He took up another stick of wood and chucked it into the stove. He slammed the stove door shut with his foot, shaking the stove on its flimsy legs. Scoggins cleared his throat. He adjusted the collar of his coat and turned to the door. "Well, sentiment maybe."

"To hell with sentiment," said Pierce.

"You're your own man."

"Then what was I doin' out on the street tonight?"

"I said I appreciated it," retorted Pierce.

"Why," drawled Scoggins, smiling in a broad, unamused way, "it doesn't matter a damn whether you do or don't. Ollie and I were there because we had to be. No man's his own man entirely. Everybody owes somebody else something."

"You paid off tonight," said Pierce. "Now you're your own man."

"Wrong again," said Scoggins. "It goes deeper than one debt or one payment. Those sort of books never come to a balance. If a man owes something to somebody, he just keeps on owing it. Never any such thing as scratching it off the slate."

"What do you figure you owe me?"

"Why, I like you. So does Ollie. I guess that makes an obligation. You like us. There's your obligation. People live that way. Be a damned cold, unfriendly world if they didn't. As for this other thing you mentioned —"

"Never mind," said Pierce. "No use talking about it. You don't need advice from me. Go ahead. That's what you'll do anyhow. It is what you should do."

"I suppose," said Scoggins. He gave Pierce a look in which doubt and irritation were mixed. He wanted to say more but presently shrugged his shoulders and left the cabin.

Wind shouldered against the log walls. Cold wind knifed through the door's bottom and through the cracks of the eaves. Pierce put the coffeepot back on the stove and sat in the chair, crouched near the stove with his hands idle across his heavy legs. Sitgreaves had disclaimed any hurry and then Sitgreaves had improved his first opportunity and had taken those two shots at him.

He was surprised at himself. He should have turned from The Pantheon and hunted out Sitgreaves and had this thing over with, fired up by the old black resentment at an unjust world. But he now sat still and didn't care. He found a cigar and lighted it and crouched forward in the chair. There was a crack in the stove's grate, through which he saw the dance of pale red flame. Now and then the flame turned to a kind of coral rose, which was the color of Diana's cheeks when the strong wind flushed them.

He had seen little of her during the last five months and yet she had never been out of his head on any day. Somewhere during each day's hours, and particularly at hours like this one, she moved before him as an actual presence and he heard the tone of her voice, sometimes deep and very gentle, sometimes lifted to a moving anger. What he remembered now was the way she had looked at him on the street, a foreign soul hating him for something he had done to her. What had he done to her?

He bent lower in the chair, the cigar clenched between his teeth and his hands locked together and a steady heartbeat of pain on his right side where the bullet had chewed its way. This night, for the first time, he had disliked Ben Scoggins' cheerful smile; it had irritated him. His thoughts slid away from that irritation, but he brought them back, as hard on himself as he was on any other man, and he made a painful search for the reason, and found it. Then he asked himself, "What kind of a claim have I got to her or to any living soul?"

He had no claim. When he realized that he took the cigar from his mouth and straightened in the chair. Lately the words of men had begun to sing a common tune at him, as though they had gotten together to talk about him, and to make it a point to warn him. These men were somehow now facing him in the room. He saw their faces, Ben's and Ollie's, and Archie Caples' who was dead, and Barney Morris, also dead — and the faces of Parris Pfouts and of Jim Williams. More or less they had all said the same thing, as Lil had said it this very night: "Nobody can live alone."

Why not? He had always lived alone. He got up from the chair again, moved by the restlessness which always came of thoughts like these. He thought of Mary Morris reading the letter he had written her concerning Barney, and he thought of Lil who was a woman, fragrant and soft and willing, and and he remembered how Archie Caples used to speak of his family; and then he was once more seeing Diana before him. It invariably came to that.

He put on his overcoat and wound a heavy muffler around his neck and ears. He got his wool gloves and his shotgun, turned down the lamp to a faint glow, and left the cabin. Wind nailed him to the wall for a moment. He had to slip the edge of his shoulder into the wind to move on, and so circled the cabin and walked on back to the lee edge of the canyon where he had stacked a pile of wood. He settled against the woodpile, sheltered from the straight drive of the weather. The world was ink-black, tortured by a wind that had not lessened for a week. Here and there on the Gulch floor miners' cabin lights made frosty points and a small glow hung over Virginia, half a mile away. All these lights were feeble man-made points of rebellion against the stark and ancient and endless emptiness of the universe. Those lights would die and the emptiness would be complete. He had been alone too long to expect anything else, or to nourish any hope.

He came into the Virginia Hotel around nine o'clock and found the ball in progress. They had gotten the musicians from The Pantheon but otherwise this was strictly for the genteel. The chandelier was decorated with pine boughs and the bracket lamps were draped with green gauze, on which wax flakes had been scattered to imitate snow. All the available proper ladies of the Gulch, from Junction to Summit were here, their gowns looking sedate in contrast to eyes accustomed to the color and flash of the hurdy-gurdy girls. Some of the men, like John Lott and W. B. Dance and Wilbur Sanders, wore broadcloth, white shirts and collars. Otherwise it was straight Gulch costume and trimmed whiskers. The music was a waltz, the fiddles and guitars bearing down heavily on the accent. Stags lined the walls, waiting their turn. One of the dance committee, Neil Howie, moved around the couples, sprinkling more wax on the floor, and at this same moment A. J. Oliver and X. Biedler were escorting a gentleman to the door, he having started his evening too early at the Senate. Oliver shrugged his shoulders, not liking the display, but the short and powerful Biedler seemed to enjoy this physical contact. He stood by the door to make sure the drunken one did not return. He said to Pierce: "Shouldn't be walking through town alone, Jeff."

Wilbur Sanders wheeled by with a lady. He was a slight, cool Eastern man short of thirty with brown hair and beard; he practiced law in Bannack. Pierce talked a moment with Biedler, meanwhile noticing that a long lunch bar had been set up in the adjoining dining room. He moved that way, sliding through the steady crowd of men. In the dining room's doorway he looked back and caught sight of Scoggins. Scoggins danced with Diana and both of them were laughing at something said, and the picture of the girl's face, so free and pleased, struck Pierce hard. He remained in the door, blocking it, and stopping the drift of the men around him. Somebody touched his back, but he didn't move. Then Diana, wheeling nearer, saw him and the smile left her face and her chin rose and over that distance he caught the half surprised look of her eyes. Scoggins, now discovering Pierce, also ceased smiling.

Pierce stopped at the big bar and got a cup of coffee; and made a sandwich from bread and a huge elk roast. Rounds arrived and stood with him, not saying much. Oliver drifted in with W. B. Dance. Presently Sanders came along and Stuart introduced him to Pierce. This group grew. Pfouts moved out of the ballroom. Pfouts put a hand on Pierce's shoulder as he talked and Pfouts looked around at the men near him until his eyes touched Ollie Rounds. Pierce, forever watchful, saw then a little change on Pfouts's face and he turned his attention to Ollie and noticed a sudden shadow come to Rounds's cheeks. In another moment Rounds drifted from the group. There wasn't anything more than this, yet it left its impress on Pierce. After a while he broke from the circle, had another cup of coffee and strolled from the dining room on through another door to the hotel's parlor. As he came into the parlor he saw Ollie and Ben and Diana before him; they were talking and all laughing and then, as before, Diana noticed him and grew serious. Pierce moved forward.

Scoggins said: "For an invalid you do a lot of spookin' around on bad nights." He grinned, and yet it lacked the old Scoggins' cheerfulness. There was a little embarrassment on him, so that he was no longer easy. The music began again, a square dance tune, and men moved toward the ballroom. Diana made a part turn to Ollie, as though to be his partner, but now Scoggins did a strange thing. He touched Ollie's arm and murmured: "Want to see you a minute, Ollie," thus taking Rounds away.

Diana gave Pierce one steady glance and turned from him to watch Scoggins and Ollie move on toward the end of the parlor. She had been surprised at this, she didn't understand it and she didn't want to be thus left alone with Pierce. Pierce said: "If you'll turn back —"

She wheeled on him, her glance direct and cold. It was the same way she had looked at him the night before when, down in the dust of Wallace, he had heard her strange poured-out bitterness. She hated him. Then he thought of their long trip together across the Bitterroots to this camp, and of the one evening when she stood before him with tears in her eyes, so full of compassion for him. The memory made an ache in his bones.

"Somewhere along the line," he said, putting one distinct word after another, "I must have hurt you." He watched her quite closely, his face showing the puzzle she made for him. "I remember how your smile was. I have not seen it lately. That is, you have not used it on me."

"You're the man," she told him, "that never asks for anything. Are you asking for sympathy now?"

He flushed, by which she knew his extremely strict sense of pride had been touched. "No," he said, "I'm not. I had my chance once —"

"Don't remind me of it," she said, as proud and as severe as he was. "Maybe it was just my way of trying to be nice to you for your trouble in helping me out in Portland. I like to pay my debts."

He went on as though he had not heard her. "I have been thinking about it lately. A woman who has been friendly to a man, and then turns against him —" He shrugged his shoulders, he shook his head. "The man's done something to make the change."

"I suppose," she countered, "you would know."

"I'd know. Hate is something I know a lot about. I've seen enough of it to recognize it anywhere. I regret seeing it in you."

"It is a little late to talk of that, isn't it?"

He closed his mouth, he set his jaw against her constant tone of disbelief and chill anger. He bowed his head, taking a steady control of himself. It was one thing he had in greater quality than most men — that power of self-discipline. Looking at him over the wide gulf which separated them, she admitted his possession of the quality, and could admire it; but as she admired it she could at the same time understand how terribly it had come between them. It was his strength to stand fast. It was his weakness as well.

"You don't understand," he said. "I am not trying to bring up old ghosts."

"Then why should we talk about it?"

"Diana," he said, "be quiet. I came here tonight to say this, and I will say it if I've got to tear this damned building down."

"Yes," she countered, "that would be your manner. You will do a thing even though you must destroy and wreck and make sinners of us all to get it done. Go ahead, Jeff."

He drew in his breath, holding back so much that he felt his will was a dam behind which the weight of all this grew. "You may be right. A man can be only what he is. If I have hurt you or destroyed any good thought you may have had about this world, I deeply regret it. That is all I came to say."

"Did you ever stop to think how it was destroyed?"

"Yes," he said, "I have. But nobody can go back over the trail and make things different. For that matter, I wouldn't want to. Maybe I'd correct one mistake, and make another that was worse. It doesn't matter, except that I wish you had met a better man in Portland. I am the wrong man for any woman to meet."

"Last night when you fell on the street —"

He showed his one stubborn reaction. "No," he said, "I didn't fall."

She made an impatient gesture. "You were on your knees and you looked at me, and for a moment I thought you were going to ask my help. You've been too proud to do that while you were strong. But last night you were weak and I thought you were going to go back on that terrible philosophy of yours and ask me for help. I would have hated you if you had. The one thing I can honestly admire you for is your consistency. I think you'll die the same man as you are now. I don't think you'll cry."

"I did my crying a long time ago."

"I know. It is too bad. . . ." She gave him

a long, suddenly aroused glance, as though wondering now what feelings he hid from her. She had a new thought about him, so strong that it made her forget her answer for a moment. "Could it be," she murmured, "that you are beginning to reap your thistles?"

He said, "Good night," and turned on his heels, going back to the lunchroom.

Meanwhile Scoggins and Rounds tarried at the far end of the parlor, discreetly observing the scene. "Both look sore as hell to me," said Rounds. "He's picking a fight, or she is. Why did you drag me away?"

"They wanted to talk."

"How did you know that?"

"Well," admitted Scoggins, "I didn't. But it seems likely, doesn't it? Why else would he want to come here tonight, with a pound of hide out of his ribs? He comes in and looks at her and she stops smiling like she's been hit in the face. It occurred to me right at that moment they had something to talk about."

Ollie Rounds considered Scoggins, and murmured, "I see."

"What do you see?" demanded Scoggins.

"You're thinking it will get worse between them, or it will get better. You'd like to know. You've got your own interests in the matter."

"Yes," said Scoggins, "I have."

Ollie shook his head. "I like you three people as well as I like anybody alive. I wish you all luck."

"The luck has got to go bad for Jeff, or for me. We can't both win."

Ollie smiled in a manner that had its shadow of regret. "That's the hell of living."

Scoggins now showed a degree of anxiety. "I would hate to lose his friendship, Ollie. But I have got to make my own try. You think I'm the kind of a man she'd like?"

Rounds shrugged his shoulders. "Who knows?"

"Ah," said Scoggins, "you don't want to say. I'd really like to know."

"Look at her," said Ollie. "She's trying to hurt him clean down to the marrow. There's your answer, Ben."

"Too bad she's turned against him like that. Makes me feel sorry for him."

"That," said Ollie, "is the wrong answer. A woman wouldn't go to that trouble with a man unless she had some other feeling about him."

Scoggins shook his head. "I don't understand."

"I do," said Ollie Rounds. "I have been through that scene. I can put myself in Jeff's boots and feel the holes she's tearing through him."

"He looks just sore to me."

"A mask," said Ollie. "We're all wearing masks, Ben."

Suddenly Scoggins turned to Rounds. He laid a hand on Ollie's shoulder and he spoke with a tremendous gravity. "Ollie," he said, "this camp's no good for you. Why don't you leave?"

Rounds stared back, his eyes completely alert. "Why?"

"Don't ask me that question."

"In the middle of winter?" said Rounds. "It would be a hell of a trip."

"I can think of a trip that might be worse."

"You shouldn't be talking to me like this," responded Rounds irritably.

"No," agreed Scoggins, "I should keep my mouth shut and let the chips fall."

"What's that?" asked Rounds, more and more intent.

"Things are happening, Ollie. I'm your friend. The time may come when I won't be." Rounds had taken a backward step, so that Scoggins' arm fell from his shoulder. His face was dark and sharp as he tried to read Ben Scoggins' expression. Scoggins met his steady stare and added, "I'd hate to think of a time —"

Now Diana moved over to the two men. The fire and fury of her talk with Pierce still remained; she was actually still facing Pierce, and seeing him. Both Scoggins and Rounds waited for it to pass and it was Scoggins who said, easy and humorous: "We're two different fellows, Diana."

Ollie Rounds excused himself, walking toward the lunchroom. As soon as he had gone Diana gave Scoggins a smileless glance. "Why did you leave me with him?"

"Was it that clear?" complained Scoggins. "I thought I was being sly about it." He dropped his head, long studying the floor; he was at the moment a big and blond-headed boy caught in his musings and so transparent in what he thought that he furnished her with an answer before he spoke. He said: "I wanted to know something."

"Did you find out?"

"I thought I did, but Ollie said I guessed wrong." He looked at her with deep care, and anxiously added, "Maybe he's right. Ollie's a pretty smart fellow."

He wanted her to answer that. She saw that he waited on edge; to him it was a moment full of importance. But she didn't answer. She took his arm and walked with him to the main room. As they came to it she looked toward the door and saw Pierce and Rounds leaving, and some of the old stormy expression came back to her. She said: "Ben, it wasn't one of the gang that shot him last night. I want you to tell him. Tell him I saw Sitgreaves in town today. He'll know."

"I guess he already knows. He said he knew it wasn't one of Ives's crowd."

As they swung into the dance she said one more thing in a deeply troubled voice. "This is different. I wish I knew —"

Scoggins put his question suddenly at her.

"Diana, you still like that fellow?"

"I'm sorry for him, Ben. His world is falling down. He just reached up and pulled it down on himself."

Pierce and Rounds moved to the Senate's bar and waited for the bottle and glasses to come. Pierce poured the glasses brimful and lifted his own glass and made his salute: —

"A warm cabin and a full meal, Ollie."

"I'm warm," said Ollie, "and I always eat well."

Pierce downed his drink and stood with one arm thrown on the bar, watching Rounds and remembering that Rounds was one of the few friends left him. Archie Caples and Barney Morris were both dead. Diana was a woman who watched him out of strange eyes. Scoggins too had changed, in the way any man must change who turns to a woman. Scoggins wanted Diana. Ollie was the only one left who was as he had always been.

"Ollie," he said, "stay as you are. Don't change."

"What would I change for?" questioned Ollie. He grinned at Pierce. "You are a damned odd fellow."

"Let's have another drink on that," said Pierce. "Everybody's odd."

"Like the Quaker who said to his wife, 'Everybody's queer but thee and me, Deborah, and sometimes I have my doubts of thee.' The dingbat birds have got you, Jeff. I know. I see 'em flying around once in a while."

"We'll drink 'em out of the place," said Pierce.

"I've tried it," said Rounds. "When you're drunk you don't hear 'em yell quite so much but their damned eyes just get bigger and bigger. What makes you think I'd change?"

"Everybody does."

Ollie considered his partner at long length. Pierce filled the glasses again. The saloon grew warmer and noisier and miners crowded to the bar: "You know, Jeff, the fellow who travels alone always travels the fastest. But it's no good. Better to be sold out by a friend than to have no friends. A preacher once left me an idea I never forgot. Man, he said, had to have the touch of other men all the way down the trail. Now look at this saloon. We'd be more comfortable at home but we wouldn't like it. Got to come here and listen to other men howl. If we propose to get drunk we're wasting time."

"Never change, Ollie," repeated Pierce, and filled the glasses again.

Jim Williams entered the Senate, looked around until he saw Pierce and made a clean track through the crowd. "Bill Palmer," he said, "just drove into town with Nick Tibault lyin' on the wagon bed. Nick's got a bullet right through the middle of his head. Turner found him in the brush. Been there a few days."

"Nick?" said Pierce and put his glass down. "Young Nick?"

"Palmer went over to that shack Charley Hildebrand and Long John Franck live in and asked them to help load Nick into the wagon. They told him to go to hell. Palmer said Long John looked mighty funny about it."

"Now," said Pierce, "somebody's got to write Anna." He turned around, a half-sick expression on his face. "That's too much, Jim. This damned miserable human race . . ." He shook his head. "You're going down there to see Long John?"

"Yes."

Pierce walked toward the door with Jim Williams. Near it he stopped to look back at Ollie Rounds. "Coming?"

"No," said Jim Williams in a flat tone, "he's not coming."

Rounds shook his head.

Pierce shrugged his shoulders and left the saloon with Williams, turning to Kasebeer's stables where Parris Pfouts and Neil Howie and John Lott and eight or nine others were waiting. The group left the stable at once. At the top of Daylight Grade the bitter wind cried against them and all before them; along the winding Gulch, cabin lights sparkled with a frosty brilliance. Williams had taken the head, and now said: "We'll move right along.

Say nothing to anybody you pass on the road."

Rounds stood a full half-hour longer at the Senate bar, steadily drinking; and then left the place and went into Tanner's. He made his way to Will Temperton's table and bent over to speak into the gambler's ear. "Lend me a hundred, Will."

Temperton lifted five gold coins from his stack and passed them back to Rounds. He stared at Rounds a moment, then said, "So-long," and returned his attention to the game.

It wasn't until Ollie reached the door that Temperton's remark struck him as being odd and so he turned. Temperton was watching him and Temperton made a short gesture that might have meant "Good-by." That too was odd. Rounds, now feeling a small chill, moved down Wallace to the Planter's and up to his room. He stood in the room a considerable while, reviewing what he knew. Scoggins had dropped a warning, and so had Temperton. These men seemed both to be trying to tell him something, and now a posse moved down the Gulch on the heels of Tibault's murder and from it the long-whispered break might come. He thought of finding Ives to tell him about it, but then remembered that Pierce was in the posse, and when he came to think of Pierce he buttoned his coat around him and left the room, taking nothing with him.

He went directly to the stable and got his horse and rode around before the Virginia Hotel a moment to listen to the music. The door was closed and the bitter cold had frosted the windowpanes. A smell of coffee came out of the Virginia. He heard a woman laugh and he heard the steady shuffle and stamp of feet, and this man who loved to laugh and to be warm listened to that music with a sudden forlorn remembrance of all the soft and kind voices of the past, with a memory of all the other places from which in haste or in shame he had fled. He wished to say good-by to Ben and to Diana, but he knew there was nothing he might say to either of them which would help. This was an old ending for him, a swift and furtive departure. Jack Gallegher passed by, hailing him. Ollie moved on without answering.

XV: Temperton's Past

THE POSSE skirted Daly's and came upon Wisconsin Creek beyond two o'clock of a sub-zero night. Dismounting to cross over the ice sheeting of the creek afoot, the party took a wetting to the knees. George Baume began to swear and was immediately stopped by Jim Williams. "Cut that out, George. No racket."

"Got to yell or freeze to death."

"Freeze to death but don't yell," said Williams laconically.

This was the other side of gentle Jim Williams, the iron-tempered side. He turned up the Stinkingwater and as he rode he talked quietly with Pierce. "I guess the time's coming for us now. Everybody liked Nick."

At three-thirty he halted the party in a black world. "Cabin's up there ahead. I'm going to scout around." He left his horse and moved forward afoot, soon disappearing. The rest of the group dismounted and stood miserably shifting in a wind that whipped over the open land and turned their wet feet and clothes frost-hard. George Baume softly groaned, "Anybody got a drink?" Burtchy turned his horse over to Pierce and tramped a steady circle to keep warm. It was a half-hour later, with some gray beginning to dilute the sky, when Williams came back.

"We've stumbled on to something," he said. "There's eight or nine men sleeping outside the cabin in the snow. That means another four or five inside the cabin — it is too small to hold more than that. So there's maybe fourteen men up there."

"Hell of a cold night to be camping out," said Burtchy.

"They wouldn't be there unless something is in the wind. Somebody called a meeting. My guess is we'll find they're all Innocents from the Gulch."

"Well, by God," groaned George Baume, "we'll find out what brought 'em here. Let's get going. I am about to the end of my rope."

But Williams waited for the light to increase. He stood by Pierce, watching the outline of the cabin rise in vague shape through the sullen, wind-ripped night. He was patient in the way a man will be who has frozen his mind beyond change; and yet even then he had his sad reflections. "You would think," he murmured, "those fellows would be content with the gold they could get out of the Gulch. Sometimes I do not understand men. When I think I do understand them, I'm ashamed."

"Let's go," insisted George Baume.

"All right," agreed Williams. "We'll close in. You fellows circle the crowd on the ground. Watch sharp. Pierce and I will go to the cabin. Franck will be inside the cabin, since it belongs to him. Henry, you stay back with the horses."

The group moved forward, their feet making some sound in the brittle snow. The cabin was a growing shape ahead of them and as Pierce stepped on with Williams he made out horses on picket near by and the shapes of men sleeping tight-rolled in their blankets. The posse spread out, circling the sleepers. Pierce followed Williams to the cabin's door and stopped while Williams lifted his gun, quietly opened the door, and called in.

"Franck — Long John Franck!"

The figures on the ground began to stir; and one man sat bolt upright. Pierce turned his revolver on that man, softly saying: "Sit still." The man's face turned to him, blurred by the heavy shadows. Meanwhile there was some commotion inside the cabin and when Williams again called Franck's name a voice growled sleepily back:

"Whut the hell's up?"

"Come out here."

"Wait'll I git my hat."

"Never mind your hat. Come out."

All the men lying on the earth now were rising and the posse closed in and made a tight ring around them. "What the hell goes on here?" asked somebody.

A figure showed at the cabin's doorway, ducked and came out. The relentless wind drove an indistinct daylight over the barren flats and Williams stepped forward, staring at the tall shape before him until he recognized Long John. "You come with us," he said, and afterwards called at the posse. "Pierce — Biedler, walk with me. Rest of you hold these lads right where you are."

He led Long John Franck a hundred feet from the cabin, Pierce and X. Biedler following. Long John Franck, all this while, was asking his steady question: "What's the matter — what you here for, Jim?"

Williams finally paused and turned. "Bill Palmer asked you to help him to get Nick Tibault in the wagon. You refused."

"Know nothin' about it," said Franck.

Pierce, meanwhile, saw a shape move up from the night and he kept his eyes carefully on it while Williams talked. "Tibault lay out here dead for a matter of days. You knew that yet you said nothing about it. What were you afraid of?"

"I didn't kill him," said Franck in a rapid, rushing way.

The shape on which Pierce had pinned his

glance now drifted into fairly distinct view, and turned out to be a straying mule. Pierce said: "Whose mule's that?"

Franck looked around, still involved in his fears. He said indifferently, "Tibault's."

"So?" softly murmured Williams.

Franck suddenly realized what he had said, and knew he had betrayed himself. His voice lifted to a half-cry. "I didn't have anything to do with it!"

"What'd you keep still about it for?" pressed Williams.

"I was afraid," said Long John, and looked at Williams and at Pierce in a close, black way. The gravity of his situation had penetrated his slow mind and at last broke his taciturnity. "I won't take the blame to save anybody's neck — not me. The fellow that killed him is sleepin' back there on the ground. George Ives did it. I saw it. Tibault had two hundred dollars. He came here to get a couple mules he had sold to Burtchy and Clark. Ives got wind of the money. Ives shot him. Didn't immediately kill him, but dragged him through the brush on a rope till Tibault died."

"What's Ives doing here? What's the crowd here for?"

"I don't know. They just drifted in last night."

Williams motioned for Franck to turn and move, and the four stepped back to the cabin.

It was now half-daylight and one of the campers had gotten a fire started in the cabin, the smoke of which fled with the wind in thin streaks. Ives was at the door, closely watching Williams and Pierce. He was a careless, quick-witted man, and showed no concern at all. Williams said: —

"What are you doing around here? What's this crowd here for?"

Ives smiled and shrugged his shoulders. "No particular reason."

"Just like to sleep out in the snow on a windy night, I suppose," suggested Burtchy with some sarcasm.

"That's as good an answer as any," replied Ives coolly. "And while we're asking questions, what the hell are you doing here?"

"We want you, George," said Williams.

"Why?"

"For killing Tibault."

"A fine pipe-dream, Jim," said Ives, betraying no concern. "Go ahead and try to prove it."

"Which we'll do," said X. Biedler. "The sooner the better. Let's hold court right here, Jim."

But Williams, who had so nourished his burning sense of retribution that he would have tracked Ives across a thousand miles, still had an impartial mind. Whatever was to be done would be properly done. "No," he said, "there will be no short shrift in this. Ives and Franck will go back to Nevada City and they will stand trial in the usual manner. It will never be said that we hang a man for fun."

"Hang?" asked Ives, and let out a short, ringing laugh. "You're away ahead of yourself, Jim." Then he turned his glance on Pierce and the false laughter ceased and Pierce felt the full and terrible force of the man's in-burning rage. "You won't be so brave in another day or two," he promised Pierce.

That afternoon the group reached Nevada City with Ives, Long John Franck, and with George Hildebrand who, suspected as an accomplice, was picked up along the road. The three were put under guard. Pierce afterwards continued on to Virginia, to find that the story of the capture had preceded him. It was then near suppertime and instead of going on to his cabin he took a meal at the Virginia Hotel. Scoggins came in to join him and presently Williams showed up for a moment. He said, "The toughs have already got all the lawyers in the Gulch retained to defend Ives. But Wilbur Sanders is still here. He had planned to take the stage back to Bannack. He will prosecute for us. Don Byam, at Nevada City, will be the judge. Tomorrow we'll settle the question of a jury." He sat by, closely thinking it out, and added, "I should not be surprised if the toughs try to take control, as they did with Stinson and Lyons." He slapped his palm on the table. "They shall not do it," he stated and looked at Pierce. "The right time has come."

"Maybe," said Pierce.

"No," insisted Williams, "it has come. We shall smash them once and for all."

"Who," said Pierce in his indifferent voice, "will write to Anna?"

"I know. Those things happen. But we'll smash them and drive them out of this country forever. We start it properly by sending George Ives to the rope."

"Jim," said Pierce, "why didn't you want Ollie along?"

Williams rose from his chair. "I have got to be going back to Nevada. We're going to watch Ives. There will be no foolishness this time." He tarried, he gave Pierce a straight glance. "I didn't want him, Jeff," he said, and left the Virginia Hotel.

Pierce grumbled. "What's the matter with Williams?"

Scoggins sat loose sprawled at the table, using his thumb nail to make idle tracks across it, writing in heavy letters, "Ollie." Pierce watched this blond man's hand slowly inscribe that name over and over again; and then he saw Ben betray his change of thought, for Ben's thumbnail printed, "Diana," and stopped. Suddenly he looked up and laid his hand over the name. He wasn't smiling and he wasn't at ease any more.

"I'll walk up the Gulch with you," he offered.

"Think I'll stay here tonight."

"Good idea," approved Scoggins. "The four walls of a cabin get damned tiresome when a man's alone." He changed the subject. "Diana wanted me to tell you she saw Sitgreaves in town. Who's he?"

"Retribution," said Pierce.

Scoggins shrugged his shoulders. He gave Pierce a smile that showed none of the old spirit. These two had lost the one fine thing which had brought and held them together. They were, Pierce realized, just two men sitting on opposite sides of the table, not the company for each other they had once been. Scoggins got up, said, "See you later," and moved out of the dining room.

Pierce signed for a room and went up to it, and stood at the window to watch men move along Wallace Street, trafficking in and out of the Senate, the California Exchange, the Pony, and other saloons and shops. It was a little early yet for the hurdy-gurdys to go into full swing. The Pantheon showed only a few lights. Scoggins was then entering Diana's bakery. A little later he came out with Diana and Lily Beth, the three bucking the wind toward Diana's cabin. Lily Beth held Scoggins' hand, and dark as it was Pierce saw

Diana turn and laugh at Scoggins. Pierce swung away from the window. He sat on the edge of the bed with his arms over his knees, a black expression crawling across his face. He got up and moved to the door. The single chair of the room was in his road; he lifted it and threw it aside and went out.

He crossed to the Senate, now in search of Ollie Rounds. The Senate, unlike Tanner's, had some pretensions of elegance and drew the genteel trade. Parris Pfouts stood at the bar with a group of Virginia City's merchants, and Parris at once drew Pierce into the circle. "The toughs will want an open jury — the whole Gulch doing the voting on Ives. That will give them a chance to swing sentiment, as they did with Stinson and Lyons. We must stick to a small jury."

Henry Touche, who ran a supply store, expressed doubt of Ives's guilt. "Ives always impressed me as a decent fellow. I think you fellows have got the wrong man."

Pfouts said: "You'll see some names brought into this you never dreamed of."

George Burtchy said: "One thing's certain. We must convict Ives, else every man who has any part with the right side of this trial will be shot down. Convict or die — that is the literal truth. Otherwise you'll see a reign of terror that will knock your eyes out."

W. B. Dance murmured, "Will the miners stand tight this time?"

X. Biedler now put in his thought. "I dug two graves to take care of Stinson and Lyons. I had my labor for nothing. This time," and he patted the shotgun he always carried, "there will be no tears to wash justice down the creek."

"It depends on the miners," repeated Dance.

Pierce saw nothing of Ollie Rounds. He tried the California Exchange, and he tried the Pony. At both places the talk of Ives's capture displaced all other talk. The general anger had grown a good deal stronger against the toughs, and men were bolder than they had been in denouncing mass lawlessness; and yet there were other men equally bold in defending Ives. Leaving the Pony he noted that Jack Gallegher came from Tanner's with Marshland and Bob Zachary, and with them also was George Brown, who ordinarily tended bar at Dempsey's, eighteen miles down the Gulch. Brown was a long way from home. Pierce stepped back into the dark wall and watched these men move toward Henly's stable on Jackson, and go into it. A little later Tanner left his saloon, following; and a few moments afterwards Clubfoot George Lane appeared from the lower quarter of town and went into the stable. These men were closeted in Henly's for a good quarter-hour; then Clubfoot rode from the stable and galloped toward Daylight, disappearing.

Pierce entered Tanner's and stopped at Will Temperton's table. "Seen Ollie?"

"No," said Temperton. "And you shouldn't be coming here, Jeff."

Gallegher, Pierce discovered, now was at the doorway watching him. Gallegher immediately moved aside, placing his back to the wall. Tanner came in and moved to the other side of the doorway. Tanner said angrily: "I don't want you in my place."

It was Gallegher Pierce watched. This Deputy was a sly man, a man who had dissembled and smiled and carried his tricky intentions close to his heart. But Pierce had handled him before and knew the limits of Gallegher's courage. He said now: "Move over, Jack. Move over toward Tanner."

"What are you worried about?" asked Gallegher.

"A bullet in the back."

"Pierce," cried out Gallegher, "I never was afraid of you!"

"Move over," said Pierce. He stepped on, straight at Gallegher. Long ago he had learned that this was the kind of pressure Gallegher could not stand; the man's nerve had its breaking point, and as he closed in he saw the desire in Gallegher's eyes grow cold. Gallegher's face screwed up and his lips pulled back from his teeth and closed again as he stepped over against Tanner. Pierce laughed at him and went through the doorway. He wheeled against the wall and waited but Gallegher didn't follow, and afterward Pierce circled town and returned to his room in the Virginia Hotel and went to bed.

By mid-morning the upper part of the Gulch was half-emptied, the miners moving down to Nevada City for the trial. Pierce spent the day on his claim, returning to Virginia for supper in the hotel. The tide had turned back from Nevada and Jim Williams came in for his meal to give out the day's proceedings as he ate. "We had a hell of a wrangle over the jury but we got it the way we wanted. We found another lawyer to help Sanders, a fellow by the name of Bagg. Sanders started his case this morning. He'll nail Ives to the cross." Then he added, "Unless the toughs stampede the crowd. They're drifting through the Gulch, talking about fair play. They're using a lot of threats on the jury."

"Maybe the crowd will stand fast. Maybe it won't."

Williams finished his meal. "We have got to make it stick this time, Jeff. Crowd or no crowd." He gave Pierce a searching look. "Forty or fifty toughs have been running this Gulch. Forty or fifty men on the other side of the fence can do likewise. How do you feel about that?"

"Yes," said Pierce. "You can do it. And I'm in on it."

Williams said: "You've changed. Was a time when you played it strictly alone."

"Still do," said Pierce. "The crowd can do its crying — I don't care. But I have been thinking of Barney and Archie Caples a lot and I've been thinking of Nick Tibault."

Williams rose. "Come with me," he said, and left the hotel. The two walked down Wallace. Parris Pfouts came along, not saying anything, and fell in step. The three turned into Kinna and Nye's store and moved on to a back room. Sanders was there with Biedler and Lott and John Nye, and Alvin Brockie and Nick Wall. Nye got up and shut the door behind the new entrants. Jim Williams said: —

"We've talked this over today. We're going to organize. It is the only way we can fight the toughs. San Francisco was cleaned out by a few Vigilantes who didn't give a damn for the consequences. That is the way it has got to be with us."

Parris Pfouts said, "Wait," and looked at Pierce. "If you do not agree to the idea it would be better if you left now. This has to be quickly done, and without anything being let out."

"Yes," said Pierce, "it's all right."

Sanders said: "The trial will take all of tomorrow and part of the next day. The danger point is when the jury turns in the verdict. If they convict Ives the toughs will

311

make a play. We must be prepared for that."

Pfouts said: "Some of the boys at Nevada City are holding such a meeting as this. We must get together as soon as possible and complete the organization. Each of you gentlemen consider an honest and thoroughly dependable man. Bring him to the next meeting."

The group broke up, Williams and Pfouts and Pierce walking together as far as the Senate. Here Williams stopped. "I have got to see Neil Howie. We must throw a ring of guns around Ives to see he's not taken and set free by the toughs."

"Maybe," said Pierce, "the jury will set him free for you."

"No, by God," said Williams. "It is in the book. He's guilty and they'll send him to the rope. I want you down there. Day after tomorrow."

Pierce moved away, bound up the Gulch. He paused in front of Scoggin's store, oppressed by a loneliness which grew like a disease. But there was no longer the old tie between himself and Scoggins; that easy friendship had gone and so he turned on his heels and moved into Wallace again and stood in front of the Senate, growing slowly irritated at his own indecision, and then went along Wallace Street, passing Diana's bakeshop. The smell of bread came strongly out and light sparkled on the window's frost.

Afterwards he walked home against the rough wind.

Peabody and Caldwell's coach came in from Bannack the following night at supper time and deposited its passengers before the Virginia Hotel — a miner, two women destined for The Pantheon, a Bannack merchant and a fashionably dressed lady with a round face and a grave mouth and a pair of blue, half-sad eyes. A roustabout came from the hotel to take her luggage and showed her into the lobby. She signed the register and stood by, watching the clerk as he reversed the book and looked at the name; and said: "Where would I find Mr. Temperton?"

"In Tanner's, I'd guess."

"That would be a saloon, and I presume Mr. Temperton is dealing a table there?"

"Yes. Should I send a runner for him?"

"No," she said. "Where is his daughter?"

"Expect you'd find her in Diana Castle's bakery. That's on Wallace — straight ahead, middle of the block, left-hand side."

She was, thought the clerk, a handsome woman on the cool and deliberate side, with considerable grit in her. She said to the handy man. "Take the luggage to my room, if you please," and moved from the hotel.

She crossed the frozen mud, reached the walk and moved down Wallace. Wind shouted around the building corners and slammed

313

against her and bits of hard dirt lifted and stung her face. She walked steadily, undisturbed by all this, fixed and resolute, and paused at the bakery's door, drawing a deep breath as she touched the knob. At that moment her resolution seemed to waver but she gathered herself, opened the door and stepped in to face Diana.

"You're Diana Castle?" she said in a voice soft and immensely determined.

"Yes," said Diana.

The woman held her gloved hands before her, the tips touching. Wind had brought color to her cheeks but it had not loosened the frozen gravity. Her eyes were dark blue, like the cold blue of high-mountain lake water. She held her lips together, placing upon Diana the steadfast and rather cruel glance of a woman reading another woman's character, and said: "I'm Lily Beth's mother."

XVI: The Trial

"I GUESSED that," replied Diana calmly. "Lily Beth looks much like you."

"Where is she now?"

"In my cabin. In bed, reading. She likes to read."

"Is the cabin warm?" asked Mrs. Temperton. "You leave her alone with a lamp on the table that might upset? With all these men, drunk and greedy, roaming the town?"

"You don't know a great deal about the men in a camp, do you?" said Diana gently.

"My knowledge of men," said Mrs. Temperton, "comes largely from one man." She was, in her smooth and soft way, incredibly hard. All her warmth and sympathy, all her feelings seemed frozen, or emptied out of her, or destroyed. Clearly, she hated Temperton. But there was no heat in the hatred; it was a passion turned bloodless by long torment.

"Shall I get Lily Beth for you?"

"Yes," said Mrs. Temperton. "When does the next stage leave Virginia?"

"In the morning."

"I wish it were sooner," said Mrs. Temperton. Then she shook her head. "No, not yet. Would you have somebody call Mr. Temperton here?"

"Yes," said Diana, and turned to the back room. But again Mrs. Temperton changed her mind. "Not for a moment, please. How is it she is in your care? Are you . . . ."

"No," said Diana. "I have my own cabin. Mr. Temperton lives at the Virginia. He asked me if I would take care of her. I have done so."

Mrs. Temperton grew visibly harder at the thought, murmuring: "How many strange hands she has passed through." She gave Diana that same prolonged inspection again and her voice grew faintly hurried. "Are you in love with him?"

"No," said Diana.

Mrs. Temperton searched Diana's face, weighing the answer and at last seeming to accept it. She dropped her eyes. "Tell me, truthfully, has he made her forget me?"

"No," said Diana. "Was that what he wished to do?"

"He took her away to break my heart."

"Then," said Diana, "he has broken his own. He has really tried to have Lily Beth love him. But she does not."

"I hope," said Mrs. Temperton, "he may suffer for it every day of his life." She tried to put live anger into her talk, she tried to put into those words the venom and fresh heat of her loss, her long torture, her blind search. But she could not. The words remained cold and therefore more terrible than fresh anger could ever make them.

"He will," said Diana. "You see, Mrs. Temperton, he loves her as much as he loves his life. But he has failed, and he knows it. You could do nothing more to hurt him."

"Yes," said Mrs. Temperton, "I can do one thing more. I can face him and tell him he has lost. That will hurt worse than you think. Please call him."

Diana moved to the inside room and spoke to her baker, and returned. She put on her coat. "I'll bring Lily Beth."

Mrs. Temperton's face showed its first uncertainty. "Don't say I'm here," she said. "Just bring her. Let her see me first."

"Why should you be worried?"

"It has been a year," said Mrs. Temperton. "A year is one tenth of her life."

After Diana had gone, Mrs. Temperton remained still. She let her hands drop beside her coat and then she brought them together again, fingers tightly interlaced. Men tramped along the walk, each nearing footstep bringing a swift, haunted expression to her eyes, each departing footstep taking the expression away. Long before Temperton opened the door she knew he was approaching, recognizing the tempo of his pacing from the past years of life with him; there was never a doubt about those steady, even steps and as they came closer and momentarily stopped at the door Mrs. Temperton sighed and lifted her shoulders and erased all vestige of expression from her face, and then he had opened the door and had stepped through.

She knew he would show no surprise. It was a matter of professional pride with him to hold hurt or misfortune or triumph or ordinary human emotion behind a fixed calm. His lips made a slight change, growing narrower, and he seemed to settle within himself. He closed the door, pushing a hand back against it without taking his eyes from her. And then, because there was one gentle-born streak in him, he removed his hat before her. In all the years of their marriage, she remembered, he had never failed to do that. That courtesy had remained even after love had gone.

"I knew," he said at last, "you would of course find me in time. You were always a steadfast woman."

"It was Lily Beth," she said.

"Even beyond Lily Beth. Had you determined to hunt me down for any other reason you would have done so, and continued until you found me. It is your character, Judith. You have a very fixed will."

"For which you have always hated me," she said.

"Perhaps," he answered, "a weak man envies those who possess the strength he does not have. Now you are happy. You have found Lily Beth."

"Happy?" she said. "Every meaning of that word was squeezed out of me long ago. But I am content."

"You should be," he said, so inflexibly polite. "You have won. Lily Beth is your daughter. There is no power on earth which could ever draw her to me."

"Yes," she said, "there is. But you do not have it."

"Ah," he said, "we have talked about that many times before, haven't we? Affection and laughter and softness. I know. But men must be what they are and if grace is not in them they can expect no grace from others."

"Tell me," she said, "was it simply to hurt me that you took her away? Or do you love her so much you could not share her with me? I have long wondered."

"If a man is not permitted to love his wife," he said, "then he must put his love somewhere."

"That," she said, and showed her first warmth, "is a lie you told yourself long ago. You loved pretty rooms and pretty furniture and a pretty wife, all to shed warmth on you, but you never cared to shed warmth back."

He made a weary gesture with his arm. "We resume the same old argument. I took you from your people, for which they have hated you and me since. I led you through shabby ways and I would not change, and I ceased to be the gallant adventurer you thought me to be and became a card sharp, nothing more."

"All of that."

"Yes, all of that. Your judgment is quite correct. You find me a year later dealing in a saloon two cuts lower than a year before. There is no regeneration, as you once thought there might be. We are two different people and God was unkind when He permitted me to touch you."

"Long ago," she said, "you found irony was the easiest way to hurt me."

"Irony," he said, "is a knife used only by scoundrels. I am a scoundrel. How different it might have been if I had used the proper words, the words you seemed to want, but which I never had."

"You didn't need words," she said. "Had you only put your hand out to me I would have seen and felt all that you could not say. That is, if these things had been truly in you. They never were."

He used a gesture that was completely like him; he raised his hands and shoulders, expressing everything and nothing. She said: "I'm leaving on tomorrow's stage with Lily

320

Beth. Will you try to stop me?"

"No," he said, and permitted his first bitterness to show in his tightening words. "The hand is played. I have lost."

She said in her distant, bell-clear voice: "You always lost easily and shrugged the loss away. You never tried very hard to win back."

"I never argue with chance."

"Love is not chance," she said.

"You see," he said, "I'm only what I am."

She started to answer him and ceased. An expression of real fright crossed her face and she started to turn away, and checked herself, and slowly brought her hands up before her. The door came open and Diana said, "Go in, Lily Beth." Lily Beth came into the bakeshop, her face red and her eyes sparkling above the heavy bundling of her coat and muffler.

She saw her mother and her mouth opened and she cried: "Mother," in a thin, rapid voice and ran forward with her hands outreached. Mrs. Temperton fell to her knees and took her daughter to her. There was no kiss. Mrs. Temperton put her face against Lily Beth's coat, her face white in the lamplight. Lily Beth's hands crept around Mrs. Temperton's neck and she said in a precise, clear tone: "I have waited a very long time for you to come."

Diana walked on until she was in the rear

room, away from this scene. Temperton looked down at his wife, his face stiffened into sharpest lines. He saw the warmth that filled and changed his wife's face, he saw Lily Beth's hands tightly caught around her mother's neck; whereupon he turned to the door. "I wish you luck," he said.

Mrs. Temperton stood up. "You see the answer for yourself, Will."

"I saw it long before this," he said.

"Lily Beth said Mrs. Temperton, "We are leaving tomorrow."

Lily Beth looked at her father. "Are we all going together?"

"No," said Temperton, "I am staying here."

A shadow crossed Lily Beth's face and, caught in the undertone of the terrible and unsaid things passing between these two people, she made the kind of answer which cut through a thousand words of explanation. She turned and reached for her mother's hand.

"Good-by," said Temperton.

"Won't you be at the stage in the morning?" said Lily Beth.

Temperton, who had his enormous pride of making his decisions clear and final, stepped out of character before his daughter. "Yes, I think so," he answered, and went into the street.

Diana entered the front room. "Lily Beth,

take your mother to our cabin. She'll pack your things."

"You'll be at the stage, too, won't you?"

"Yes," said Diana.

Mrs. Temperton moved to the door and there paused. "We should hurry, Lily Beth, or we'll miss supper at the hotel." But, as she went through the door, she looked back at Diana a long moment, and said: "I know."

Diana remained alone in the room, openly crying.

Temperton stood at the window of his room next morning and watched the stage in front of the hotel. His wife and Lily Beth stood by the coach with Diana, and presently Scoggins appeared and handed Mrs. Temperton a package. The package contained a small gold locket and chain in which Lily Beth's daguerreotype rested. This had been his wife's present to Temperton on Lily Beth's second birthday, and his one treasure. But he had wrapped it and had given it to Scoggins, with instructions, and now Scoggins handed it over. Temperton saw his wife open the package and afterwards lift her head and look along the street, as if in search of him. Diana bent to kiss Lily Beth and a group of merchants, all old friends of Lily Beth's, arrived to pay their compliments. Pierce came forward and now Temperton saw this big man's face break into one of its rare smiles as he said good-by to the girl. Afterwards Lily Beth and his wife got into the coach and the door closed, and the coach moved on and turned the corner of Wallace Street.

Everything that had been his life, important and gentle and possessing hope, moved around the corner with the coach. He remained by the window and in a little while caught one more view of the coach as it reached the summit of Daylight, paused against winter's sunlight and thereafter vanished.

He moved back from the window, a grave and thoughtful man; he removed his coat and shirt and shaved, taking considerable care with the chore. He replaced his shirt and coat and brushed his hair, and he lighted a cigar and sat down before the room's table with a pack of cards and dealt out a game of solitaire. The game, presently, went bad. He let the cards lay and put both arms on the table and went back over his career and thought of Lily Beth and then of his wife, and remembered, in a slow and searching way, every incident between them through the years.

At eleven o'clock the clerk in the hotel heard a small report and judged it to be a board somewhere falling. A little afterwards the chamber girl came down and called the clerk. Going upstairs he found Will Temperton still seated in the chair, with his arms and head on the table.

The unbeatable solitaire game remained as he had played it and had left it; and he lay dead with a bullet hole through his heart.

The clerk made an observation about that. "Man usually shoots himself in the region he considers most important. He was a cool one but I never knew he considered himself to have a heart."

Pierce walked down the Gulch to Nevada City a little beyond noon and found five hundred or more men standing in a street churned to deep greasy mud. Don Byam sat as judge on a wagon drawn up in front of Lott Brothers' store; and as the lawyers for defense or prosecution rose to speak they mounted to the wagon to command the crowd. A space had been roped off in front of the wagons for prisoners' dock, jury box and witness stand. Bob Hereford and Adriel Davis, sheriffs of Nevada and Junction respectively, acted together as bailiffs.

Going through the crowd Pierce met many men he knew and exchanged words with them; and other men he did not know called his name, they remembering him for his part in the stage holdup as well as for his carrying Barney Morris' gold to Bannack, and for his fight with Gallegher. News like this traveled swiftly in the Gulch and marked a man overnight. It warmed him, it thawed the increasingly lonesome spot in him. At the roped circle he found X. Biedler and Jim

Williams standing together. Williams leaned over to whisper to him.

"We've got twenty men standing by this rope. If there's a rush to set Ives free they'll turn and make a stand against the crowd. That's your job, too."

The trial was about over, with Sanders, a slight and polished man in these robustly rough surroundings, now on the wagon making his final argument. He had a strong voice and he controlled it effectively as he spoke of the murdered Tibault, of the young man's likeable ways, of his honesty and his simplicity, of the way he saved his money and stayed away from the honky-tonks in order to go back to the girl he planned to marry — to Anna. It was a telling point, for many men in the Gulch had heard Tibault speak of Anna.

Then Sanders, warming to his task, summoned anger to his side and called the roll of the dead — Hilton murdered in cold blood during the stage holdup, Barney Morris shot down on the Bannack — Horse Prairie road, Archie Caples assassinated in his cabin. There were many other men now sleeping in the Gulch cemeteries who had come to the same kind of end and he named them with a monotone relentlessness which left a visible effect with the crowd. Pierce saw men shift under the strain, he saw them grow restless. Perhaps, went on Sanders, it was not Ives who had held the gun on all these. He was not debating that proposition. But Ives was a brainy, conscienceless killer. Ives was a leader of organized banditry in the Gulch. Ives was a star example of a system of brutal rapine and pillage which, unless stopped now and forever, would carry the Gulch to ruin. Human beasts prowled by day and by night and times grew worse and there was no safety for any honest man with a grain of gold in his poke, and there would never be any safety until all honest men rose and smashed this villainy to the ground. It was time for law to come.

"There is," he said to the jury and to the crowd, "no shred of defense for George Ives. We have torn down the deliberate lies of his witnesses. We have seen them contradict each other. We have had Long John Franck's stated testimony that Ives, knowing Tibault had $200 in his pocket, went out and met Tibault in the brush, Tibault being unarmed, and called to Tibault to turn around and then put a bullet in Tibault's head. He was not instantly killed. As further torture Ives roped him and dragged him through the brush, God only knowing what beast savagery prompting Ives to do this, and left him at last a victim. There are no words in our language to describe the full infamy, the degraded and unspeakably vile character of a man who piles that kind of torture upon that kind of a crime.

You should find him guilty, and he should be hung."

He was through, to be replaced by the defense lawyer. This man had defended Stinson and Lyons previously and by his subsequent associations had lost the confidence of the Gulch's thoughtful ones. He seemed to be laboring under deep emotion, or under the spell of whisky, so that his words were labored and thick-spoken and deeply sentimental. It was too bad that Tibault was dead. Tibault was a fine lad. Nobody loved Tibault more than he. But Tibault was dead and nothing could bring him back to life. And who could be sure George Ives had done it? All the evidence was flimsy. The testimony of Long John Franck could scarcely be believed. Franck was supposed to be a friend of Ives. What kind of a man would squeal on a friend? George Ives was reckless, but he was not a bad one. He had done many good things and if he lived he would do many more good things. George Ives deserved a chance to prove it. "Gentlemen," said the defense lawyer, "don't let passion sway you. Be fair. Be just, be gentle. Remember the injunction of the Good Book, which is to judge not that ye be not judged."

He came down from the wagon, sweating and unsteady. Here and there in the crowd a single voice called: "Never mind that cryin'!"

"Give Ives another chance!"

Judge Byam said only a few words to the jury. "You will retire to Lott Brothers' store, arrive at your verdict and return."

Suppertime had come and daylight was gone from the Gulch, with a moon rising above the Bitterroots wan-white in the dustless winter air. Men broke away from the crowd to cook supper and campfires sprang up along the creek. Ives sat on a keg inside the roped circle, as calm as any man in the group. His supporters came near him and he laughed and carried on his low, cheerful conversation. Byam remained on the wagon and Sanders walked slowly back and forth, his head dropped in thought. Williams and X. Biedler watched the crowd with a vigilant attention.

"Where's Franck and Hildebrand?" asked Pierce.

"In that cabin," said Williams, "under guard. They'll be tried separately. Probably they'll be let off. Not much real stuff against them."

The jury, out less than a half-hour, came from Lott's store and re-entered the circle. With their appearance men ran from their cook fires and a murmur, running like a low long swell of water, moved through all this waiting mass; and the pressure of the crowd pushed Pierce into the rope which marked off the center area. George Ives lifted his head to stare at the jury with a drawn brightness.

Don Byam said: "Reached it, gentlemen?"

The jury foreman knew his answer meant something and he took his time making it. Every set of eyes in the Gulch was on him and the silence grew heavier and heavier until it seemed to flow like a soft-thick substance. This was the moment. Ives knew it, and all his kind. Looking over the heads of the nearest men, Pierce discovered Jack Gallegher. Gallegher's head was pushed forward a little and on his face was a solemn, rapt expression. Sanders had come to a stand in the middle of the roped-off place and here he waited without showing anything of his feelings. Yet Pierce understood what was in the slight, indomitable man's mind. If the jury set George Ives free, then Sanders and all these others with him would go down in a flood of vengeance. It was George Ives's life against Sanders' life. It was the toughs against the little, resolute group. Everything locked into the answer. The foreman stepped forward and handed a slip up to Byam. "We signed this verdict, all except one man. Guilty."

Sound started small, and rustled and murmured and swelled back through the crowd; and then men were crying out their private beliefs. Sanders wheeled swiftly and went up to the wagon. He lifted his hand, his voice resonant: "The trial has been fair, the judgment duly returned. I now move that the verdict of the jury be approved by the miners here assembled!"

"Second!" yelled X. Biedler.

Byam's voice came in at once. "All in favor . . . !"

A roar erupted through the pale dark. Sanders listened to its sustained reverberation until he was sure of its meaning, then waved his arm for silence. "I further move that George Ives be hanged!"

A dozen men called, "Second!" Byam started to put the motion but his voice was drowned by the tumultuous shouting all around him. He nodded his head and he waited until the sound fell away. "I direct Adriel Davis and Bob Hereford to make the arrangements. Court will stay in session until they report back."

Davis and Hereford shoved themselves out through the edges of the crowd and disappeared. The steady, hollow tone of talk kept on, but here and there single voices began to cry. "What's the hurry? Give a man decent time . . . !"

"Bring up Long John Franck! Hang him too! He peached!"

"Let's hear from that jury! Let each one of 'em get up and vote out loud!"

These voices came from different parts of the crowd. The toughs had placed themselves this way, to bring fear to the men around them, to raise doubt, to harry and to change.

Pierce turned to the crowd and Biedler and Williams were both alert. Pfouts and some of the rest of the trustworthies had moved in to the rope. This was the second tight moment, as they all realized. The crowd had made its decision, but it was a formless mass to be swayed either by terror or pity; and now the voices of the toughs grew greater and more arrogant and men hurled themselves through the tight-packed ranks, colliding and cursing. Biedler nursed his shotgun and spoke at Pierce and Williams. "Watch for the tears! This time, by God, we will not be cheated."

Ives, who had sat like stone through the verdict and through the subsequent confusion, now mounted the wagon to face Sanders. The miners, arrested by this byplay, quit talking. Biedler suddenly moved out of the open area and disappeared behind a small log house near by.

"Colonel Sanders," said Ives, formal and polite, "I should like to ask a favor, one gentleman to another. This is pretty rough on me. I will not ask for sympathy but I've got a mother and some sisters back East and I'd like time to write them. I give you my word of honor to make no attempt to escape if you'll put this business off until tomorrow."

Sanders showed feeling. He dropped his head, deeply thinking. There was scarcely a sound in the packed audience, for this was a strange and dangerous and dramatic moment and the crowd, sensing it, let him have his silence. He lifted his head to look at Ives. Against Ives he was a slighter and less colorful man, educated and civilized and therefore at a handicap before the wild, half-sinister yet intensely attractive Ives. "I am not insensible to your position, Ives," he said. "I —"

Suddenly a voice said, "Wait," and all eyes turned to find X. Biedler mounted on the roof of the nearby cabin. X. Biedler stood up on the roof peak, short and heavy in the shadows, the shotgun cradled. "Sanders," he spoke in a voice that boomed up and down the Gulch, "ask Ives how much time he gave Tibault."

He had said the one right thing. That taunt, that practical and vengeful reminder, broke the tension. Somebody called: "Damned right!"

Sanders was obviously relieved. "Get down and write your letter," he said. "You'll have time enough before the rope is rigged."

He stepped from the wagon. The defense attorney came at him swearing. "It is a damned outrage to cut short a man's most sacred moments —"

Davis and Hereford pushed through the crowd and Hereford called at Byam: "Can't find a suitable place."

One of the miners near by called: "There's a place good enough," and pointed to a log house under construction hard by the wagons.

The walls were up but the roof not yet constructed. The miner pulled himself to the top of the wall, unseated a log and threw one end of it down inside the house. Other men now assisting, the log's high end was placed over the rim of the house wall, making an out-thrown arm on the street. Somebody, long prepared for the hanging, brought up a rope and tossed it over the extended log. This same man laid nine turns around the standing end and formed the hangman's knot.

"There's your rope!"

Judge Byam made a motion to Davis and Hereford. These two took Ives by the arms, moving him forward to the rope. It was X. Biedler, with the unflagging memory of the earlier trial, who found a box for Ives to stand on. Adriel Davis tied Ives's hands behind while Hereford slipped the noose around Ives's neck. Both men helped him up to the box. Hereford suddenly turned to speak to Byam. "Who's going to knock the box from under him?" This particular duty, for some reason of his own, displeased him.

The crowd now found voice again. The toughs, Pierce noticed, were making their last desperate effort. He watched Gallegher push through the miners with his gun raised. Gallegher had lost his hat and he was cursing and shoving his elbows into men. All through the crowd other toughs kept shouting:

"You can't railroad a man like that!

Let him go!"

"The man that kills Ives will never live out the night!"

"Let him write to his mother!"

"Shoot the fellow that touches the box! Pull down that rope somebody!"

Hereford was still undecided about the box and Byam had not spoken. There was this delay, with the cries of the toughs growing louder and louder. Ives stood on the small top of the box, holding himself rigid for fear of falling. Davis had taken the slack from the rope and had tied its free end to the cabin, its pressure holding Ives straight. He was marble pale and his eyes stared out before him, wild and full open. He seemed to search the crowd for help, glancing from man to man; and in a moment he saw Pierce directly below him and the wildness turned to pure hate. "I wish to God," he ground out, "I'd settled with you!" Then he lifted his voice so that everybody might hear him. "I am Innocent!"

Jim Williams, hard by Pierce, muttered: "That's the roadagent password!"

The toughs were in full yell; and, gaining courage, they were pushing forward. Pierce swung on them, and Williams. This was the last moment of danger, this was the final gamble.

It was Sanders, watching from the background who, having sensed the turning of the tide before, now sensed it again. He said in his clear, cold voice. "Men — do your duty!"

There was a stir in the front ranks and at once all the men stationed around the rope's circle wheeled against the crowd and flung up their guns. This blue steel gleamed in the deepening night and iron clicked on iron, and these muzzles made a barrier against the crowd. Suddenly a pair of men rushed forward and knocked the box from under George Ives's teetering feet. Pierce, his back turned to the outlaw, heard that strange whining thump of the sudden-strained rope, and he heard Ives's gasp. Every sound stopped in the crowd and every body ceased to move. Then Hereford said: "He's dead." Far back in the crowd a woman set up a piercing blood-chilling scream.

XVII: Vigilantes

THE GULCH awoke Christmas Day to find two feet of snow on the ground. The creek was frozen hard enough to support a wagon; the shop windows had half an inch of rippled ice adhering to the panes. Smoke rose straight from chimney tops through a windless air and in this wintry atmosphere all sounds carried far. Sunlight came down through a crystal-wool fog, bringing no heat.

These people were, for the most part, two thousand miles or better from family firesides. Yet this was Christmas Day with its old memories and its old, strong and undying customs, so that the shops put up pine greens at their doors and the Virginia Hotel advertised, by word of mouth, a steak and oyster dinner with sweet potatoes, canned tomatoes, brandy pudding and "French bon-bons especially freighted in for this occasion," at ten dollars the plate. Beginning at noon the Virginia's dining room did a land-office business.

Men moved from cabin to cabin exchanging the ancient phrase, "Merry Christmas," and miners snow-bound in the upper reaches of the Gulch tracked into town on snowshoes to break a cabin-confined monotony. On this morning a town loafer was found frozen in the hay pile of Nolan's stable, whereupon Nolan, who knew something of the man's past, walked down Wallace to take up a collection for the man's wife in the East and raised five hundred dollars before he got farther than the Senate. This day old grudges were absolved and old debts paid over eggnogs and Tom and Jerries at one saloon or another; and as early dusk came to the Gulch and lights gleamed through doorway apertures and windows and tent walls, four heavy-cloaked miners moved from saloon to saloon with the fiddlers and guitar players from The Pantheon, singing carols. This was the day of sentiment and regret and tears, and strong recollections bearing everybody in the Gulch back through time.

Pierce came into town after dark and stopped at Scoggins'. Finding Ben gone, Pierce made a search of the saloons for Ollie. When he reached Tanner's he noticed that the chairs at Temperton's poker table had been reversed; and a pine bough lay on the table. Tomorrow another dealer would sit in Temperton's chair and the table would again be in use, but on this Christmas Day Will Temperton had his tribute. Pierce found no trace of Ollie. Going along Wallace, he felt as much alone as he ever had; he had no part in any of this holiday.

He moved on to the Virginia Hotel and ate his meal. A little later Scoggins came in with Diana and took a table at the far end of the room. When Pierce finished he rose and moved over to them. Scoggins showed a small surprise, and then the surprise faded but his smile lacked the old warmth, the old closeness; and once again Pierce had the sensation of being closed out. He said: "Merry Christmas."

"Why," said Scoggins, "the same to you."

Diana looked up at Pierce, her face dark, her eyes suddenly reserved. He had expected nothing else from her but his memory this day was very clear and made him recall how different it once had been. He said gravely, "I'm sorry about Lily Beth. Leaves you a little lonesome, I'd imagine."

"Yes," she said, and continued to watch him. Somewhere in her was a lasting judgment of him, like a scar burned in; and so she sat, still unmoved — but hating him deeply. He said, "Merry Christmas again," and moved to the lobby. He stood in the lobby, lighting up a cigar. He found his coat and slid into it. He stood irresolute and tall and bulky and taciturn as people stirred steadily around him. From her place in the dining room Diana observed him, noticing again how little he seemed to need anything from other people. He was alone and seemed to wish for no other thing. Yet she had her suspicion. He had gone out of his way to come to this table and wish Scoggins and herself a Merry Christmas; and he had expressed his regret to her concerning Lily Beth. He had understood her feelings. Below the iron crust of this man, as she had long known, was a capacity for understanding. He had always had it but had never permitted himself to show it. Hardness and distrust were his faith. And now, she told herself, he was reaping the barren crop; this day he was really lonely.

She was still watching him when Lil Shannon entered the lobby with a huge, tawny-bearded miner. Lil at once came over to Pierce and smiled and placed a hand on his arm. Diana marveled at the long, easy smile Pierce showed back. These two talked a moment, the big miner forgotten by them. Lil laughed at Pierce and a rose color showed on her face and she was then an attractive woman, eager and anxious to please this one man alone. Pierce said something to her, and afterwards Diana noticed the little answering shrug of regret from the dance-hall girl. The miner at last grew weary of his neglect and claimed Lil, who walked into the dining room with him; but as Lil took her place at a table she lifted her head and smiled across the room at Pierce. None of this did Diana miss. She watched Pierce straighten himself and leave the hotel; afterwards she turned her attention to Lil and gave the woman a long, close study.

"Here's your steak, Diana," said Scoggins.

She put Pierce out of her mind; she closed a door on him, but when she did so she was smaller than she had been, for it was not only Pierce she put beyond the wall but a part of her life which had once been so eager and so gay.

Scoggins said again gently: "Better eat, Diana."

She settled to her meal. "Christmas is a time for memories, isn't it?"

"Sure. Nice things ahead — and mistakes behind."

She cast a swift glance at him. "Now and then you strike deep, Ben."

"Don't think too long of what's behind. Tomorrow's the way to look."

"You can't cross out the past. Who would really want to do it, anyway? All the nice things and bitter things are mixed together in the past. The times we cried and the times we laughed go together. To look ahead is to be young, and that is right for us. But it is the things we did yesterday, or didn't do, which make us wise."

They talked idly through the meal; and afterwards left the hotel, walking along through Wallace. Somewhere past the bakery Diana caught Scoggins' arm and drew him against a house wall. "Wait," she said and looked at something diagonally over the street. When he stared that way he saw a man, heavy-bundled in his coat, standing in the shadows beyond The Pantheon. "Sitgreaves," she murmured.

"What about him?"

She shook her head. "This is something that happened before I knew you, Ben."

She hadn't meant to close him out but nevertheless she had lifted a fence on part of her life. He was outside that part, well knowing that her own thoughts were all of Pierce, either remembering him with hatred, or with some kind of love, or perhaps simply tied by some obligation of old companionship. He didn't know, and he wanted to know; and he felt his keen jealousy.

Sitgreaves was watching something on Van Buren. Diana said, "All right, Ben," and walked toward Van Buren Street rapidly. There was nothing to be seen either way and Diana, after scanning the street carefully and anxiously, shrugged her shoulders and crossed with Scoggins to her cabin. Scoggins followed in and waited until she had lighted a lamp.

"A little lonesome without Lily Beth," he said.

He was sorry he had said it. She had taken the parting hard and now he observed that she could easily cry. "Well," he said, "things like that happen."

"I remember you warned me, Ben. You told me not to love her too much."

"Maybe you'd better put your heart on something else."

"You can't just trade your love around."

"Why, I suppose that's so," he answered. She wasn't a woman to surrender things at the drop of a hat. She never would quit loving Lily Beth. Then the rest of that thought moved in on him. Nor would she ever quit loving Pierce, if she had ever loved him. He didn't know about that, and now he realized he had to know; and since he had no other way of going about it he simply dropped his question flatly at her.

"How about me, Diana?"

She lifted her eyes at him, those expressive eyes of an expressive woman. She could knock a man down with her eyes, as she had done with Pierce; or she could be tender and soft. She seemed to feel that way now, giving Scoggins a sudden thrust of hope.

"You've been quite a while coming to that, Ben."

"Didn't want to rush in on another man's ground. I wasn't certain about it. I'm still not. But if it means the end of friendship between me and Jeff, that's how it will have to be. I can't help it. I'll ask for myself."

"I remember how you came aboard the

343

boat at Celilo. You didn't fight. You just argued the purser down. You get what you're after without making a fuss."

"I can fight, too, if I have to fight."

She still watched him, but he felt that he no longer had her full attention. She had an expression which mirrored other thoughts, she looked at him and saw other faces. It made him say with his gentle stubbornness: "Diana, how about me?"

Her voice ran along wistful notes. "I ran away from safety and comfort. I said I'd never go back to those things. I'd feel ashamed of myself now if I did."

He spoke in a tremendously fallen voice: "Is that all I mean?"

She answered him with a swift kindness. "I don't think so. Yet —"

"Diana," he said, and put aside his loyalty to Jeff Pierce with a painful, stinging effort, "You'll get no happiness from Pierce."

"Why did you say that? He wouldn't have said it of you."

"I fought for that man once. I'd fight for him again. But I know him well. Things have got to be his way. He'll break anything that's against him — even a woman. That's what I'd tell you, regardless of what you thought about me."

She asked a question which seemed beside the point to him. "Where's Ollie?"

"I think he skipped."

"Then he has no friends left, has he? Jeff, I mean."

"I'm his friend. But I am your friend first."

"No," she said, "he has no close friends left. Now he knows what it is to be quite alone. That had to come to him."

"He always was that way. There's no difference."

"Now he's feeling it. He didn't before. As long as he never knew anything else it didn't matter. It couldn't hurt him. But he found out there was something else, and now it hurts."

"Where'd he learn about something else?" asked Ben.

"From me," she said and turned her face to him. What he saw shocked him. Her expression was close to being cruel and her eyes held that stirring anger he had witnessed only once before. "From me. He knows how different life could be. Now," and her voice fell in full, hard weight on Ben Scoggins, "let him learn."

The scene had gotten away from Scoggins. Once he had her interest. He no longer had it. The bitter and passionate relations between these two people — of which he knew nothing definite — simply swamped every other thing. He could not have been more completely out of Diana's mind had Jeff Pierce been in the room before her. There was in Scoggins a certain amount of pride and a certain amount of jealousy, now making him stiffly say: "I will let you alone with your quarrel."

She put a hand on his arm. "It is a good deal different than you think, Ben. Jeff and I will never be nearer to each other than we are now."

"Of course not," he said. "You ain't the same kind of people."

"You're wrong. We're exactly the same kind of people. It is all or nothing with each of us." She saw that, keen mind as he was, he could not follow her reasoning and so she added, "I want to be honest with you, Ben. I don't know what I feel about you. Let's not talk of this again for a while."

He said, "Good night," and left the cabin. Sitgreaves, he noticed, had crossed over and stood in another shadowed area on Wallace Street; he gave it no particular thought, his mind being full upon the girl. She was full of unfathomed contradictions, possessing all the sweetness and kindness a woman could have, yet how swift her anger had risen and how resonant her voice had become upon mention of Pierce! She was controlled by a deeply passionate temper that would never grow less until it had been satisfied. Scoggins, being a calm and temperate man with his own standards of womanhood, looked upon this astonishing revelation of Diana Castle's nature with an increasing thoughtfulness. The fire he had seen made him uncomfortable.

Next day Pierce moved around the cabin half-heartedly planning an addition to accommo-date his horse which he had been keeping in town. There was little else to do, the ground being too solidly frozen for mining: and idle-ness increasingly bored him. Later in the day he moved up-Gulch to borrow a pair of snow-shoes, returned to his cabin and made up a small pack of grub, and thereafter struck into the hills with his gun. The taint of town was on him, as old George Noon had prophesied it would be, and the staleness and the increasing restlessness of a cabin-bound man came upon him. That night, high back in the Tobacco Roots, he made camp and watched the distant lights of the Gulch, and felt grateful for the release which seemed to come to him. The physical weariness of the climb into the hills dulled the steady irritation he had been feeling, it diminished the thoughts that circled endlessly through his head. Half-asleep and half-awake before his fire, he had his old feeling of cleansed and simplified aloneness; crouched in his blankets and attentive to all the small sounds in the starkly bitter night, he reached out and caught at the edges of his old content. A frozen moon stood in the sky and the tree shadows lay black against the surrounding snow; once four elk passed him in file. It was always better to be this way, braced against the natural world and listening to it, than to be any other way. And yet even then, grasping for that simplicity of his earlier years, and feeling its relief, he knew it was not enough. Once it had been; but now it was not.

On that same night Sanders and Jim Williams and Lott and Pfouts and eight or nine other men met in Fox's house in Virginia City and signed the Vigilante oath. Pfouts was to be president, Lott the treasurer, Sanders the counsel, Jim Williams the executive officer. There were to be companies, with a captain for each company. Each company, out on the trail, had complete judgment and authority to pass sentence. The only sentence was to be death, although it was within their power to banish a man if they saw fit. Upon them all was pressed the inviolable oath of secrecy.

Sanders stressed that. "We are working largely in the dark. We know, or suspect, certain of the Innocents. Others we do not know. They are all around us and they will be watching. Anything we let drop will be picked up, either resulting in their escape or in our own assassination. The hanging of Ives has not seemed to impress them much. Gallegher and Tanner and Marshland are talking big."

"There must be no delay," said Lott. "Speed is the essence of this thing."

Jim Williams had an answer for that. "Ives

was not alone in the Tibault matter. Long John Franck mentioned Alec Carter. We'll find him and put him to question."

"Include Dutch John Wagner and Steve Marshland, Jim. They were involved in the last robbery on Moody's pack train. Some of the boys recognized them."

"Marshland's left town, so's Carter," said Williams. "I hear they went over to the Deer Lodge Valley. I'll get a group and go after them."

It was nearing New Year's and Williams delayed until after the first, meanwhile building up the Vigilante organization with members from Nevada City and the other Gulch settlements. When he was ready to leave for his scout he sent word up to Pierce's cabin but found Pierce still gone; and so the group, consisting of about twenty men, moved down the Gulch, passed Daly's, crossed the Beaverhead and moved through the McCarty Mountains. Coming down the Deer Lodge Valley they met Red Yeager riding the opposite direction. Red was known by most of them as a man of various occupations in the Gulch — and was liked by the Gulch.

"Seen Alec Carter?" questioned Williams.

"Whole gang up at Deer Lodge on a New Year's drunk," said Yeager, anxious to please. "Billy Bunton's there, too, and Whisky Bill Graves." He traveled on, throwing casual advice to other men in the column.

"Seems like we'll bag our game," said Jim Williams. But when at dusk two days later the group came into Reilly's Ranch at Cottonwood they found their game gone. Reilly said: "Red Yeager came in here on the gallop with a letter warning the crowd to get out of sight. Bill Bunton threw that letter somewhere around here." Reilly moved around the ranch house and finally discovered the note under a corner chair. He brought it back. When Williams saw it he said: "That's George Brown's writing — George Brown who tends bar for Dempsey."

"Bunton said it was from Brown," agreed Reilly.

"Yeager," said Biedler, "was returning from that chore when he passed us."

The group fought its way back through a bitter three-day blizzard. At the Beaverhead Ranch they heard that Yeager was twenty miles farther up the river at a cabin. Williams set out with five men, raced on through the snow and caught Yeager in the act of rolling his blanket roll for further travel. When he saw Williams' gun leveled on him he shook his head and all the spirit went out of him. Stripped of his gun he returned with Williams to the main crowd at the Beaverhead. Williams said: "We'll pick up Brown at Dempsey's," and put his group immediately into motion. Frostbitten, hungry and red-eyed for want of sleep, the posse came into Dempsey's and nailed Brown.

Brown was a man without sand. When Williams passed him the letter, he showed the group one pale, agonized expression and bowed his head. "Yes," he said, "I wrote it."

Williams turned to Biedler: "Few of you fellows take Brown over in that corner and question him. Red, you come with us." He took Yeager into another room of Dempsey's house, the rest of the posse following. "Red," he said, "you carried the letter that warned Alec Carter. That puts you in it. You know what we are, don't you?"

"I've heard," said Yeager, calmly. He stared at the floor, dismally contemplating his past and his future. "I had an idea of leavin' the Gulch a week ago. Wish to God I had. I'm done for and I know it." He hit one hand against the other, crying out: "Bill Bunton got me into this! I wish he was dead!"

"May get your wish," said Williams tersely, and moved back into the main room. He left Brown and Yeager under guard, calling the rest of the party outside. They stood around in the crackling cold, comparing the stories of Yeager and Brown, until Williams said: "That's the case. Vote your convictions just as you see them. All for hanging step this way. All against, step the other way."

There was no dissent. The entire party

moved over to the hanging side.

"So be it," said Williams. But he considered his new duties with some gravity and at last came to a decision. "I'd rather know what Sanders and Pfouts think of this. We'll move on to Laurin's Ranch for the night. I'll stay there with six or seven men. The rest of you go on home. One of you see Sanders and Pfouts and bring back what they say."

They put up at Laurin's. The next morning before daybreak, Neil Howie returned from Virginia City and aroused Williams from a sound sleep. "They say you're on the right track. Go ahead."

Williams woke the rest of the party. Yeager and Brown stood backed against Laurin's fireplace, both men drawn and silent. "Guess you know what's comin'," said Williams. "I'm sorry for it. Some of you boys go out and fix the ropes to those cottonwoods."

Brown suddenly dropped to his knees and began to cry. "Just give me a chance to get out that door! Let me get on a horse! You'll never see me in this country . . . !"

Yeager reached over and kicked his partner in the ribs. "Buck up!" He dropped his head and went through his terrible thoughts and when he looked up he spoke Bill Bunton's name again. "If you never do anything else, get him. He's not the only one, but get him."

"Who's the others, Red?" asked Williams. "It won't help you any but it would be doing the Gulch a favor. It would be on the credit side of your book."

Yeager, as steady as any of the posse, shrugged his shoulders. "I could stand a little credit where I'm going. Well —" he looked at Williams intently, and dropped his first name into the complete silence. "The leader is Henry Plummer."

"Don't start lying, Red!" warned Biedler.

"I know what I'm talking about. He pulled the wool over everybody's eyes, but he's the reddest dog in the lot. He came into this country with half a dozen killings on his hands. He married a fine woman and he fooled Sanders and all the respectable ones. But his woman left him, didn't she? He's the brains. He organized this whole thing."

Williams slowly shook his head, saying nothing. The rest of the posse stood in complete stillness. "Well," went on Yeager, "here they are. You can take 'em down. There ain't a man that's got a clean spot in his soul. I ought to know."

Williams found a pencil and rummaged up a piece of paper and noted the names as Red Yeager intoned them one by one. Plummer and Bunton and Ives. Ives had been second in command, as smart as Plummer and as crafty. Cy Skinner and Steve Marshland, Dutch John Wagner, Alec Carter and Whisky Bill Graves. Stinson and Gallegher and Ned Ray, all Deputies. George Shears and Johnny

Cooper and Mex Grant and Bob Zachary. Boon Helm. Hayes Lyons. Clubfoot George Lane . . .

"Him?" said John Fetherstone in surprise.

"Him," said Yeager. "Then there's Rube Ketchum, who's dead, and George Lowry, Billy Page, Doc Howard, Jem Romaine, Billy Terwilliger, Gad Moore. The country's shot with them, boys. And there's another fellow nobody trusted much, but he was in on the stage holdup when Hilton was killed. That's Ollie Rounds."

Williams looked at his list. "That's all Red?"

"There it is," said Yeager. "I did my good turn, didn't I?"

"All right," said Williams. "Let's get this done."

Yeager turned through the doorway but Brown fell on his knees, making it necessary for some of the posse to drag him by the arms. They crossed the yard to the cottonwoods; here Yeager turned and poured his contempt on Brown. "Damned shame I've got to go to hell beside a yellowback like you."

Biedler had brought out a pair of chairs; on these the two men were placed and the loops thrown about their necks. The Vigilante affixing the noose to Yeager suddenly lost footing in the snow and fell, carrying Yeager with him. He rose, angry at himself and apologizing to Yeager. "We've got to do better than that, Red."

There was, then, the last long silence. Brown trembled so greatly that a Vigilante had to hold him by the coat. Yeager looked down on the crowd, thinking his way slowly up to this moment, framing some last thought in his head. Then he said: "Get the rest of them, Jim. I'll feel better."

"We'll try," said Williams.

Suddenly two men rushed at the chairs and knocked them aside. Williams took off his hat and looked down. He was an indomitable man, truly savage when aroused, and he would have followed Red Yeager a thousand miles to satisfy his own deep sense of justice. Yet he held his head down while the two men died at the ropes' ends. Not until Biedler said: "They're dead," did he look up, and then it was to turn his eyes on the stocky Dutchman. Biedler had watched the two drop with his gray face showing its seamy pleasure; there was that strain of barbarism in Biedler, honest as he was.

"I liked Red," said Williams. "He had some good in him." He turned back to the house, and he stood inside by the fire with his eyes fastened to the list Yeager had furnished him. It was the last name, the name of Ollie Rounds, that held his attention. Laurin had cooked up some coffee. Williams drank two cups of it while he pondered. He had known a long time ago that this clean-up would come and he had known it would be a dirty chore; but he was a man who would flinch no part of it until it was at last done — no single part from beginning to end. And there was still another moment to come which he knew would be more brutal than what had gone before.

Biedler said: "Home now?"

"No," said Williams, "we have got something more to do. I'm going to Virginia City. I'll be back. You fellows stay here and catch up on your sleep." He left the house. White frost stood on the whiskers of his horse and its breath turned to shallow white steam in the air. The saddle leather, when he sat upon it, was cold as ice.

He changed horses at Virginia and rode directly on to Pierce's cabin, and found Pierce splitting wood. He said: "We've been on a hunt and had some luck. We're going on another hunt. Come along."

It was a command rather than an invitation. They had all subscribed to the Vigilante oath — Pierce tacitly at the first meeting — and they were all obligated to serve when called. Pierce accepted it as such and stopped in his cabin only long enough to put away the shotgun which had been leaning outside the cabin wall and to buckle on his revolver. He followed on foot behind Williams, reached town and saddled his horse. Together the two moved southward through foot-deep snow churned and scarred and flecked with the frozen mud of traffic.

"We hung Yeager and Brown this morning," said Williams. "Yeager did some talking and left a list."

"Who's on it?"

"Plummer for one. He's the chief. That surprise you?"

"No," said Pierce, "not much. I never liked the way he scouted around me in Bannack. Something wrong in the feel of the man." He looked down the trail, half-closing his eyes. "I have met men like Plummer before, smooth outside and rotten inside."

"Occurs to me," commented Williams, "you have met many kinds of men."

"Most kinds. I am not much of a hand to be surprised at whatever turns up."

Williams murmured: "Good way to be."

Williams stopped in Nevada City to pick up John Lott, the three rode on without conversation. Down by Junction Parris Pfouts came by on his horse. He turned about and joined them at Williams' signal. Williams explained what had already taken place, and mentioned the list. He went about halfway through the list; then he said in a noncommittal way, "a few others," and that was all he said between Junction and Laurin's Ranch. At the ranch he called out the waiting crowd.

"Where we going?" asked Biedler.

"Past the Beaverhead. Up to that cabin beyond where Bain's horse ranch was."

"Who's there?"

"I don't really know," said Williams. "Billy Southmayd's reported a man holing up there the last five-six days. We'll look."

When they left the mouth of the Gulch the wind began to sweep steadily at them. They reached the Cold Springs' Ranch and noted a horse standing there; and Williams, who had a retentive memory, suddenly said, "Pull up," and got down. The crowd followed suit and part of the men came behind him as he moved on the door and flung it open. Bill Hughes, who ran the ranch, was in the room with one other man. That other man was Sitgreaves.

Williams said: "Where'd you get that horse?"

Sitgreaves said: "Bought it at Virginia City. From a fellow named Marshland."

"Yes," said Williams. "That's Marshland's extra horse. He must have needed money. When I saw the horse I figured maybe Steve was in here. We're looking for him."

"Come on," said Pfouts. "It'll be dark before we get to the Beaverhead."

But Williams watched Sitgreaves coolly. "What brings you here?"

"Scouting the country," said Sitgreaves.

"Come on," said Pfouts again.

Williams gave Pfouts a half-irritated glance. "We've got business here, Parris." He swung to Pierce. "This man took two shots at you in Virginia, didn't he?"

The crowd, so far disinterested, now centered full attention on Sitgreaves, who stood with his back to the fireplace, both hands laced behind. He had a full square beard above which his eyes showed a black-bright glint. He said nothing and showed no fear.

"I was on the street that night," commented Williams. "The fellow was in the crack between the Pony and Pete Recken's tent store. He wore a blue coat with brass buttons. I saw the brass buttons shinin'. Those are the same buttons."

Sitgreaves gravely listened to Williams and thereafter passed his attention to Pierce. He remained close-mouthed and outwardly disturbed. Looking at this man's weathered face with its Yankee tenacity and its fixed zeal, Pierce doubted if any power on earth could bend Sitgreaves from his purpose save the sudden burst of a bullet or the swift closure of a rope around his neck. This man was a bloodhound who knew no other purpose than pursuit and vengeance.

Williams was a patient man but he now turned impatient. The crowd also grew restive. Pfouts said: "That the man, Jeff?" Yet none of these people counted; and it were as if they had not been in the room. Pierce faced Sitgreaves, thinking of the thousand miles or more over which Sitgreaves had followed him, and he was also thinking of the master of the *Panama Chief* as the latter roared and rushed at him, and his mind jumped and stopped at scenes along the succeeding way, at the wagon on which he had smuggled himself and Diana, at Lewiston and on the long road over the Bitterroots, at the miners' camp near the McCarty Mountains when, near tears, she had stood before him with her whole heart open. There his thinking ceased. He shook his head.

"No, not the man."

Williams gave him a sharp stare. "How would you know?"

"I know who the man was."

"Who was it?" pressed Williams.

Pierce said, "That's altogether my business, Jim, and I will take care of it."

He watched Sitgreaves as he said it. He was saving this man from a hanging, as Sitgreaves should be realizing. He was avoiding a showdown with Sitgreaves as he had done before, wanting none of the man's blood upon his hands. Sitgreaves, staring so steadily back, showed no expression. There was no break, no recognition, no silent admission of the charity given.

Williams was wholly unsatisfied but Pfouts said, "That should settle it. Now let's get on the way," and led the crowd out of the ranch house. They were soon in the saddle, fording the Stinkingwater and rising from the valley to the barren land lying between this river and the Beaverhead. Even then grayness had come upon the country and the wind drove at them with its needle-keen cold. At full dark they swung from the stage road, moved two miles north and picked up a light in a shallow coulee ahead. Williams stopped here.

"Some of you circle behind. Some of you stick in front. Pierce and Biedler and Howie and I will tackle the door."

These four dismounted and walked straight on, their feet slipping and squealing in the snow. Biedler fell and rose with a disgusted curse. There was a window covered over by an oiled hide, through which light yellowly seeped, and flakes of fire whipped up from a tin chimney and fled in the wind. Pierce and Williams came upon the door together, and it was Pierce who reached for the latch and held it a moment. He looked behind him, seeing the crowd shift in the snow. Williams gave Pierce a short stare and nodded, whereupon Pierce softly lifted the latch, pushed open the door and stepped into the cabin.

A single man occupied the room, his back turned from the door; at the first sound of entry he flung himself around and threw out a hand toward a revolver lying on the table. But before he completed the motion he checked himself and looked at Pierce, and then a half-smile replaced the first visible shock of fear.

"Hello, Jeff."

Pierce said: "What are you doing down here, Ollie?"

XVIII: "Let Me Live!"

OTHER MEN crowded into the small cabin. Rounds looked at them with keenest speculation, but that first show of fear had vanished and now he displayed a careless grin.

"Waiting for the wind to die down," he said. "I never did like to be cold."

Pierce said: "What's the matter with Virginia City? This is a hell of a place to spend the winter. I wondered about you. Been looking for you."

Ollie said: "Got restless. I never stay in one place long. You know that."

Pierce shook his head, neither understanding Ollie nor the reason for Williams' leading the Vigilantes here. He turned to Williams and observed the leader's steady stare to be on him. "Water haul, Jim. Who'd you think you'd find here?"

Williams said: "Ollie Rounds."

"All right," grumbled Pierce, "he's here. What of it?"

"You're slow on the catch, Jeff. Red Yeager gave us a list. This man's name is on it."

"Don't be a damned fool," said Pierce. "I know Ollie."

"So do other men," said Williams.

"Ollie," said Pierce, "speak up."

"Let Williams talk," said Rounds, maintaining his self-assurance. "What do you think I've done?"

"You were with Ives and Ketchum and Marshland when Hilton was killed at the stage holdup."

"I was in Virginia City," said Rounds. "How could I have been across the Beaverhead?"

"You're quick on the answer," commented Williams. "Most innocent men couldn't be so sure of where they were four or five months ago."

"That's easy," said Rounds. "I haven't left Virginia half a dozen times in that many months."

Williams spoke over his shoulder. "Southmayd."

Billy Southmayd moved through the door and came abreast Pierce and Williams.

"Billy," said Williams, "what do you know? You drove that stage."

"There were four of them," said Southmayd. "Ives and Ketchum and this man — and one I never recognized. I knew Rounds right off. He wore a big buffalo coat that had the fur partly worn from the lapel. Yellow hair, blue eyes. His horse was a solid bay with big ears and a callus just above the off rear fetlock."

Pierce turned on Southmayd. He gave the man a black stare. "Be careful, Billy."

"I'm apt to be careful when I'm helping to hang a man, Jeff. It was Ollie."

Williams said: "Where's the buffalo coat, Ollie?"

"Somebody held me up and took it, on Daylight Grade."

Biedler, planted in a corner of the room now added his bit of information. "Tack McGuire found that coat, day after the holdup, chucked behind a couple boulders near the mouth of Alder, beyond Laurin's. Why would a man steal your coat on Daylight, then carry it clean beyond Laurin's and throw it away?"

Williams said: "Red named you on the list, Ollie."

The silence fell. Pierce watched Ollie's face take its dark and fatal stain. Light went out of Ollie's eyes and hope went out of him. He faced the crowd and betrayed a fear too deep to hide. His lip corners tightened and his nostrils swelled to deeper breathing. Little by little the irony and rashness and the smiling humor — all those things which gave Ollie his flavor — died away and left him colorless.

"Ollie," said Pierce, "speak up!"

"Why did you come along?" asked Ollie Rounds sullenly.

Pierce shook his head. "I didn't know." He turned to Jim Williams, as dangerous to Williams then as a man might be. "Why did you bring me along?"

"I knew this was coming," said Williams. "I wanted you to see for yourself, so you'd get it first hand and not second hand. He's one of the Innocents, but he's got his right to have somebody talk for him. Go ahead, talk for him."

"Red," said Pierce, "was a scoundrel. You believe what he told you?"

Williams said in his unstirred voice: "Cross out Red's testimony then. But Billy Southmayd's testimony still remains. You know Billy to be a square man."

Pierce said: "Billy, how sure could you be in a situation like that? Other men have got blue eyes and light hair and buffalo overcoats."

Southmayd said: "Maybe. You know Ollie's horse?"

"Yes."

"Got a scar on its off rear fetlock?"

Pierce fell silent as he remembered back. There were gaps in Ollie's Virginia City career which, now that he recalled them, were bad. How had the man lived, flush enough to play poker at Temperton's, to eat and sleep well? He remembered the overcoat and the rubbed lapel. And he remembered the horse. "Yes," he said.

"There you are," said Southmayd. "I might be mistaken in one thing. I couldn't be mistaken in three or four things."

Pierce put his eyes on Ollie. "What were you doing down here, Ollie?"

"I meant to pull out," said Ollie Rounds, and then he shrugged his shoulders. "I always stay a little too long."

"This man," said Pierce, "is a friend of mine, Jim."

"Not enough," said Williams. "There'll be others of us with friends like that, before this thing is done. And they'll hang. It is not enough, Jeff."

"You will recall," said Pierce, "that he stepped out from the walk and put himself between me and Ives and Marshland, when I was down on my knees in the middle of the street. He stood so they couldn't shoot."

"There's some good in every man," said Williams. "But it is still not enough. He rode with Ives and he spent other men's money at Tanner's bar. But go ahead, Jeff. He's your friend."

"He took my part against Ives and Ketchum in Lewiston," said Pierce.

"The devil was an angel once," said Williams.

Pierce stepped forward and circled the table

367

so that he was beside Ollie Rounds. He looked at the dozen men packed into this small room. "I suppose —" he said in a soft voice, and gave his intentions away by the expression that ran over his face. Suddenly Williams murmured a word and all these men flung up their guns on him and blue light danced along those barrels. "No," said Williams, "don't do it, Jeff."

"All right," Pierce said, grinding the answer between his teeth. "All right."

Williams spoke to Biedler and Fetherstone. "Stay here," and led the rest of the crowd outside. They went a short distance from the cabin, their talk coming back in murmured spurts of sound through the chill air. Ollie Rounds said, "If you don't mind, gentlemen, I'd like to put on my coat. It is cold."

"Go ahead," said Biedler.

Rounds moved to the corner of the cabin and slid into his coat. He buttoned the collar around his neck. "Sorry, Jeff," he said.

Pierce listened to the rise and fall of talk in the yard; and he heard the talk quit. Moonlight was strong enough for him to notice a pair of men move away and by that he knew how the decision went. Rounds knew it too. He paled and a little wincing sound came from him as his fertile mind ran ahead to embrace the last blow of pain and the last agony. He pulled his lips together and moistened them and he thrust one mutely terrible appeal at

Pierce. Pierce shook his head. "I guess that's all, Ollie."

Rounds stiffened his shoulders. "What the hell?" he whispered. "It happens sometime."

Pierce said: "What do you want me to do, Ollie?"

"Nothing," said Rounds. "No letters East, lying about my brave end against the Indians. I've got nothing to leave except a few bad memories. There was another time or two, Jeff, when I helped you against Ives. Just want you to know that. I would help you again. It really doesn't matter. There is only one thing on my mind. I set out a long time ago to be the sort of a fellow you are — just tough and not giving a damn. I never quite made it, because I never had enough leather in me. But I found out one thing which you should know. Tough or not tough, no man's got a hole card big enough to play this damned funny game of living alone. You'll find that out."

Williams came in. "Sorry, Ollie. I guess we're ready."

The agony of fear went through Ollie Rounds again, shrinking him and chilling him; cursed with a vivid mind, he saw too clearly the picture of his own end. He opened his mouth and a strange sigh came out. He put his hand on the table and for a moment stared at his feet. From some deep source he seemed to be calling on his last remnant of pride, and succeeded and straightened. "I have got to do this in proper shape," he said. "I'd be damned ashamed to make a poor show." He had then, one final flare of irony as he looked at the crowd half inside and half outside the cabin. "I'm on the receiving end of this business. You're not. Just pause a moment once in awhile and consider if you could do it any better."

"All right, Ollie," said Williams and pointed to the door.

Ollie tried to smile at Pierce. "My love to Ben — my love to Diana."

Pierce nodded. He said, "Luck, Ollie," and watched Rounds move through the doorway. On the threshold Rounds turned, even then his face turning indistinct to Pierce. "Jeff," he said hurriedly, "don't let me hang out there in the wind too long. I can't stand the thought."

"All right," said Pierce, and watched him march on with the crowd. Biedler ran back and took the cabin's only chair, which was a canned-goods box. Pierce moved to the stove. He put his hands over it, and he held his head down, watching the color of the fire flicker through the warped lid. Presently he moved from the stove and stood with his back to the door. Time dragged on and there was no sound; but he beat his hand slowly against the wall, making a noise that would drown out the outer noise he didn't want to hear.

Part of the crowd returned. Biedler came in with Williams, who said, "All over."

Biedler, always practical, said: "I brought along a pick and shovel. This ground's hard as rock."

"Bring him in here," asked Pierce. "We'll bury him under this floor."

"No use spoiling a good cabin," objected Biedler.

Pierce stared at Biedler. "God damn you, shut up!"

Biedler's gray jaws set and he would have started a quarrel had not Williams immediately checked it. "All right, Jeff. We'll bring him in here."

Pierce threw the table to a corner of the room. He kicked at the loose floor puncheons with his boot and reached down and dislodged them and tossed them aside. Biedler disappeared, to return with the pick and shovel. A pair of men brought Ollie Rounds in and laid him on the floor.

"Now," said Pierce, "get the hell out of here."

Williams nodded at the others, sending them out. He paused in the doorway. "Too bad," he said, "but that's how it goes."

"Shut the door," said Pierce.

When they had gone he took up the pick and broke the soil, and thereafter began to shovel out the grave. The room grew warm. He removed his coat and shirt and, stripped

371

to his heavy undershirt, continued the digging. Sweat ran down his face and dropped into the deepening hole.

The hanging of Ives and the banishment of Hildebrand and Franck had sharpened the attention of the toughs, but it had not shaken their confidence. Gallegher and Marshland and Zachary and those others who headquartered in Virginia City continued to gather at Tanner's and to make their open boasts. The capture and execution of Brown and Yeager and Rounds stirred them, though it did not awaken them to their danger. Long triumphant in the Gulch they remained blind to the signs about them until it became known that Yeager had revealed the roster of the Innocents.

By that time it was too late. Acting in swiftest secrecy, the Vigilantes now struck their hammer blows one after another. In the first half of January Lott and Sanders led a party to Bannack, rounded up Stinson, Ray and Sheriff Plummer and hung them side by side to a shed rafter on the edge of town, with Plummer — the chief and the symbol of all that was lawless — falling to his knees and crying out his abject terror: "Cut off my arms, cut off my ears — but let me live!"

Scarcely had the news of this traveled to Virginia City when Jim Williams threw a ring of Vigilantes around the town and took into custody Gallegher, Skinner, Clubfoot Lane, Boone Helm and Frank Parrish. There was no formal trial, for these men had long since convicted themselves by their record. Each had his moment to confess or deny, to curse and beg, and thereafter was led to the ceiling joist of a new building on Wallace Street. Gallegher, who, as Plummer's Deputy, had made a travesty and a joke of the star he wore, maintained his character to the last. His final request was for a drink and when he received it he laid the full bitter venom of his soul upon the world and died defiantly.

Fear left the Gulch and sentimental pity vanished. All the accumulated memories of injustice, all the thwarted righteousness, all the recollections of good men murdered gathered in terrible momentum. The Vigilantes rode through January's storms, hunting down their men one by one in canyons and remote settlements and isolated cabins, and pulled them out and passed sentence upon them, by day or by late night, and hung them at whatever tree or corral arch happened to be handy. In this fashion passed Steve Marshland, Bunton, Alec Carter, Zachary, Johnny Cooper. Ranging far over to the Gallatin Valley, to Fort Owen, and to the Bitterroot Valley, the Vigilantes also caught George Shears, Whisky Bill Graves and Bill Hunter. Jim Williams carried a list of these men in his pocket and scratched them out one at a time until at last late in February he drew a line through the last name. All those who had been active Innocents were accounted for and disposed of. In this corner of Montana gray-yellow mounds of earth, unmarked for the most part, testified to a terror and to an evil power come to an end. That same month Oliver's stage left Virginia City with forty thousand dollars of gold dust and reached Bannack without incident. In little more than twenty days the malignant thing of six months' growth had been completely removed in clean, cruel excisions.

Watching that stage roll down Wallace Street with its treasure, W. B. Dance spoke regretfully to his partner Stuart of other treasures unrecovered: "Too bad to think of all the money Ives and his crowd got away with."

"It brought 'em nothing," said Stuart. "Liquor took it, and women, and the poker tables. All they got was a grave."

Pierce came into Dance and Stuart's during late afternoon to take his dust from the safe and walk over to Oliver's express office, there consigning it to Mary Morris. Afterwards he dropped in at the Virginia Hotel and spent the best part of a half-hour writing a letter to her, explaining his stewardship.

He had never met this woman, and never would. Yet the obligation laid down by Barney was cemented not only by one man's faith in another but by the memory of a woman at the entire mercy of someone two thousand miles removed. His own mother, long ago, had been thus left alone to suffer in a thoughtless, unmerciful world. He remembered that as he wrote to Mary Morris. Mary Morris was the receiver of a fidelity his own mother had never had from any living soul.

In full dark the sound of wind drummed Virginia's walls and snow began to race by. He left his letter with the clerk and moved down to Doc Steele's cabin. He sat with Steele awhile, discussing the claim he now shared with Mary Morris.

"If it were entirely mine," he said, "I'd feel free to dispose of it as I saw fit. It is her half-interest that bothers me. She could be bilked by a dishonest man."

"What does this lead up to?" asked Steele.

"I'm leaving the Gulch."

"Winter's a hell of a time to be traveling," said Steele. That was his first, practical reaction. Then he added: "Why leave? Spring's coming, the toughs are wiped out and you'll see the biggest camp in the West."

"It may be," agreed Pierce, not interested.

"Not many times in a century," reflected Steele, "when a man can start at scratch with a country that's starting at scratch. I wish I were as young as you. Like to think that maybe fifty years from now I could stand on this street and look back to everything that happened, knowing I saw it start." He remembered his classics and drew out an appropriate phrase. " 'All of it I saw and some of it I was.' That's a rare thing. Gives a man a feeling having lived a full and useful life."

Knowing Pierce's skeptical streak he expected to hear some half amused and half bitter retort on the general nonsense of a man's hoping to leave any permanent mark behind him. But Pierce only shrugged his shoulders. "Perhaps," he said. The old bubble of vinegar and alum was missing. Pierce had turned quiet. And, the doctor reflected, when a man in the full prime of an exceptional vigor turned quiet it augured a pretty deep disturbance. Perhaps it was the death of Ollie Rounds, perhaps it had something to do with Diana Castle. The talk around town was that she was marrying Scoggins. Virginia was like that, a labyrinth of gossip; everybody knew everybody else's affairs.

"You know of a good man we could trust with the claim?" asked Pierce.

"What you want for your half?"

"I'll just turn it over, same way it was turned over to me."

"Hell," said Steele, "it is worth five thousand dollars any day."

"Don't need five thousand dollars very

much. How about Mark Tyson?"

"He'd do," agreed Steele.

"I'll talk to Mark," said Pierce and rose.

"Have supper. Those are damned good elk steaks in the fryin' pan."

"Not tonight, Will," said Pierce and went out. He took a quick tour of the saloons and saw nothing of Tyson, and afterwards dropped into Pfouts and Russell's and spent a good deal of time on a pair of snowshoes and a light pack sack. He owned both a shotgun and revolver, neither of which would be the best weapon on a long trail, and so he bought a second-hand Spencer. That was all. The lighter a man traveled the better it went. One man, one campfire, one set of blankets — and no obligations. He stood at the counter, more or less looking ahead at the trail while the clerk patiently waited. The clerk was a small man. Pierce stared over his head, eyes narrowed into the future, receiving the impressions of the fore-ordained trail, the smell of wet wood burning, the white hillsides and the pine boughs whose snow dropped as he touched them, and the ghostly glow of moonlight and the thin crack of a creek coursing between its ice and margins, with the print of game tracks leading down to it; and the black, ragged edge of mountains breaking against the skyline, and the wild drums of the wind.

"That's all?" asked the clerk.

"Yes," said Pierce. Usually there was a feeling about breaking camp and moving on to new country. Usually everything went off his shoulders, all the old cares and memories, so that for a little while a man got back to simplicity and was content to ride and sleep, and ride again. It wasn't quite that clear or that fresh this time. The old anticipation didn't stir alive. A man was like a wagon which, starting empty, accumulated freight as it traveled, the burden getting greater and the hills seeming tougher to climb. Nor could a man stop and dump out the load. He came to this camp empty-handed but he left it with heavy things and couldn't dump them.

He tucked his new possessions under an arm and moved to the Senate for a drink. Lott and Pfouts and Williams were at a corner table, heads together. They got up and joined Pierce at the bar. Percy Fadden, who ran the Senate, set up a bottle and glasses. He said, "On the house, gentlemen." Scoggins arrived and they drank a round. They talked a little, but nothing said was important; they were like men relaxed after a hard chore, saying little about it but content with it.

Pierce said: "What's the trail over to Deer Lodge look like now?"

"Lot of snow," said Williams.

"Have another," said Pierce, "on me."

"Celebration?" asked Pfouts.

"I guess," said Pierce. He lifted his glass

at Williams. "It's all right, Jim."

"That makes it better," said Williams.

They drank on it. Then Williams said, "Well, supper," and moved away with Lotts and Pfouts. Scoggins scanned Pierce with a dry, thorough glance.

Pierce said: "You're putting on weight, Ben. Country agrees with you."

"I guess it does. I'm always a hand to take things as they come. My people all settled down and got fat with good living. Joined the church and the town council. New England is full of Scogginses who have got to be eighty years old. What you want to know about the Deer Lodge trail for?"

"Going out that way."

Scoggins looked down at his feet. He had a fair and ruddy face, an easy-going, steady face. Thought made a flurry across it and he said: "Have one on me, Jeff," and poured from the bottle. "How far you going?"

"Until something stops me."

Scoggins leaned on the bar with both elbows. He took a finger and traced out a pattern on it. He said in a mild, slow way: "Sorry you couldn't stay on long enough to see Diana and me married."

"A fact?" murmured Pierce.

"Yes."

"That deserves another," said Pierce and reached for the bottle.

Scoggins said, "Well, wait. I had to talk

against you with her. I said you would bust anything that was in your way. You couldn't help it. That's what I said. I like you both, but I'd have to tell her that."

"You may be right," said Pierce. "Here's your drink."

Scoggins pushed the glass away. "Things don't seem right. What's happened — what's happened?"

Pierce said: "You knew about Ollie a long time back, didn't you?"

"I knew he was on the crooked side two months ago. I warned him to get out of town before this happened. Well, he started, but he didn't get far enough."

"I didn't know about him," said Pierce.

"I guess most people knew — except you. That is the hell of it. You liked Ollie a lot. So nobody said anything." He sighed again. "Something is wrong as hell."

"Sun's gone down," said Pierce.

"It'll come up tomorrow."

"Not on the same things," said Pierce and turned from the bar. "See you sometime."

Scoggins didn't answer at all. At the door Pierce turned to find his partner scowling across the room at him. He went out with his snowshoes and pack and rifle under an arm. He moved down Wallace until he got opposite the bakeshop, and here he stopped, long looking at the light shining through its window. A miner went in, and later came out.

Presently Pierce crossed the street, pushed the door open and entered.

When she saw him the color of her eyes changed; they filled with the shadow he always brought, they were hardened by the memory of what lay so solidly between them. He stood at the door; he closed it and put his back to it.

"My best wishes," he said. "Ben just told me."

Ben, she thought, had been right about Jeff. He wished her well, but he hated the thought with all his tremendous power of feeling. He could not be mild, he could not stand defeat. He was a tall black-shaped man in the room, half threatening. Against him her softness had never helped. In another moment, she realized, they would be openly quarreling.

"Is that all?" she asked.

"Yes," he said, "that's all. I'm leaving in the morning. Good-by."

"Leaving?" she said and watched him with a full wide glance. "For where?"

"Some place. Maybe another town with another woman I can take on another boat."

"I wouldn't wish another woman that experience," she said.

"Why not?" he said, and seemed then anxious to know. He shifted the things under his arm and she noticed the break of trouble and one gray, empty glimpse of inner perplexity. "Why not? What have I done

381

that's wrong?"

"According to your lights, nothing."

"I am not as proud as you might think. I am more humble than you think."

She threw her strong cry at him: "You have needed a beating! You have needed to be knocked in the dust and bruised, and left with the life half out of you! That never came to you. But someday it will!"

"That's happened to me," he said.

"When?"

He started to tell her, and changed his mind. He thought of Ollie and he thought of her, and of the feeling of emptiness that came to him now. He was so much muscle and bone wrapped around hollowness. But if he spoke he would seem to her to be crying over failure, asking for a pity he had no reason to ask for. Before her he had stood for certain things. Maybe he no longer stood for them, but he could not admit that now. She hated weakness no less than he; and her scorn would grow. So he pushed all the explanations aside. "I remember how you smiled at me in that Portland rooming house."

She cried out: "If you remember so well, remember when I stopped smiling at you!"

"For that," he said, "I have nothing but regret. I told you so, didn't I?"

"But you never really understood, Jeff. When I —" She ceased talking, the memory of that one scene returning, so tragic for her, so unbearably humiliating. She had opened her arms and she had offered him everything, trusting him to understand how full her heart was, how faithful and everlasting the offer was. He had not understood. By one cool glance he had shamed her and scorched away the moment's fineness; and had left her bare and full of hate.

"Good-by" she said.

He nodded and left the room. She stood at the counter, listening to his steps strike the wall and afterwards grow silent on the snow-packed ground. Wind shouldered against the cabin and her baker stepped in from the back room. "Bread's done."

"Go on home, Max."

There was a shout and a shot in the wind and the wind flung these sounds against the wall of the shop. She said, "Oh, my God!" and rushed at the door and wrenched it open. The freezing wind roughed against her; snow made a thickly flittering screen all along the street, through which the shop lights spread vague and round-yellow stains. Beyond her, near Van Buren, Pierce slowly turned and dropped his snowshoes and his carbine and pack and called down Wallace: "Sitgreaves — I don't want to touch you!"

Sitgreaves, having come out of an alley near the Senate, now lifted his revolver, took aim and fired again. Wind shook him, the gun's explosion swayed him. Then Diana's glance raced back to Pierce and she watched him draw and call again: "Go on away — damn you!" Agony got into her, so that she silently cried out to him: "Fire!" He was not firing. He held the gun half-poised while he faced Sitgreaves in the mealy shadows at the other end of the street. Having poor sight of his target, Sitgreaves now paced forward with his nerveless patience, aiming as he marched. Pierce shouted once more: "Put down the gun!" Sitgreaves fired, and stopped long enough to stare at Pierce still on his feet and still untouched. Sitgreaves shook his head, again advancing.

Diana could no longer look toward Pierce. She listened for his voice to come and, waiting, she watched Sitgreaves deliberately steady his revolver for another careful shot. This, Diana thought, engrossed in her terror, would be the fourth bullet. Sitgreaves braced his feet in the snow, he brought up his free arm to support the gun. People stood along the building walls in the ice-blast and Scoggins was at the Senate's door, his hand half lifted. One round echo raced with the wind, louder to her than the others. It was not Sitgreaves' gun. Sitgreaves' gun became a weight too heavy for his hand and dropped to the ground and the man tipped his face, shocked and unbelieving, to the sky and fell into the street's muddy snow.

Pierce came by her, reached Sitgreaves and

fell to his knees. She heard him say: "I'm sorry. I didn't want to do this. Lift up your head."

But Sitgreaves was dead and Scoggins and Williams and X. Biedler moved forward and stood around Pierce and Biedler patted Pierce on the back. Pierce threw Biedler's hand away; he rose and swung on his heels. This was only twenty feet from her so that she saw then the futile remorse, the deep despair he revealed. He had forgotten to be hard, he had forgotten to be strong — and it was this loss in him that shattered her reserve. When he arrived abreast the bakeshop she stepped out to him. "Jeff," she said, "Jeff —"

"Well," he said, "this should please you, Diana."

She gave him a thorough and penetrating glance. She witnessed the break of his spirit, she heard in his voice the cry of emptiness and the misery of emptiness. "Now you know," she murmured and caught his arm and firmly held him.

"Why," he said, "the joke is on me. I saw all this coming and I could do nothing about it."

She never ceased to watch him with her stern composure. "So now you'll run away from it, and you'll keep on running and hating and you'll wear yourself out fighting the world you think is so blind and unjust, and the world will have you as its victim after all."

"No," he said, "there's no hate left in me. I have seen too much of it. And I am not running. I'm just leaving some bad mistakes and some damned painful recollections behind me."

"One of them," she said, making it as hard for him as she knew how, "is the recollection of what you did to me."

"Yes," he said. "That's one of them."

"How far do you think you must go to forget me? How many hills will you have to put between us, how many rivers, how many miles? I'm in your head and I'm in your body. I put myself there and I'll be a misery in your bones as long as you live. That's paying you back for what you did to me. I'm a lot like you. I can wreck your dreams as much as you have wrecked mine."

"Sure," he said, and drew beyond the touch of her arm. "Good-by — and I wish you luck. You and Ben."

"No," she said, "I don't want it that way. We have hurt each other too much to be enemies or friends. It is more than that. If you've got to go, take me along."

He straightened before her and he looked at her with his powerful and disturbing thoughts. "Another chance, Diana?"

"We could never live apart. Everything would be so dull, so empty."

"Yes," he told her, "damned empty," and moved back to her. She was not quite smiling but he saw on her face the expression which had first puzzled him in Portland — the flurry of excitement and laughter and the inexhaustible capacity for living. She was a woman who could not fold her hands and be placid; she would always hunger, as he hungered, for inexpressible things. When he drew her forward in this night's colder and colder wind and kissed her, some part of that hunger had appeasement, and he knew then what real wonders the world held.

She drew away, now laughing and showing him the old gay streak of temper. She caught his arm and drew him toward the bakeshop. She said: "This is why I left Portland, Jeff. I was born for this and every moment of my life I have been waiting for it. Come inside."

Scoggins, still at Tanner's doorway, watched the door close upon those two; and thereafter he shrugged his shoulders and dismissed his own hopes. Now that he came to think of it he realized he had never been very sure of Diana. The big fellow — the big fellow's shadow — had always been present whenever he and Diana had been together. Maybe it was something written in the book; if so there was no use nursing sorrow, and perhaps the old friendship and the old strong loyalties would bloom again. That, he thought, would be mighty nice. Upon this note he turned into Tanner's for another drink, being the kind of man to adjust himself reasonably to misfortune. It was, though, odd about those two people. How could a man like Jeff, capable of such fury and destruction, make his peace with a woman with so passionate a temper? How did love come out of brimstone and sulphur? It confused him. But then, he thought, he was a different kind of a man and liked life to be simple. They did not.

One other person on this street had been a spectator to the scene, and when the bakeshop door closed upon Diana and Jeff, Lil Shannon returned to The Pantheon. The music was in full swing and a miner waited with a ticket. He claimed her and moved with her to the floor. "And whut's so serious?" he asked. "Smile for me, Lil."

That was her profession — to smile and please. She put the tip of her finger to her eyes and drew it swiftly across them, and lifted her face to the miner and smiled.

The publishers hope that this
Large Print Book has brought
you pleasurable reading.
Each title is designed to make
the text as easy to see as possible.
G. K. Hall Large Print Books are
available from your library and
your local bookstore. Or you can
receive information on upcoming
and current Large Print Books by
mail and order directly from the
publisher. Just send your name
and address to:

G. K. Hall & Co.
70 Lincoln Street
Boston, Mass. 02111

or call, toll-free:

1–800–343–2806

A note on the text
Large print edition designed by
Fred Welden.
Composed in 16 pt Times Roman
on a Mergenthaler Linotron 202
by Modern Graphics, Inc.